Riding the Unicorn

By the same author

THE WAY TO BABYLON

A DIFFERENT KINGDOM

Riding the Unicorn

PAUL KEARNEY

VICTOR GOLLANCZ

LONDON

First published in Great Britain 1994
by Victor Gollancz
A Division of the Cassell group
Villiers House, 41/47 Strand, London WC2N 5JE

© Paul Kearney 1994

A catalogue record for this book is
available from the British Library.

ISBN 0 575 05767 X

Typeset at The Spartan Press Ltd,
Lymington, Hants
Printed in Great Britain by
St Edmundsbury Press Ltd, Bury St Edmunds, Suffolk

For Marie

Acknowledgements

To John Wilkinson, as always,
John McLaughlin and Richard Evans,
still fighting my corner, and
Superintendent Eugene Kearney, RUC.

'Schizophrenia, like the Unicorn, is described in various ways by various people. And its elimination, like the capture of the Unicorn, appears to require some special conditions, not all of which have yet been specified. Finally, whether or not these conditions exist, belief in their existence has had significant consequences.'

Schizophrenia, Behavioural Aspects
Salzinger, 1972

Prologue

He sees them in his dreams . . .

A column which extends for miles. It comes down from the mountains, a snake of people marching south with the rime and bite of the high passes written on their wind-burnt faces. Warriors in furs with iron swords, leading tall horses. Women crammed in the few wagons that have survived, or stumbling along beside their mates. Children hollow-eyed and silent, tramping with their elders or carried on bent backs. An entire people is on the move, their faces set towards the green world of the south whilst behind them the huge snow-covered peaks and ridges pierce the sky as far as the edge of sight – mountains they once deemed impassable. Tens of thousands march south bruising the grass and scattering the wild things as they go. Thousands more lie frozen and still on the road behind them. They march like an army intent on conquest.

At night he hears the stamp of their feet, the thunder of a hundred thousand hooves. In his sleep they move ever farther south, and he can smell the close-packed smell of the Host at their campfires. They are never stilled. They eat away at his reason.

PART ONE

Willoby's Madness

One

The early shift – the one he hated most. A dark, just-birthing morning, and the whole wing was filled with the sluice and clatter of buckets, brushes, the catwalks crawling with the pail-emptying queues, the smell already inching out of their covered containers. All the excrement of the night was being poured away by men still half asleep. They shuffled in blue-clad lines, yawning, grinding the slumber from their eyes or staring stupidly into space. Unlit cigarettes dangled from the lips of a few. They were pasty, grey-yellow in the light of the overheads.

'Come on, Greggs, we haven't all fucking day.'

'I dropped me fag in the bucket – me morning fag!'

A ripple of laughter. 'Shouldn't have been sticking your nose into it, then! What were you looking for, your breakfast?'

'Screw you!', but said without conviction.

'Move along and shut your mouth.'

They shuffled past endlessly. Most did not look at Willoby as he stood, a black, silver-flecked statue, but some raised eyes filled with blank hatred, flicking away just before his own locked with them. A few, a very few, smiled or winked at him.

Mawson the Mass-Murderer paused beside Willoby with his mop and pail. He was a tiny, wizened broomstick of a man, his bald head as pale and pitted as a golf ball.

'Morning, Mr Willoby – another fine day in our salubrious establishment.'

Willoby only grunted in reply. Mawson made his flesh creep. Despite his nickname, he was only in for one murder: that of a pretty young man on a London to Edinburgh train. But he had been in so long and behaved so well that he had become a trusty of sorts. Christ knew the Governor made some odd decisions in that line.

'A nice film lined up for tonight we have, and ping-pong for those as likes it. I'm thinking we— '

'Fuck off back to work Mawson,' Willoby said mildly, and the man shuffled away, mopping as he went, face expressionless.

Some screws cultivated Mawson, for he knew all that went on in the wing – in the whole prison. But he was a queer, a right fucking nut-case in Willoby's opinion. When he got out, whenever that might be, he would be chatting up pretty boys in trains again.

Christ, the smell. The piss smell in the morning, the unwashed smell, the old food smell. It had sunk into the very bricks and boards of this place. It had clotted in the mortar. High time they pulled the shithole down, built something new. Something different, for God's sake.

He snatched a glance at his watch. Eight hours to go. Purgatory passing. Looking up, he saw the blackened skylights high above. Still dark. Still night. Somewhere beyond the glass the stars wheeled; Canopus the Dog was rising and Venus was a last gleam on the lightening horizon, but not a man in here would see them until the steel gate of Her Majesty's pleasure had banged shut on his back. Years hence it would be, for some of them.

The prison tang caught in his throat for a second and the sweat popped out along the rim of his cap as he fought the panic, the screaming pressure of the walls and the creeping queues.

Oh, Jesus, not here.

But it passed, and he was Willoby the big bad screw again. Willoby the hard bastard with the flint eyes.

My luck won't last for ever, he thought as the last of the trembling died away. One day it'll hit me as I stand here, and they'll laugh their fucking heads off as I go down.

The thought steeled him. His face stiffened further. Passing prisoners avoided the fish-cold stare, affording him a grim kind of pleasure. He was lucky in being a big man, with a prize-fighter's nose and shoulders broad as a door. The years were thickening his middle, but by Christ he could still hospitalize any bastard that tried it on with him. Oh, yes.

They were filtering back to their cells now, preparing for breakfast. He jangled the chain of keys in his pocket gently. When this shift finished he would not go straight home. He would drive out of the city, up to the moors, and he would sit with the windows open and listen to the wind and the silence.

Except that he would not. He knew he would go homewards, and pick up Maria from school, and crack jokes she never understood on the way. And he would doze in front of the telly until Jo came back from work and cooked his dinner.

Just there, hovering still – the panic and the blackness at the edge of vision. The need for violence, shouting and running. He closed his eyes momentarily, hoping to see something else when they were open again, some other world, perhaps. Mawson slopped water on the shining boots from his mop and went ashen, but Willoby did not even see him.

Close – so close.

But no cigar. Not this time. He had sweated through it again, and the inmates had not even noticed.

'You all right, Will?' another black-uniformed figure asked, striding up.

'In the pink, Howard. These bloody early shifts, though – I hate them. It's a God-awful hour to be awake.'

'The dog watch, I know.' Both Howard and Willoby had been in the army before this, and they knew the limb-leaden weariness of the last hours before dawn, when the body was at its lowest ebb.

'Still, finishing at three isn't so bad. I get a lot done around the house after an early, and the wife likes the dinner cooked for her for a change.'

Willoby looked at him quickly. Howard was a purple-faced, corpulent man, the kind who would accumulate weight with every year he made it past thirty until the first heart attack at forty. He liked his grub. So did Willoby, but that did not necessitate cooking it himself.

'Things to do.' And Willoby walked away with his hands behind his back. He was blind to the line of prisoners; the last of the slopping-out line. Breakfast smells wafted from the mess hall below overlaid with a rancid veneer, like greasy fingerprints on a glass. His own stomach was knotted and closed. He was not a breakfast person. A tot of whisky, though — that would be welcome now, by Christ. A little pick-me-up. And he glanced around as though the thought had been audible. But the kitchen clatters and the talk and the feet on the metal catwalks were enough to drown out a storm.

What is wrong with me?

The notion popped into his head, as startling and unwelcome as a whore at a wedding. It sat there with the early morning racket playing around it.

'Give us a fag, Bromley!'

'Fuck off — smoke your own!'

'You tight bastard!'

'That's enough there, Sykes.'

Nothing wrong that a stiff drink and a bit of quiet wouldn't cure. The wind-rushing stillness of the moors, with only the buzzards for company.

'Move along there. We don't want our breakfasts to get cold, do we lads?'

'It's always bloody cold anyway.'

'Yesterday's bloody leftovers, I shouldn't wonder.'

Oh, Christ, that fucking noise! Couldn't they shut their mouths just for one morning — just once?

The sweat was trickling down his face and his back felt like sun-heated sand under the heavy tunic and shirt. Too warm — too warm in here. Too many people, all of them fucking scum, criminals, wasters. Wouldn't they love it if hard man Willoby cracked up in front of their eyes? They'd fucking cheer.

Here it comes again.

Mustn't, mustn't. Must not. All that money spent keeping them here, just so John Willoby could walk up and down this brick and iron hell in a stifling coat, with a black hat squeezing down on the bones of his skull.

He groaned aloud, the sound lost in the morning cacophony. The world blurred, and he had to grip the metal handrail that bordered the catwalk with both hands.

Sweet Christ, what's wrong with me?

It was the voices again, the voices in his head, except that they were louder this time, more insistent. He could never understand the words. They were speaking foreign gobbledygook.

No one else heard them. They were his alone. He had carried them for months now, as some men carried a hidden cancer. Ghosts, spirits, demons – they haunted him like a conversation heard through a thin wall.

Like maggots squirming through his brain.

He lurched into motion. He had to get off the wing, back to the staff quarters. He had to get away to where he would not be seen.

A prisoner in his path was shouldered aside and left sprawling, shouting obscenities. Willoby was almost running.

He hit the bars and wire of the catwalk door with a crash, and for a second a scream was gagging in his throat, his eyes wide and white, the voices crawling across his mind; incomprehensible, alien, impossible. He scrabbled frantically at the bars, then remembered his keys. The voices were shouting now, shrieking – and underlying the unknown words was the growing thunder of hoofbeats. Galloping horses, a squadron of them coming up behind him. He heard a high, aching whine, like that of a child, but never thought of it as coming from his own, tightening throat.

His keys, his keys. He jabbed a shaking hand into his pocket, dropped them to the length of their chain, got them again, stabbed them clattering against the lock.

'Open, open, Christ God. *Open you bastard . . .*'

The hoofbeats were right at his back. They were an earth-trembling roar.

The key turned, the door opened and he fell through it, crawled forward and kicked it shut behind him with a clang. Shutting them out.

17

Safe now. Safe here.

His cap was off, lying beside him. His chest was easing. He felt as soaked and racked as a sprinter. The voices were a final, whispering echo that died into soothing silence. Nothing. Nothing there but the prison noises.

Oh my God, what is wrong with me?

'What have you done to him?' the Prince asked curiously. 'What was it you put into his mind to make him act so?'

'What was it I asked you to think of, sire?'

'Why, the – the manhunt, the pursuit of the traitor Carberran. Is that then what he was seeing?'

'Partly. The link is tenuous yet. This is a shadowed land we walk in, my Prince. Best we tread slowly, and as softly as a cat's footfall.'

'Indeed. It is a hideous land also. This man, though, he interests me. We will stay with him. He may suit our purpose.'

For the first time in fourteen years Willoby did not complete his shift, and the occasion was like a mark of shame, following him as surely as the puzzled looks of his colleagues. He had walked these corridors hung-over, bronchitic and exhausted, but hitherto had always lasted out his eight or twelve hours, even if it meant Howard covering for him whilst he groaned over a toilet rim. Not this time. His ailment was different, and no longer possible to ignore.

The prison receded. It was a cold winter's morning, the keen air spearing in through the open car windows and watering his eyes, clearing the fug from his brain. He had a few miles of open countryside to motor through before plunging into the sprawl of the city where he had his home.

And he had time, time to play with. The thought made him pause with his lighter halfway to his mouth, the cigarette drooping and forgotten.

Why, then, was he hurrying?

To get back to Jo? She was still at work. Maria was at school. There was no one else.

The novelty of the situation fascinated him. He slowed down, lit the cigarette, dragged deeply.

Open moorland, the end heights of the western Pennines. It was all around him, a bleak, sombre bowl of vast emptiness, populated only by sheep and stone walls. He stopped the car, opened the door and laboured out.

Cold, bloody cold. The wind caressed his thinning hair, sped the glow of his cigarette into a tiny, bright hell.

This is better. This is better for the head, for everything.

The morning's events slid to the back of his mind. There was something about this country that soothed him. The city scab was a distant blur on the horizon. Here the fells swelled from streams and rivers to green slopes, then up to tops purple-grey with heather and rock, desolate.

This feeds my soul, he thought, and tossed away the cigarette, drew in a big lungful of the sharp air.

Someone on a horse behind him.

He turned, *feeling* the hoofbeats through his soles. They drew near, then faded again. The chink of harness had been audible, and the animal's breathing.

Except that there was nothing there.

Strangely, he was not alarmed. Nothing threatened him here. The noise was not burrowing into his head in the same way it had in the prison.

Ghosts? Poltergeists? Hallucinations?

Madness?

And the calm broke. A car flew past, the passenger's face a white blur. Willoby felt the first hard spots of rain.

Am I going mad?

No answer in the rain or the flanks of the fells. He smiled; an expression that, unknown to him, chilled prisoners and fellow warders alike.

Big Will, a basket case.

Visions of himself strait-jacketed and drooling, banging his head against a padded wall.

The smile faded.

I need a drink. Several.

And then drive Maria home from school? She'd love that, her dad smelling like a brewery. Fucking teenagers. You give them the best days of your life but nothing is ever enough.

'My daughter hates me,' he said aloud. The smile again. Several drinks. Several and several. Maybe Jo would be in the mood tonight.

Quite suddenly, he ached to hold his wife, be held by her. And he laughed, running his big fingers over his face. I must be mad, he thought. When had he last screwed his wife? No—

When did we last make *love*?

What was in his head, messing up his thoughts like this? These stupid questions.

A vision of Jo as a fresh-faced girl, dark, cropped hair and that upturned nose. The light in the brown eyes, long ago. She was blonde now, for she had hated the grey hairs. Blonde and tired, and she wore too much make-up.

He shook his head, a big mountain of a man running to seed, standing baffled by the roadside with the rain pelting down on him unheeded.

Get a grip, Willoby.

Just for an instant, he caught a glimpse of some internal desolation, his mind's skeleton parading across a wide expanse of pallid years. The rain dripped into his eyes and he knuckled them dry.

Wasting fucking time, here. Good drinking time. He climbed back into the car, puffing slightly as he fastened his seatbelt, and slammed the door.

See a doctor?

The rain pattered tinnily on the roof, blurred the view beyond the windscreen. An odd sound came out of Willoby's throat, a strangled sob, a whimper. He choked it into silence. His face as he started the car was that of a maniac.

Two

Cold air ripping past my face. I am on a horse, full gallop, the ground an undulating blur below the stirrups, my ears full of hoofed thunder. In my right hand is a heavy sword. I am pursuing something.

A man, stumbling among the heather ahead.

Words shouted back over my shoulder — unknown words full of exultation. I bend over in the saddle, predatory, eager.

– Swing the sword at the man's head and feel the jar and click of impact, the blade wrenching free of the skull as I rein in, laughing.

Other riders — a crowd of tall figures on champing horses, sun glittering off metal everywhere.

They dismount, hack at the body and toss the bleeding chunks aside until there is nothing left — a slick, broken place in the heather, the shine of entrails, the white glint of bone.

And I laugh again, kiss my bloody sword blade and taste the coppery shine of man's-blood.

'*Tallimon!*' the others are shouting. '*Tallimon First Prince!*'

And he was awake, open-eyed in the darkness of the conjugal bed, Jo breathing softly with her back to him.

He licked his lips, fully expecting the butcher smear to be there still, but they were dry as cotton.

Tallimon.

The click and crunch of steel in bone . . .

Jesus.

He sat up, pressed his fingers into his eyes and watched the spangled lights dance in the darkness.

'Bastard dreams,' he said softly. A solitary car whooshed

past below the bedroom window. The streetlights cast an amber rectangle into the room.

He got out of bed and padded out of the door in his underpants, silent as a cat despite his size.

And paused on the dark landing, suddenly fearful.

What was out there, in the dark – what lurked in the lightless corners?

Damn!

The electric light banished the shadows. He screwed up his eyes against it, cursing under his breath. Another broken night – what he'd give for a blank night's sleep: ten hours of nothingness to restore the thinning fibre of his nerves.

See a doctor?

Yes – and get a bottle of pills and a pat on the head, some medical gibberish about stress, or insomnia. Bollocks, all of it.

It's my *mind*, he thought. Nothing belongs in there but me. My problem alone.

His throat rasped, parched as cardboard.

What the hell time was it? Three, four? Time to get up soon, get ready for another early shift.

And his spirits plummeted. Back to that bloody madhouse. He grinned weakly at his mind's choice of words.

I could take the day off. Ring in sick.

See a doctor.

Like hell.

'*Well?*' *the old man asked.*

'*Yes. He suits our purpose admirably. There is that under-current of desperation in him. It will see him through it. Such men do not greatly care whether they live or die, so long as they can do something different to what they have been doing.*'

'*Such men are dangerous, unpredictable – this one at least is not easy to control. Can you be so sure you will master him?*'

'*I am the King's heir.*' *Sneering.* '*Am I not fit for anything?*'

'*All the same, sire, he troubles me, this man. He is like a mountain cat pacing a cage.*'

'He is past his best. His youth is gone, but he has enough strength for what we want.'

'He may yet surprise us with his strength.'

'I may yet surprise you with the finity of my patience. This is the man. He is mine.'

Later in the dark morning Willoby did ring in sick, said he had caught a bug of some kind – even held his nose as he spoke to the phone, like a schoolboy intent on truancy. Howard would cover for him, he told the duty officer. Howard was a good man.

Relief washed over him in a tepid wave. A free day. It was what he needed to set him on his feet.

The winter sun had not yet risen when he rejoined his wife in bed. He was freezing, his feet numb with pacing the cold living room downstairs, and he pushed up against her until her warmth oozed into him through the nightdress. She shifted in her sleep at the cold under the duvet. A heavy sleeper, Jo – not a morning person, whereas he had always been easy to wake, bright as the sun in the mornings. In the beginning it had been a game of his, to wake her with touches, caresses. He burrowed closer, until they were lying like spoons in the big bed and her buttocks were pressing against his groin. He felt the first stirring, and edged his hand under the nightdress as furtively as an adolescent. Warm, smooth skin, the curve of her hip, the spreading bulge of her belly with the deepening navel.

She twitched like a horse with a fly on it. 'God's sake,' she mumbled, and pushed his exploratory hand away, turning in on herself in the bed.

His erection faded as he drew away, still cold. He felt the familiar surge of anger and sadness, and lay flat on his back with his hard eyes fixed on the ceiling.

But she was awake now, and turned to look at him.

'What time is it?' Muzzily, pale hair covering her forehead.

'Just gone seven.'

'You're late. You've slept in.' She blinked, coming slowly to life.

'I'm not going. I called in sick.' And yesterday I left early. She did not know that yet.

'What's wrong with you – a cold? Don't give it to me, for God's sake.'

'I . . . just didn't want to go in this morning,' he said lamely, on the defensive. Anger, irritation at her questions.

She sat up, rubbing her eyes, and asked what was wrong with him again.

I hear things that aren't there, he thought. I dream of killing people. I can't ever sleep a night through. And my wife will not let me touch her.

'Nothing. I'll get breakfast.'

If there was a thing he liked about early shifts, it was the solitary breakfasts he made himself – breakfast in his case being coffee strong enough to walk on and at least two cigarettes. He loved the peace and silence of the early hours, though it was better in summer when he could watch the sun come up. At such times the city would be almost as quiet as a country village.

But he had barely finished his first cup when Jo came down in a pink dressing gown, yawning and looking frowsty, sleepy. She shouted back up the stairs for Maria to get up for school, and Willoby's morning quiet died instantly. The television was switched on and began its meaningless noise in a corner. No one looked at it in the mornings; it was just a necessary noise. Jo needed noise, voices, activity around her all the time. She could not stay in a silent room without switching something on. Now she was clattering with the teapot and the toaster, still yawning.

Maria came down. Willoby's daughter was a slim, pale girl with dark, straight hair she had cropped short. She reminded Willoby of the wife he had married. Fourteen – the worst age in life – she spoke to him rarely, and then mostly in a mixture of wariness and defiance. Willoby was not sure if it was entirely their fault, but there was a wall between his family and himself. It had been growing silently for years, a little at a time, and the little things that would have helped break it down had been too much trouble. Now it was a high, massive, thing. He was no longer sure there was a way through it. Worse, he was no longer sure he cared.

'Home sweet home,' he said quietly, draining his cup. No one heard him.

'Maybe you should see a doctor. You've not been sleeping lately,' Jo said over her shoulder.

'You noticed, then.'

'Of course I noticed. You need a pill or something, something to knock you out at nights.'

His face darkened. 'I don't need any fucking pills.'

'You watch your language in front of the child!'

Willoby looked at his daughter. Maria was smiling into her cornflakes – the same smile, had he known it, that he used himself. It was unpleasant on her young mouth.

'I don't need a doctor, just a – a rest for a while, that's all.'

'You'll not get much of that without a line from the GP.'

'I know, I know.' He stared at her as she buttered her toast. His wife's face was small, oval. Without make-up the deep lines at the corners of her mouth were more visible and her lips were thinner. She plucked her eyebrows, which he hated. When they had met she had possessed thick, dark brows, wonderfully expressive. She had looked like a cross between a pixie and a witch.

'What's wrong?'

'Nothing.' He poured himself more coffee. No one else in the house drank it. Jo preferred tea and Maria drank only milk and water – and cider, he suspected.

'What are you going to do all day?'

He looked up, surprised. 'I don't know. I never thought— '

'You can take Maria to school, then. It'll save me a journey, and you know I've never liked that road in the mornings.'

He nodded. By God, if the prisoners could only see him now. Big hard Willoby bobbing his head to this shrill woman as though he was a schoolboy. His fingers tightened round the coffee cup.

Wind in my hair, cold and fresh as spring – thundered hoofbeats – the sound of a cavalry squadron at the canter; and a guidon cracking in the air. What is the device upon it? A mountain?

'John – *John*; are you listening to me?'

He shook his head, baffled. 'What was that?'

'I said Maria's got something to tell you. Go on, love.'

'It doesn't matter – he doesn't care.'

'Of course he does, love.'

Willoby collected his unravelling wits with an effort. 'What? Tell me, for God's sake.'

His daughter looked at him sullenly. 'I've been picked for the netball team, so I'm staying on this evening for the training.'

'There you are,' Jo said triumphantly, but Willoby stared closely at his daughter and she dropped her eyes.

'Netball is it? Mind if I watch the game?'

Her eyes were huge, outraged. 'No you *can't* – no one else's parents will be there. It's only a try-out.'

Willoby smiled at her. She lied well, like himself. To his surprise he found that he did not care about this, either. He leaned forward into his daughter's face.

'I hope he's *nice*.'

Maria flushed crimson, and her glare turned into an icy smile.

'I'll be late for school.' She swept out of the kitchen like a princess.

'I don't know why you do it to the girl,' Jo complained, eating toast.

Willoby looked at her, full of sardonic amusement. 'Maria can take care of herself, I think.'

'She's only fourteen! And I don't like the crowd she hangs about with.'

What parent ever did?

'When I was her age all I wanted was to be a soldier,' Willoby said. Jo rolled her eyes with a here-he-goes-again look.

Maybe it would have been easier if he had had a son. Maybe

not. Knowing Willoby's luck his son would have been a mincing little faggot. He laughed at the thought, and the laugh turned into a churning cough. He swore.

'They'll kill you yet, those things,' Jo told him, nodding at the cigarette.

'Probably.' He paused, and asked, genuinely curious, 'Would that make you happy?'

She blinked. 'What?'

'Me turning up my toes.'

'My God, John! What a thing to ask.'

'Just wondered, dear.' He leaned over the table and kissed her crumb-grained lips. She wiped her mouth, staring at him. He grinned. There was an odd sense of carelessness in him this morning. He truly didn't give a monkey's, and he had a day of his own stretching out before him like a jewel in the dark of a mine.

'Don't forget to take Maria to school.'

See a doctor.

'I won't.'

'What are you going to do all day?' This time she was genuinely curious.

'Frankly my dear, I have no idea.' Thank Christ, he thought.

Three

'It is time,' said the Prince. 'Time to give him a look at the world he is to enter.'

'It's too soon, sire. You do not have enough influence over his will. There is no telling what may happen. The melding is still in its early stages.'

'I have had my will thus far, have I not? We will take him somewhere lonely, away from distractions, and then continue. It is time he saw our own mountains.'

'Then he must come through you, for the moment. We cannot yet bring him here entirely, for there is no way to send him back, and the time is not yet ripe.'

'So be it. Let him look through my eyes, and see what a Prince sees when he surveys his kingdom.'

Howard, the perfect family man, the all-round nice guy, had once told Willoby that there was an unspoken rule in his house: it being that if he had a Sunday off – a rare thing with the shifts they worked – then it was tacitly recognized that it was Dad's Day. He walked the dog, read the paper, drank a lot of tea and had a few pints in the evening. No one, not his beloved wife or perfect children, ever intruded. He needed that kind of thing to look forward to, he said. A day of his own.

Damn right.

There were no such rules in Willoby's household. He knew that he let Jo browbeat him out of an obscure sense of guilt, a recognition that he had not done particularly well by her. For years she had dragged round the world after him, living in a succession of crummy married quarters, and when Willoby had finally left the army, they had found themselves strangers, unable to support the idea of days in and out together. Hence her job, dinner lady in a local prep school. Hence his shift work. They had forgotten how to hold a conversation with each other. But that was life.

There had been the odd fling, the nights with the business-like whores in Germany, other soldiers' wives. Nothing that amounted to much. They were still together. A powerful thing, thought Willoby, is habit.

But now there was this wild card in the pack. This creeping . . . illness? These dreams which he half enjoyed.

'Fucking weird,' he muttered.

There was no one to hear him. He was up on the moors, alone but for the wind and the rain.

Memories of the sucking mud on Dartmoor, himself a young lance-jack, struggling for that second stripe on his arm. It had been his whole world back then.

He opened the boot of the car, feeling the chill prick of the ubiquitous rain on his neck, and rummaged through the crap that always seemed to fill his car. Grunting, he hauled forth a faded green rucksack, its straps frayed and worn. Someone had scrawled on it in large letters *Willoby 21233245*, but the ink was washed out and faint. He slammed the boot, locked it, and took off.

I'll ring her later, he thought, let her know I won't be back tonight. There's a phone box on the road.

That thin worm of guilt coiling in him. She'd think he was shacked up with some tart in a B and B somewhere. Well, tough titty. He needed to breathe, to get his feet dirty once in a while. Time she understood that – she'd had long enough to try.

The heavy rucksack bit into his shoulders, oozing his boots into the thickening mud, whilst the rain picked up to chill his face.

Maybe this was a daft idea. What was it he had once said? *If it ain't raining, it ain't training.* And he chuckled aloud at the blast from the past. Getting too soft was his problem.

The sky darkened, the morning taking on the sombre blue

aspect of late afternoon. He could see the swells and anvils of cumulo-nimbus powering their way across the sky's face, and knew he was in for a dirty night. There was an odd prescience in him, a clear-sightedness unclouded by cares of home or work, so that for a moment he felt almost as though the rain were passing uninterrupted through him. Dimly he realized that there was a crux on the horizon, a crisis approaching. He felt it as clearly as the loom of the thunderheads piling down from the northern sky. And he did not greatly care.

The rain harried him throughout the day, seeping through his cheap waterproof and the worn leather of his boots. His hip flask kept him insulated, however, and he took a grim satisfaction in the rain-swept bluster of the weather. It kept other people off the moors. The pale tracks were empty. The only evidence of man up here apart from the tracks were the regular lines of grouse butts, U-shaped stone breastworks for the toffs to shoot behind, that dotted the bleak landscape. As the afternoon came round, and the clouds closed in further, Willoby saw lights in the valleys that huddled under the steep flanks of the fells. Then the mist closed in – or it might have been low cloud, he could not tell – and he was alone in a drifting whiteout, the water vapour standing in beads on his sodden clothing, all sounds cut off. It was getting dark.

'Terrific.'

He left the track, the whisky from his flask hazing his brain a little, and after twenty yards he saw the dark loom of a grouse butt to his left. It looked like a burial mound, ancient as a dolmen in the mist, and for a moment Willoby hung back.

Stupid bugger, wandering about here alone. No one knows where I am, even. What brought me out here?

He threw off the rucksack with a grunt of relief and set his back to the drystone bulk of the butt. He'd wait out the mist for a few hours, then head for the nearest valley, some pub which would put him up for the night. It was too lonely here, too dark and wet – and night was coming.

He slugged at his flask. It was almost empty.

Tired. Fresh air and exercise, the first for ages. His body

ached, and he knew his feet were blistered inside the soaked boots.

He was on the verge of dozing off when the images hit him and his head jerked upright, eyes wide.

The smells are different, somehow more vivid. If they were to be made visible, they would be in colours brighter than he has ever seen. Dung and woodsmoke, new grass, cooking meat, wet soil; and horses – many horses.

The sounds come: the talk and laughter of a numerous people, the clang of the hammer on hot iron and hiss of quenched sparks. The murmurous rumble of hooves and rattle of metal.

He feels the heat of an alien sun on his face, and stands on the earth of another world.

High mountains, tall as Alps. They tower and reach clear across the northern sky, their flanks pale with snow, the foothills dusted with it despite the warm sunlight. All around, the world is a vast rolling expanse of hills clad in long grass. The wind plays over it, making the meads a green, wave-rippled ocean studded with wild flowers. Here and there a lonely fist of rock thrusts out of the soil, a reminder that the hard bones of the land are near the surface. And here and there a copse, a wood, a small forest will darken the hills. Birdsong everywhere, and on the farthest slopes the moving shapes of animal herds.

But this is in the background. Set against the awesome hugeness of the country, there is a busier scene close at hand. He is standing on a tor that butts on to a wide river which flashes in the sun. A high knoll, almost a small mountain, rises before him with the river lapping at its stony foot. Other knolls and buttes are scattered in a wide crescent along the banks of the river. And they are covered with people.

Smoke rises from cooking fires, but also from the clangour of forges. Lopped trees lie by the hundred with gangs of men shaping and chopping at them. Stone blocks are tumbled here

31

and there, masons at work rearing them into walls. Leather tents are pitched with no apparent order. Thousands of men are at work here, a great hive of labour and construction, and the herds on the hills he can now see are cattle, sheep, guarded by patrols of watchful horsemen. A rough track has been beaten from the river into the hills, and heavy ox-drawn wagons are convoying along it, their beds full of lumber and stone.

The scene is as bright and as clear as a sunlit jewel. The very air seems transparent, and he can feel the breeze moving on his skin, playing in his hair.

My hair.

It is strangely thick, falling down over the collar of his leather tunic. His sword baldric weighs down his right shoulder and his left hand rests on the pommel of the weapon as though accustomed to its presence.

Other things. Horses behind him, their riders laughing and bantering. The press of sun-warmed gold on his forehead.

Gold?

He is thinner, harder. The energy he feels in this younger body is almost too much to bear. It is a form made for running, for fighting. But it is not John Willoby.

And as the realization hits him, he is aware that there is something else here – some other thoughts lining his mind. There is a moment of panicky fear before he is shunted aside. The sensations do not change, but he realizes that he is removed from the wind and the ground and the smells. He is a stranger. And then the alien thoughts come crowding his brain.

Tallimon. I am a Prince of this proud people, the First Prince of the Kingdom. This is my inheritance.

Pride, hauteur cold as frost. And there is savagery lurking there, also – a barbarism that makes him recoil. He is part of another man, staring through a window to his soul. He is peering into the mind of a killer.

No – he is not just an onlooker. He is becoming part of this other man. His soul is soaking up this Tallimon's essence like blotting paper.

Memories of murder clot the edges of his mind.

Can you see them? Can you remember even my memories?

Who are you?

Tallimon, soon to be a king.

Where am I? What is this place, these people?

We name it the Green World, after the white hell of the mountains we traversed to come here. We are the Kristill, the First Men, and this world is ours, now.

The questions became absurd as the memories began to trickle into place. The bodies in the whipping snow, the vast column of people struggling through the drifts, a nation on the move. And the first glad sight of the wide warm world of the lands beyond, the plains and hills green with grass, rolling to meet the blue sky on an infinitely far horizon. His heart soared at the memory.

Yes! You see it also. The passage of the Greshorn Mountains, the Mankillers. We left one in ten of our folk there, frozen in the high passes or crushed in falls from the precipices.

Willoby felt that he had knocked back a huge swallow of potent wine. His head – if it was his head – was spinning with the grandeur of the sight before him, the feral eagerness of the voice that seemed to be inside his head with him, an impossible bedfellow. He rubbed his young, hard hand over his face and stopped as he came across the bristle of a moustache on his upper lip.

'Ho-Tallimon! Cadye? An whil ne smaenna Greshir n-itai?'

What? Willoby, or this new version of him, turned round to face a body of men on the slope behind. Some were mounted, others held reins in their fists while their steeds cropped grass, the crunching sound loud in the clear quiet of the day. The men were tall, dressed in furs and cured skins, rough linen and wool. Gold glinted in torcs at their necks and on the pommels of long swords that hung by their hips. They were bearded and shaggy, hard-faced men with hollow cheeks and bright eyes, the colour flaming and alive over their cheekbones. They were out-of-doors men. They had that vibrant, lean look that

33

Willoby had seen in the best of soldiers. And that, he realized, was what these were. Fighting men.

'*Is that not what every man should be?*' the voice in his head said. And abruptly, Willoby was shut out of this new body again. It spoke. Willoby could feel his own mouth working, the lungs powering, and he could hear the words, but was not responsible for them, nor did he understand them. A cold shiver of panic went through him.

This is madness. This is what insanity is like.

The body turned round again, and Willoby was able to feel his own will flooding its fingertips.

Who the hell are you people?

You will find out more about us in time. Indeed, you will become an expert before you are done. Look well on this world. It will become as familiar to you as your own – and far more attractive, I feel. Here there is none of that bad air, the black smoke, the stone streets, that you have in your own world. This land is a blank slate, untouched since the creation, and we the First Men of the world. Use my mind – seek out the memories that are there, the knowledge of this place.

Pictures flooded his reeling mind. He physically staggered, and felt himself leave the nerve-endings of the body again. He became a nebulous thing, a pane of thin glass for light to shine through. Around him there was a nothing world of images from a past that did not exist.

A forest, vast and dark, the deep woods swarming with beasts. Fire in the doorway of a hut with darkness outside, and the black quadrupedal shapes milling and snarling beyond the flames.

The clink of iron against his young teeth as he is fed from a sword-point.

The joy flooding his brain as he stabs home the spear at the springing wolf, and the collapsing animal buries him in rank fur.

The face of a girl, dark-haired and pale; heart-wrenching in her loveliness. She is running through a sunlit wood with her tresses streaming behind her like a banner, and the sun shines

34

through her robe to reveal the silhouetted perfection of her limbs. He feels the pain of someone else's love in his breast as if it were his own.

Then the cold, terrifying slide of iron into his flesh, the snarling face of the enemy, and his exultation as he twists free of the impaling spear and brings his own blade down, shattering the face of his attacker.

The smoky torchlit length of a great hall crowded with men, the roasting meat and rough beer bringing the water into his mouth. He is sat at the King's end of the firepit, its light a red hell below the bearded faces of the warriors. Dogs fight for the bones in the shadow, men haul serving maids on to their knees, grease shines on mouths and fingers. And the King is there – a great broad barrel of a man, thickly bearded, the rugged handsomeness of his face marred by one torn and empty eye socket. He stands up to shout laughter at his men, and seems like some firelit god about to rain lightning down on mankind.

Courberall, the High King. My father.

And with that the pictures falter. There is one last glimpse of the girl's face – she wears a garland of honeysuckle and forget-me-not on her raven head – and then there is only darkness.

Who is she? Her face haunts him.

Let me see more.

No. Enough for now. You will see more in time. It is best we return you to your own world, and give you back the body you left behind.

He does not want to go back. This wide, green world has reached into his veins and fired his blood. He wants to ride a horse across its hills, to be a young man again and find the dark girl with her garland of flowers.

Amusement, mockery from the voice in his mind.

Those things you may yet do, if you have the strength. For now, my hulking Turnkey, you must make sure you survive in the world you call your own.

'No!'

35

But it was too late. He could feel himself slipping away, the voice of Tallimon fading from his brain. An awful chill settled into him as he felt himself sinking back into his own heavy limbs. Suddenly, the impression of lightness, of vibrancy, was gone. He felt the laboured heaving of his lungs, the catch in his breath that was the legacy of cigarettes, the lumpen sluggishness of age.

Rain on his face, and mud sucking at his dead weight. A shudder convulsed him, and he dragged open his eyes.

Grey morning on the moors. His clothes were wet through, the dampness settling in his very bones. He twitched and groaned with the raw, agonizing discomfort of it.

A dream – was that all?

Madness.

And he screamed into the dank rain, screamed until his throat hoarsened and closed, and the cords on his thick neck stood out like bloodshot wires.

'Jesus Christ, John! What's happened to you? What do you think you're playing at? You look as though you've been lying in a ditch all night. Do you know how worried we've been . . . ?'

Caked mud fell from him as he slumped into a chair. Maria was staring at him with curious wonder. Jo, meanwhile, went on with her tirade.

Home again, home again, jiggedy-jig.

'Well?'

He remembered a sight of high mountains, their flanks pristine with snow. That girl – the sun shining through her dress and her dark hair flying.

Impossible. Hallucinations.

Madness.

'I'm going mad,' he said quietly. No one heard him.

'What were you trying to prove? That you're still a young man or something? My God, John, you could have caught your death. You look like a tramp. You're not in the army any more, you know . . .'

Something like a sob inched hotly up his throat, and he closed his eyes momentarily. Shut up, please . . .

It had been wholly desolate on the moors, a grey dawn. It had taken him the better part of two hours to retrace his steps to the car, and on the way home he had dozed off twice, producing frenzied honks from other drivers. And now he was back to the same morning routine. The shuddering futility of it boiled up and up in his brain.

'You phone, tell me you won't be home, that you'll be out sleeping on the moors. What am I supposed to think? How am I supposed to feel? You could have been anywhere. What if you had fallen down and broken a leg? You'd have lain there till you died . . .'

'*Shut up!*' His roar filled the kitchen.

The colour fled her face. She backed a step from the fire in his glare. Maria looked on, fascinated.

'You'll be late for work,' he said then, mildly. When he stood up she jerked away as if he had lunged at her. He had not struck her in years, and never sober. Her sudden fear irritated him beyond measure.

'I said you'll be late for work.' He let his hulking frame dominate her, the red unblinking eyes stare her down.

'I – we'll . . . talk, when I get back.' Her voice shook. 'Make yourself something. Have a bath. Come on, Maria.' She had to drag her daughter with her. Maria's face had the avid look of a spectator at the circus.

The door slammed, and the house was empty. He listened to the car crunch and whine its way out of the drive, and knew he was alone.

'Tallimon?' Was that the name? But there was no answer. What did they call voices in the head – hallucinations? Was there a name for it? Or a cure?

'Oh, this is great, just great.' And he chuckled harshly. Old Will has finally flipped his lid. The boys will love it. The crowds go wild.

He coughed, and suddenly his whole body was craving a cigarette.

The memory of that other body, lithe and hard as a greyhound, with bottomless lungs. The body of a young man.

'Fucking good dream,' he said to the empty house. Better than this, anyway.

Four

'Well, Aimon, what think you? Have I chosen well?'

The old man leaned back against the leather wall of the tent, his eyes two glints of jet in the thick whiskers of his face. He looked like a particularly ancient rodent.

'You saw and heard what went on between the Turnkey and I, did you not? You were able to eavesdrop?'

'I was able,' Aimon said heavily.

'So speak to me! You are one of the few whose opinion I value. Will he suffice?'

'You are less sure than you were before, my Prince. Has this foray into another's mind taught you something?'

'It has taught me the value of patience, it seems. Now answer my question.'

The old man brought a fist down to slap on to his withered thigh. For a second fury flooded his wizened face. 'Moon and stars! We are talking treason here, parricide no less. We are in the throes of breaking every law of nature and magic we have ever known, and you chafe and smart, prating to me of *patience*! You will end up on an impaler's spike yet, sire. You push too hard, too fast. Do you realize what we are doing here – the consequences it will have?'

The Prince's face was white, dangerous. 'I understand we are talking of the killing of a king – the man who is my father. I know well the stakes we gamble for.'

'Do you? Do you? I talk not only of this kingdom, this kingship – even of the lordship of this New World. Do you and the other nobles truly think we are the only folk to abide here? What of the sightings in the mountains, the encounters with the stunted people in the snows? Your own father's brother died raving of snow giants, of dwarves. This land is not empty, nor is it yet wholly ours.'

'It is. None shall gainsay twenty thousand Kristillic swords. There is nothing here to challenge us but fairy tales and the shadows that men see before sleep.'

The old man, Aimon, closed his eyes for a second. 'I do not, in any case, speak only of this world, this kingdom, or this kingship. Have you no idea of the enormity of the thing we have done? We have broken through the wall that separates this world from another. We – you – have spoken to a man from a world alien to us. We have seen an unimaginable place; and the link between him in that place and you in this is still open. I cannot close it. Who knows what might wander through from that world of stone and smoke and steel – into your very mind? Could we withstand the chariots these folk ride in, that need no horses?'

'You are an old woman, Aimon. None know of this world except our Turnkey, and he believes he is losing his mind. Theirs is not a credulous land. Even if he speaks of what he has seen to others, they will not believe him.'

Aimon stared fixedly at his Prince. Tallimon, the bastard eldest son of the High King. A young man, not yet thirty, lean and fast as a hunting hound. If he shaved off his thin moustache he could pass for a girl – and a comely one at that. But Aimon had seen him ride into winter camps with the bleeding heads of his enemies garlanding his saddle. Men admired him. Women adored him. And he cared for none of them.

Not even I, he thought, who am so close to him in this treachery. I also he would slay without a qualm if it suited his ends. Everyone is expendable but Tallimon. Around him the world revolves. What monster's coat tails am I clinging to?

'It seems I asked you a question, old man. What think you of our protégé? Will he suit?'

'If you do not drive him out of his mind first. He is a warrior. I sense that from him. Violence is nothing new to him. And he has a . . . hardness, a steel in him that few men have. It is deeply buried but I believe it to be there still.'

40

Tallimon grinned. 'I know. I recognized it. Something there is in him which reminds me of myself. I like him.'

'Which is why, as I have said, he will not be easily mastered. Nor is he the very type of an assassin. I would have him beside me in the front rank of a battle line, but whether his courage, or his inclination, is of the type for dark deeds in the shadows, I am not so sure.'

Tallimon grinned again. 'You think I cannot control him. Let me tell you this, Aimon; I have already begun planting an idea in his mind which will bind him to us more firmly than any spell you could devise.'

'And what might that be, my Prince?'

Tallimon hesitated – oddly for him. 'Love, old man. The love of a fair lady.' And his face became as grim as stone.

Later, he and Aimon supped with his father, the High King, and the other nobles in the newly built Great Hall. It had been one of the first structures of the new city to be raised on the hill beside the river, and some of its planks oozed resin, making the diners curse under their breath as it stuck to their breeches.

The firepit glowed and flickered, an entire boar spitted and turning above the flames, a dark shining shape attended to by the royal pages. Fat hissed and spat as it hit the fire, and the heady woodsmoke and roasting smell filled the entirety of the hall, along with the stink of sweating humanity. They might be seated in the hall of their fathers back in the Wildwood, Tallimon thought. The crossing of the mountains has changed nothing in them; the sight of this Green World spreading out before them has not widened their horizons at all.

He picked meat from a bone with slender fingers and carved it into unrecognizable shreds with his belt knife, ignoring the attendants who refilled his drinking horn. A neighbour, indulging in horseplay with his fellows, gave Tallimon a nudge that sent the knife point scoring across the broad table. Tallimon merely glanced at him, and the man blenched and turned away.

He smiled, an expression many men had seen in the moment before their death.

He has it also, that fat man from the Iron World. The Look. The Something in the eyes that men fear. We are brothers in many ways, he and I.

He looked up along to the head of the firepit, where the King and his sons dined along with the elder nobles. Tallimon did not eat with his father. They ruined each other's appetites.

The King looked down the long trestles, and his good eye caught that of his eldest son's. For a moment the dark one-eyed stare held Tallimon's; then the King looked away, calling loudly for more beer. Tallimon felt an odd pain, a momentary regret, wondering why it had come to be this way, who or what had laid the foundations of the barrier between them.

But, of course, he knew the answer to that. It lay in a shallow grave on the other side of the Greshorn Mountains, rotting in the leaf-mould of the forest. His mother had been only a concubine, captured from some forest tribe and kept to service the needs of the King. She had loved him for a while, in her own way. Perhaps he had felt something for her too – for the son she bore him whom he named Tallimon. But there had been other women in the King's life, and one of them had become his queen. The Queen's sons, Idramon and Madavar, sat at the King's side, and any idea that the bastard Tallimon might once have been the rightful heir had been tactfully forgotten, like the unmarked grave in the deeps of the forest. Call him a prince, yes – even let him call himself First Prince when he is with his friends – but never recognize him as such publicly. Give him estates and a small retinue, and let him devote his energies to carving out a niche for himself in this new land. Whilst the King's legitimate sons . . . for them the kingship is being saved.

And once Madavar is King, my life must be forfeit. Tallimon smiled again as he met the glance of the elder of his half-brothers. Madavar was quick and dark, lean as a cat, his wit as keen as the point of a sword. In another life, Tallimon could have loved this half-brother of his – and again, the momentary regret, swiftly stifled.

42

Madavar raised his horn, unsmiling, and Tallimon returned the salute. They each knew how the land lay. Already some of their retainers had clashed. The old tensions were stirring, now that they had fought their way through the mountains.

He remembered an arctic night in the peaks, the fluttering fires of the people burning over miles of the lower passes, and he seated by one such fire with his father and Madavar. They had shared barley spirit and doctored each other's frost nips; and in the night Tallimon and Madavar had woken their father and pummelled him back to life from the cold death sleep he had slipped into. There had been no distance then, for they had had the mountains to fight against. In this fat land, however, there was time and space for ambition.

An attendant refilled his horn. He seized the youth's wrist before he could go.

'It's Farlad, isn't it? You know the lady Merrin?'

'Aye, sire.'

'Have her sent to my tent ere the end of the feast.'

'I will, sire.'

The boy hurried off. One did not tarry on Tallimon's errands.

'So it is Merrin, is it?' Aimon asked beside him.

'What about her?'

'She is the lady whom this Turnkey of ours is to love. I wonder at you, Prince. I thought you prized her.'

'I do, old man. She is the bait I am setting. It does not mean our prey must taste her, though.' He said this though he knew it was not true. If that is what it took, then so be it.

'She has been tasted before,' Aimon said.

Tallimon glared at him but did not reply. Merrin was his concubine, her mother a captive from a long-ago war, but she had belonged to other men before him. She had been a present from Courberall the High King, in the days when his bastard son had been in favour. And, of course, the King had tasted his gift beforehand, to break her in for his son. To bind himself to her would be to ruin any faint hope of becoming King by legitimate means. The bastard who married the concubine – a

43

fitting King indeed! But he could not let Merrin go. He had never been able to fathom whether his father's gesture had been thoughtless generosity or calculated cruelty. Either way, he hated him for it. And he hated himself for what he was about to do to her.

'When do we summon our man?' he asked Aimon in an undertone. At the High Table the nobles were singing. The King was banging his beer horn on the table, sending the liquid flying. In the red firelight it looked as though he were scattering blood over himself and his sons.

'Give it time.' The old Mage sounded worried, ill at ease. 'I have told you, Tallimon – that channel we have opened is not yet closed. Be wary. He may come through when you least expect it. Your minds are still linked.'

'So be it,' the Prince said off-handedly. 'But when can we bring *him* here, himself? If he is to do what we want him to do then he must be a man, whole and solid, not some vaporous presence in my head. I want to see this Turnkey of ours standing on the soil of this world, Aimon. Then we can begin readying him for the tasks ahead. Until that happens we are drifting, and with every day that passes there is more chance of my father or Madavar finding out.'

Aimon was jostled by the antics of his fellow diners. Someone was dancing on one of the tables. Presently some of the slave women would be called in, and then the feast would disintegrate. Nobility, Tallimon thought. We are no better than the savages we conquered in the Wildwood.

There was no chance of their being overheard in the rising din. The noise blanketed them like a curtain.

'It will take time, sire. It is one thing to summon a spirit, another to bring a living breathing man from another world to this . . . You killed Carberran because he knew, didn't you?'

Tallimon hesitated. 'He talked too much. He would have doomed us all.'

'He was not a bad man, and he would have sided with you.'

'Such men I can do without. *You must be swift*, Aimon. In three days' time I take a single Rimon from my command out on a clearance patrol to the south. My father's orders. It is a calculated insult of his, a way of cutting me down to size, to make me lead out a fifty-man patrol like a common Rimarch instead of letting me delegate it to one of my junior officers. But I dare not disobey. It is his way of testing me. The Turnkey must be here by then – before I go. I may be away for a week or more.'

The old man shook his head. 'Too soon. Far too soon. Would you have me bring a raving imbecile across, or a corpse?'

'Bring him here, and soon, or I will send you to join Carberran,' Tallimon hissed. Aimon looked at him.

'The snake bares his fangs. Kill me, my Prince, and no one will ever come through the door that I have opened, but this man will be forever in your mind, to drive you mad.'

'I . . . am sorry. But we stand on a sword's edge here, Aimon. We cannot balance for ever.'

Then Tallimon noticed his father's eye on him again, and raised his horn in toast to the King.

He left the noisy torchlight of the hall an hour later. Except for the sentries, the great camp slept. From the summit of the hill he could look out to see the moonlit glitter on the Great River. Walls stood half finished around the foot of the high ground, like the ruins of an older fortress. Here and there light flickered out of the open flap of a tent. A baby cried, but mostly there was silence, the soft wind soughing from the dark peaks of the high mountains in the north. Most of the people were in the main camp, away from the city site.

There will be a great city here one day, he thought. And it will be of stone. Men will speak of it all over this world. Courbisker, my father would call it, but when I am King it shall be named after me, and I shall found a line of kings to hold it after me.

The exaltation in him faded. He stepped down from the height where the citadel would one day be, threading through the tents, speaking softly to the watchful dogs, and at last found his way to the shadowed loom of his own tent, black under the faint starlight. There was no light within, and he frowned. The boy had neglected his errand.

But then a shape moved away from the side of the tent, hooded and cloaked to the ground.

'Why did you not go in?'

'I was watching the stars. They are strange, some of them. They make shapes I have never seen before. Someone will have to name them soon.'

He smiled, a real smile, and felt the ease in his chest that always seemed to come when Merrin was near. 'There are many nameless things in this new land, but they will have to wait a while for their names, I think.'

'Courberall the King called the river the Courbering, after himself, but men still call it the Great River because that is what it is. Perhaps names will come in time, come to everything.'

'If Courberall does not try to name the whole world after himself first.'

She laughed softly in the night, and he moved closer to her tall hooded shape. The night air was cool, and he could sense her warmth under the cloak, the faint hint of lavender and honeysuckle she set her clothes to store in. It wheeled through his head more potently than all the beer he had consumed that evening.

'A great man, your father,' she said.

'My father.' He could not keep the sourness out of his voice.

'You loved him once, Tallimon, and he you. It is ambition and pride that sets you at each other's throats. It was never like this in the mountains.'

'The mountains . . .' Already many of the people were looking back with a kind of nostalgia to their ordeal in the high passes. They had died by the hundred up there, and finally by the thousand, but Tallimon knew that in thirty years' time veterans would be boasting of the passage of the Greshorns to make the young men feel small.

But there had been no intrigue, no time for plotting in the mountains.

Enough. They were out of the mountains now. The past was dead. He had the present standing shadowed before him, fragrant with lavender.

'Let me see you, Merrin.'

And she threw back the cloak, her raven hair a second hood, her face pale under it and the starlight catching in her eyes.

He moved closer yet, slid his cold hands in under the cloak, and found her naked. She did not flinch at his chilled fingers, but let them scale the firm curve of her hips and back. Her skin broke out into gooseflesh at his touch.

'Let me warm you,' she said in a low voice, and set his hands on her breasts, the nipples hard under his palms. He pressed his lips against her neck.

'Merrin, my lady Merrin . . .' The pain was seeping in. He wanted to weep, knowing what he was to do with her.

'Take me inside,' she said, and he swung her into his arms and carried her into the privacy of the tent.

Willoby woke to find the streetlight filtering through the blinds in wands and bars. The green digits of the clock told him it was four a.m. But no work to go to. He was taking a week off. He was going to sort out his mind without the benefit of doctors. He had bullied Jo into letting him do that.

But what had woken him?

Nothing. The pictures were not there. His mind was as empty as an eggshell. Winning the battle, then.

Beside him, Jo stirred, turned on to her back. Surprised, he realized that her eyes were open.

'Awake?' he whispered.

'Can't sleep tonight. It's too quiet.' The city was in the lull before dawn, the only time he ever knew it to be peaceful.

His wife's face was all amber and shadow from the light outside, a reflecting glint lighting her nearer eye.

'What's wrong with you, John?' Still she did not look at him. 'Is there someone else?'

The image of a dark girl with flowers in her hair – adolescent fantasy. *Hallucination.*

'There's no one else, honest.' He placed his hand on her shoulder, rolled towards her across the no-man's land between them. She did not protest.

'Then what's going on? Are you – are you sick or something?'

He paused, the swimmer poised for the dive.

'I think I am. I think it's in my head. Jo, I think there's something wrong with my *mind.*'

Her hand grasped his, moving his absurdly. It had been so long.

'Are you sure? Is it stress, the work?'

'Maybe. I don't know. But it's weird, Jo. There's these voices in my head. I see things, and they seem real. Christ, I think I'm losing it.'

She clutched his hand. He felt her body press against his, the soft swell of her breast under the thin nightdress.

'You have to see someone, then. A doctor, or a – a psychiatrist.'

'A head-shrinker!' He bit short the anger in him, aware that this moment, this closeness, was rare and fragile, a thing to be nurtured.

'You can't go on the way you have been, John. And you'll have to get some kind of sick note for work.'

'I know, I know.'

They lay still, both suddenly aware of their closeness. He bent and kissed her as though she were a stranger he was unsure of, but the kiss was returned. He moved lower, kissing her neck. His thumb skimmed a nipple and he felt her start.

'No John, we have to talk . . .'

But he silenced her. Slowly his wife's arms came up around his neck and she pushed her pelvis against him. He slid the nightdress over her thighs, caressed the birthing wetness at the crux of her legs. She moaned, and he moved between them, careful of his weight.

And was inside her, moving in her. She muffled her mouth against his shoulder, aware of Maria in the next room.

'Oh God, Jo— '

He moved faster. Her fingers sank into the flesh of his back. Sweat started out all over him and glued their bodies together.

'Oh, God.'

The girl's face was staring into his, her mouth open, the dark hair falling back from her temples. She was beautiful, perfect, her skin flawless in the bloom of the candlelight. He moved inside her, felt her thighs about his waist, her nails scoring his back.

'Tallimon.'

He thrust harder into her, stirred by her beauty. He possessed her – she was his, and she owned him utterly.

The crisis came. He cried out, burst into her and heard her own glad cry. As he sank down on her breast she kissed his eyes, smiling.

'Merrin,' he said in a breath. 'My lovely Merrin.'

Jo heaved him bodily off her, throwing his heavy weight across the bed.

'You bastard!'

He felt like a man struggling out of deep water. For a moment he could not recall where he was. Where had Merrin gone – the tent and the candlelight?

'You couldn't even stop yourself saying her name. It was her you wanted, and you were fucking *me*. You bastard!'

'Jo?' Dazed. He struggled to collect his wits, still lulled by the aftermath of loving. He was slick with sweat and the by-products of sex. His penis oozed.

'Oh, Christ, Jo.'

He had been someone else. The dark girl . . . for a second all he could feel was the pain and the loss of being torn from her. Jo's voice passed over him like an unheeded breeze.

A knocking on the door. 'Mum, are you all right?'

'I married a faithless bastard. He can't even fuck me without

49

thinking of some other tart!' She was sobbing as she screamed. Willoby felt like a lion in a cage. His head spun. He needed quiet, to collect his wits.

'Please Jo, it was in my head. I saw someone else —'

She slapped him, hard, her nails ripping the flesh of his cheek.

'Jo— ' warningly.

'Get out, get out of here. *Mad*, is it? going mad, are you? You lying shit! All you want is time off work to see this slut of yours, to shack up with her somewhere.'

Maria was pounding the door. 'Mum! Mum!'

Willoby knew with cold intuition that she wanted in to spectate, to lap it up.

'Jo, listen.'

The alarm clock sailed across the bed and struck him above the eye. He toppled on to the floor, utterly bewildered.

Maria burst in, nightgown streaming.

Willoby staggered drunkenly to his feet with the warm blood sliding down his face, clogging up one eye. He saw his daughter eyeing him. Jo was in sobs on the bed.

'Get fucking *out!*' he yelled at his daughter, one hand trying to cover his slick nakedness. She smiled at him eye to eye, then fled.

'Little bitch!'

Fury and tears contorted Jo's face. 'Don't you dare! Don't you dare call her that, you dirty bastard!'

Something gave way in him. He snarled and back-handed her across the room. Silence fell, heavy as stone.

No – not this.

His wife looked almost puzzled. Then her eyes met his, and the coldness seeped into his belly.

'Jo, are you all right? I'm sorry – I'm so sorry.' His blood intagliated the bedsheets. It was ribboning down over his collarbone.

His wife's face was a white mask. His blow seemed to have knocked the noise out of her.

'Get out,' she whispered. 'Get out of here, now.'

'Jo – no, wait.' He felt the constriction of tears in his throat. He could have shrieked for the unfairness of it.

'Get out of here.' Her voice was as cold as a dawn frost, her eyes black holes in a chalk face. Even in the dim light, he could see the swelling mark where he had struck her.

'Leave me alone.'

He stumbled naked from the room. On the landing, Maria stood watching. Coolly, she looked him up and down, but when she caught his stare her face changed. She bolted into her room. Willoby went down the stairs like a punch-drunk fighter, insanity glowing in his eyes.

'Tallimon,' Merrin asked. 'Tallimon, what is wrong?'

He let the forearm fall from his eyes and saw her dark shadow beside him. The candle had burned to a stub, guttered and gone out.

The air clicked in his throat. It had been so different. The light had been strange, saffron and splintered, and the woman below him had been old and worn, deep lines running from the corners of her nose. He had been able to feel the unresisting flesh of her under him, so unlike Merrin's tautness. The memory made him shudder.

That was him, he thought. I was him for a few moments. Who then was the woman? His wife? His skin crawled. Aimon had been right – they were meddling with monstrous forces here.

'Tallimon?' Softly. A hand brushed his chest.

He felt a stab of fear. What if Aimon is unable to bring this Willoby across – would he then be forever the ghost in my mind?

He shook his head. Madness lay in that line of thought. Better to push Aimon, make him bring the Turnkey over as soon as he could.

He caressed Merrin's rich hair, and smiled at her enquiring eyes. 'I'm all right. It was nothing.'

'You said someone's name.'

'Did I? No matter. It is done with now.' She continued

staring at him. Soon he would have to prepare her for her role,
but he was too tired this night. He pulled her close.

'Come, let's sleep.'

Jo found her husband later, asleep at the kitchen table, wrapped in towels. His head rested on his arms and the blood from his temple was a black bar down the side of his face. He appeared younger in sleep, boyish almost, and her eyes filled with tears; even the one that was swollen shut. She touched it gingerly, and then even more gingerly caressed his thinning hair.

'What's wrong with you?' she whispered.

But her face hardened at the memory of earlier that morning. Willoby had other fish to fry. This talk of insanity . . .

What? A cover-up? Or was it real? Was her husband going mad, or simply covering up for an affair?

The bastard hit me, she thought. He hasn't done that in years – and sober too. She glanced at the thick stripe of blood that lined Willoby's face. I asked for it, maybe.

There had been a bewilderment, a desperation in her husband's face that she could not remember having remarked before. She had seen him hangdog, guilty and shifty, but never so lost.

'It's the bloody job,' she said aloud.

He was awake. He had always been a light sleeper. His eyes peered over his forearm, one half shut by gumming blood. He winced, and straightened.

'Hello, love.' At another time it would have been almost comical to hear the diffidence in the big man's voice. But he still looked like a lost child.

'Is there another woman?' she asked.

He blinked. 'No.'

She nodded thoughtfully. 'You're going to see a doctor, John. Or psychiatrist. Someone who'll sort you out. We can't keep on doing this.'

He agreed heavily. The life seemed to have leached out of him. His arms were as white and heavy as uncooked dough, his fingers puffed around the rings he wore. The boy had vanished, and he was old, unfit, worn out. She could still feel pity for him.

'I'll ring and set an appointment this afternoon,' she said, watching his face fall, the protest stifled. Her pity did not stop her from savouring the moral high ground.

Five

The date was set, the appointment made. Willoby was referred by his doctor to a psychiatrist while Jo sat primly by his side. The doctor had glanced at the dark glasses which almost but not quite hid her bruising, and then at the sticking plaster on Willoby's temple, and had let well enough alone.

They walked the street together afterwards, weaving in and out of weekday morning shoppers. Jo was talking, something about getting him on his feet and having a long talk, getting back to work – the usual crap. He nodded in approximately the right places, following another agenda in his mind. Jo was milking this for all it was worth, he thought. The fact of illness – real illness – had not sunk into her. She was too taken up with its trappings and ramifications. For Willoby, a throwaway comment of the doctor had seeped into his very marrow.

'Sounds a bit like schizophrenic symptoms,' he had murmured, scribbling on his little pad with his flashing fountain pen. The bastard.

Schizophrenia: a fancy word for madness, in Willoby's book. It had other meanings also – unemployment being one of them.

Bastard, bastard, bastard.

Not one of them gave a damn. Jo just wanted to be certain he wasn't screwing someone else. Maria would smirk if she knew her dad was a nutter – as she had smirked at Willoby's nakedness, after the fight. That little madam needed a lesson taught. And work. Once they found out he was being treated for a psychiatric disorder, they'd drop him like a hot potato, pension him off as another casualty of the stress of the job.

'Are you all right, dear?' Jo asked him. *Dear*. She was so charmingly solicitous now she knew she had him by the balls.

54

'In the pink, dear.'

The shopping crowds irritated him. He was taking big steps and small ones, shuffling through the crowds, checking his stride to keep pace with his wife.

Momentarily, a vision came to him of mountains and hills, the shining expanse of a huge river. He could smell wood-smoke and horses. Then it was gone. A second only, but it had made the cold sweat prick out all over him.

I could murder a pint.

His dry throat cried out for a drink. Jo was gravitating towards some shop windows. She had taken the morning off to see him safe and sound to the doctor's door. It was, he guessed, a minor holiday for her.

'Want to do some shopping?' he asked her.

'I wouldn't mind. I've no money, though. We ought to be getting home, John.'

Sweat was trickling down the small of his back. The crowds jostled him, and the traffic noise crawled up the walls. The street seemed suddenly to have narrowed and the sky was an impossibly long way off, hedged in by overhanging buildings. It reminded him of somewhere else, some other time.

Christ.

He jammed a thick hand into his pocket, pulled out some crumpled notes.

'Here, take these – do some shopping. Buy something.'

Her face lit up and remained distrustful at the same time.

'We can't really afford— '

'Please Jo, a treat, on me. I'll wait for you, meet you somewhere.'

She thought he was trying to make amends. Well, let her – it didn't matter. What mattered was to get away from the crowd and the noise.

At last she went, promising to meet him later. He plunged into the crowd like a swimmer taking to a mill-race. His size made it easier to forge through, and resentful looks at his rough passage twitched away when they saw the expression on his face.

At last he got a door closed behind him, and was in a dark, cool pub. An old man's place, it lacked jukebox and gaming machines. He leant his forearms on the bar and bent his head as though he had just finished a sprint. It felt like it. He fumbled for his cigarettes and ordered a beer with a Scotch to chase it down.

Schizophrenia. That was great, just great.

'You never had much luck, Will, but this takes the cake.' And he chuckled, the sound turning into a racking cough. A few old eyes stared at him curiously, the florid-faced giant at the bar standing talking to himself. But they soon wandered away again.

Those . . . visions he had been having. The girl's face, that memory of being young – of being someone else in some other time. So that was madness. He shook his head and laughed harshly. A pity; it had had its points.

Merrin. Yes, that had been the name. His throat tightened at the memory and he swallowed raw Scotch to loosen it.

If I went there, to that place – if I was in the vision, would that be the end? Would I really be drooling in some cell somewhere, and all of it in my head?'

And would that be so bad?

The thought chilled him. It seemed unlucky, or prophetic perhaps.

Got to keep a fucking lid on this, or I'm finished. I'd lose everything.

He ordered another Scotch. Already he had a hazy intention of staying here and drinking away the afternoon. Alcoholic agoraphobia he and Howard had labelled it; fear of wide open spaces without a bar. He smiled at the memory of past drinking sessions – stag nights, Saturday nights, or nights when they had both wanted to blot out some lurid incident from the prison.

There had been suicides, over the years, quite a few of them. Willoby remembered the dangling body of one, the protruding tongue and the smell of shit. Or the young lad who had slashed his wrists with a broken glass because a pair of older prisoners had raped him. Willoby wrinkled up his nose. There had to be a better way.

More whisky. The barman was beginning to look askance at the big, silent man with the closed face. Willoby knew the signs. He had been thrown out of more pubs than he could remember, mostly when he had been in the army. There had been glorious fights in those days, mainly against rival regiments. The locals had hated them, while needing their custom. Squaddies; the scum of the earth until they went to war, when they became Britain's finest.

And then he remembered what he had been thinking of, what the narrow streets brought from his memory. He remembered way back, to a morning in Aden long ago . . .

A hot, still morning. The transport had fucked up again and so here they were, though the op had been meant to start just before dawn. Bloody great. The town was already coming alive. The streets would be hiving with activity soon, and they'd never get through. Impossible to do a cordon and search when the bazaars had started.

White light, glare, reflected heat that hurt his eyes. He could feel the sun seeping up from the very ground through the soles of his boots. The webbing straps were soaking his shoulders. He could see the uniforms of the other lads darkening with sweat. Fucking desert. Fucking Arabs.

The order came to move. They were going in on foot, at the double. The men bitched and moaned, hitching up their kit and shouldering their SLRs.

'With a magazine of twenty rounds, *load*!'

A volley of metallic snaps as the magazines were slotted home.

'Make ready!'

The satisfying double clicks down the line as the weapons were cocked.

'Safeties on. Follow me.'

The officer set off at a jog, the platoon trundling along behind him. Fresh out of bloody Sandhurst, keen as mustard and totally bloody useless. Willoby could see that the back of his neck was red and peeling.

They laboured on through the narrow streets, grubby boys calling out at them derisively, dark men in robes eyeing them from shut faces. Willoby became uneasy. They were running along here like a bunch of blind chickens. He hated the blank streets, the white walls blaring with heat, the sky so far away above them.

'Good-spot-for-a-fucking-ambush,' he grated out to his corporal. The man rolled his eyes. 'Donkey's leading lions, Will.'

They slowed down to a march, the men breathing like winded horses, rifles hanging by their straps when they should have had them in the shoulder.

Then it happened. There was a crack, sharp and loud between the echoing walls, and the platoon commander seemed to jerk backwards and fall. There was blood, shockingly scarlet in the pale dust and sun-bleached dirt.

'Jesus Christ! Take cover!'

More cracks. Figures moving along the rooftops.

'Ambush! Take cover and return fire!'

But there was nowhere to go. Men raised their rifles and fired. Suddenly the little street was deafeningly loud, and Willoby's ears were ringing. He felt no fear, only a kind of heightened awareness, as though the blood thrilling through him were coursing in quick time. He fired the SLR, feeling the heavy thump of the recoil knock his shoulder back. Men were beating down doors to get into the houses and under cover. A soldier in front of Willoby tripped and fell on his face, and did not rise. There was a hole the size of a fist in his back.

Shouting, screaming, the ear-aching rifle fire. They seemed to be in a bright, dust-choked oven, and were milling about like cattle. The platoon sergeant was wounded, someone said. Still Willoby was not afraid. He was firing calmly at the flickering shapes above, watching where his bullets ripped chunks of whitewashed masonry.

'Keep their fucking heads down! Win the firefight. Come on,

you bastards!' It was his own voice, hoarse and furious, almost unrecognizable. The volume of fire increased. Willoby changed his spent magazine. He saw a corporal firing from a doorway.

'Get in the house! Get up on to the roof!' The corporal disappeared.

I can do this, he thought. *I'm good at this.* He began shouting fire control orders, just as they'd been taught in the lectures.

I love it, by God.

Without warning, everything changed.

The horse bucked and circled under him and he jerked savagely on the reins. 'Wolves!' someone shouted, but they were not wolves. He slid his sword out of the saddle scabbard. The other riders milled round him, horses shrieking. There was a musk in the air, a gagging potency. It came from the encircling pack.

They were the size of boars, grey as granite, with long, hairless tails. Great rough crests of fur ran along their backs. Their feet were clawed, and they had yellow tusks curving out of their maws. They screeched like rabbits caught in a trap, a high squealing that hurt his ears.

'On me!' he yelled. 'Ride through them — break through!' And he kicked his terrified mount from a stand into a gallop.

They rushed him. His horse trampled on one and he saw its pale underside as it rolled over. Another leapt for his bridle arm but he kicked it away with his left foot. A third made for the horse's belly but a swing of the longsword broke open its skull.

The rest of the squadron were thundering behind him, lances levelled. He cursed the luck that had made him take only a sword on this patrol.

'Form line! Form line on me!'

The horses laboured abreast in the familiar tactic. The fifty-man Rimon formed two successive lines. They had slowed to a canter. He could see blood on the lances; on the horses also, but so far there were no empty saddles.

The pack had retreated. The squadron was between the horns of a crescent, perhaps three or four hundred of the beasts, and the pack was uphill of them.

'Left wheel!' he shouted, jabbing with his sword. Best to hit a flank and break out rather than be encircled by them.

The line grew ragged as the riders changed direction. He had a glimpse of a livid, snarling mass to his front, and then the line struck home.

They destroyed scores in the first onslaught, the lances dipping and coming up again and again, ribboned with streamers of gore. But there were riders down now, the beasts hauling them from the saddle and engulfing them. They were losing speed.

He hacked frenziedly to right and left, felt the stallion rear under him to brain an opponent, kick out at others to the rear. A rip opened like magic on his steed's neck, and then the beast was underneath, going for the vitals. He slewed the horse round, collided with another rider, stabbed at a raging animal face and felt the jar of impact numb his fingers. The charge had been halted by sheer bodyweight.

We're losing, he had time to realize. There was no fear at the thought, only anger, frustration. There would never be a city called Tallisker on the hill beside the river.

'Break through! Keep moving!' If they halted for long they would be massacred.

The line seemed to shudder. There were riderless horses aplenty, but the beasts were still attacking the men. It must be now. They could still get through.

Knots of warriors were forging ahead, most using their longswords. In one and twos, threes and fours they drove wedges in the enemy mass, the blades creating nightmare shimmers of steel and flesh all around them. The horses' terror lent them new strength. They bowled through the beasts by main force, riding them down.

– And were through, at the hilltop beyond. He raised his sword.

'Rally on me – on me!'

'Gather on the Rimarch,' someone shouted, and they were struggling through the press towards him. Some horses carried two riders. Other men were trailed along by the stirrups, running at the horses' sides. The pack was slaughtering those in the bowl below.

'What *are* they?' his second-in-command, a grizzled veteran of a dozen battles asked, clearly shocked by the carnage in the bowl.

What, indeed? Aimon had been right – they did not possess this world merely by virtue of riding through it.

The pack was reforming. There was no one left alive on the slope below. He glanced round at the survivors. Half his men had died down there. He set his teeth as he saw the grey hordes start up the hill towards them. No funeral for what was left of those warriors; no high pyre to send their souls skywards.

'Here they come again,' someone said. The voice shook. Tallimon made his features into a mask. He must grip them, hold them together.

'Collect yourselves! You are Kristillic horse-soldiers, not peasant rabble!' he barked. He looked down into the bowl. The beasts were mindless. Perhaps nine score of them had been killed, and still the rest were bent on pursuit.

'This land has its own rules, it seems.' He shook his head. His entire being cried out to run away, to gallop from the approaching beasts, but he held in his frantic mount a moment, let the men see he was in control of himself.

'Retreat – back to the river. Godorin, I will take your Pennon in rearguard. The rest of you double up if you have no horse. We can do no more here.' They spun round their mounts as one, and began beating their flagging horses along.

He looked at the rearguard Pennon – eight men with round eyes under their helms – and forced himself to smile.

'For us, there is a little more fighting to do.'

He hardly had time to make his dispositions before the pack was on them again, and the savagery of the running fight had begun.

*

Willoby reeled and cried out. They were on him – he was down among them. He lashed out with fists and feet and felt them connect. Someone grunted with pain. There was a crash of breaking glass, a woman yelping in fear.

They were holding him down. There was a circle of faces thrust into his own. He struggled, but they had him firmly pinioned. Confusion flooded his mind. He blinked.

'Godorin?' Have they drawn off? Am I wounded?' But the words came out as odd-sounding and weird.

'Easy, son, it's all right . . . It's over.'

'Will I phone for an ambulance?' a voice asked.

'No, I think he's OK. It's over.'

'What the fuck?' Willoby asked.

'It's all right, mate. You went into a sort of trance, and came out of it kicking and shouting stuff. But you're fine now.' It was the barman. Willoby was on the floor of the pub with a knot of customers gathered round him. To one side a table had been overturned. Other people stood watching and whispering, their drinks forgotten in their hands.

It came back to him. He felt himself slipping into his own mind once more. He sat up. 'I'm all right. It's OK.' He dropped the stub of the glass that was clenched in one fist, grimacing. The barman helped him to his feet.

'You're sure? You gave us a fright there – standing so still and then falling over like that.'

'You gave me a right thump on the head,' someone else said, smiling.

'Get the man a drink, Jeff. A brandy will set him up.'

Willoby allowed himself to be set in a chair and another glass was put into his hand. He drank down the fiery stuff and his head seemed to solidify somewhat.

'Epilepsy is it?' an old man asked gently.

Not knowing what else to do, he nodded. Some of the customers nodded with him, happy that their suspicions were justified.

'My brother had it,' the old man confided. 'Did for him in the end.' Then he sank his pint in embarrassment.

'I have to go,' Willoby said, and pushed himself to his feet. He could not stand their concern. He was not used to sympathy.

'Are you sure?'

'Will you be OK?'

He waved away their words and staggered out on to the street. He needed air.

Mad. I'm going mad. That's what it's about.

He swung off into the shopping crowds, looking for an empty place, somewhere he could lie with his back on grass and let his whirling mind stop its careering.

Did I die? he couldn't help wondering. Was that me? Did the beasts kill them all? But that was phantasm, a picture from some shadowed corner of a tormented mind. The street and the scurrying people were all that was real.

Days passed in a forgettable blur. He did not tell Jo about the episode in the pub; he was still chewing over it himself. He remained at home, though there was an inchoate longing in him for the isolation of the moors, the high fells with their solitude and horizons. To disappear again would be to court disaster, however. It seemed that he and his wife had signed a shaky truce; she would not voice her suspicions and mistrusts so long as he remained within sight and sound and ready to do her bidding. He became therefore the family shopper, chauffeur and handyman. It was a new experience for him and one he did not relish in the least, but if he needed a prod to keep him on the tracks he needed only to look at the bruise on his wife's cheek, fading to yellow now and not so easy to discern through the layers of make-up. It would not have been so hard were he not able to sense that Jo was enjoying her newfound power. She had always been able to pressurize him into doing her bidding, but it had never been so easy.

He found himself missing work, also. The days seemed purposeless and crammed with too many hours. He felt continually that he should be going somewhere, doing something. There was an odd guilt at not driving out to the prison every morning. He realized that the job had given him moral stature. He had come home after work and felt justified in sitting down in front of the telly and waiting for his tea. There had been days when he was virtually incapable of doing anything else, and he had dozed off over his egg and chips. He hated this sensation of drifting; it gave him too much time to think, and made him feel vulnerable. He had a conviction that the more he thought about his condition the worse it would get, whereas if he simply plunged back into the old routine it would fade away. The forthcoming visit to the psychiatric specialist terrified him especially: it was making his sickness *official*. Once that stage was reached it could never be argued away or ignored again, and he would bear it with him, in the form of files or records, for the rest of his life.

And Jo did not see that. She did not care. As for Maria – well, his daughter was a creature from another world, which spoke a different language. Willoby found it difficult to manage even breakfast-table civilities with her. He could not forget the way she had looked at him when he and Jo had argued. It had chilled him to the bone. He knew he and his daughter hated each other – it had become a fact of life – but he would have felt easier if he could have put a finger on the point where it had begun, found a concrete reason behind it. That he could not, that the dislike was motiveless, disturbed him more.

It's going down the toilet at a rate of knots, he told himself; fucking unravelling like a badly made cardigan. His own simile made him crack a grin. He was standing at the kitchen sink doing the breakfast dishes, but was staring at his stilled hands in the soapy water whilst drizzle beat at the window beside him.

Unless it isn't madness. Unless it's real somehow.

He went on washing. That idea was almost worse than its alternative.

Maybe it's a sign I'm really losing it – the fact that I'm beginning to believe in it.

The grin again, not so wide this time.

There are mountains in that land, and hills that roll on for ever to the edge of sight. It is spring there, and no one wanders the slopes but the wild things.

He shut his eyes, fists clenched in the dishwater. A wholly unexpected grief had him by the throat, and he bowed his head whilst the rain tap-tap-tapped on the glass beside him and the dim roar of the traffic howled on in the street beyond.

I wish it was *real. I wish I could go there, and leave this shit behind. If I could, I wouldn't mind being mad.*

That girl's face in his mind. But overriding it came the memory of the battle, the horror of the misshapen beasts that sought to tear him from his saddle, the screams of the men who fell, the shrieks of the maimed horses. It made the hair rise on the back of his neck. *Not all roses, then, in that place. It had its horrors too.*

He looked out of the window. Though mid-morning, the air had a blue quality to it, a gloom intensified by the clinging rain. Rows of car lights trickled down the street like some torchlit procession, and people were struggling along the pavements, hunched against the rain and jostling one another.

I have two more mornings like this before the appointment. And then – what? Off to a funny farm to crayon the walls?

Jo wants that, he thought unwillingly. *She'd be happy enough with that. Me out of the way and the invalidity coming in. The odd visit at weekends, maybe.*

He shook his head. *Get a grip, Willoby. She's still your wife.*

She could sign forms, have me locked away as dangerous. He could see it now. '*He beats me, your honour, he's violent, he has these fits – he sees things. And he hates my daughter.*'

Face it, Will; you're no model hubby.

He brought his fists crashing down into the sink to send up a fountain of water. Crockery shattered under his hands and he felt the sharp edges slice his flesh.

'Fucking bitch!'

Dishwater dripped from his eyebrows and puddled the floor. He looked at the scarlet spread through the water in bewilderment, and jerked away.

'I need a drink.'

He dripped his way to the living room cabinet and poured himself a generous whisky. His blood smeared the outside of the glass as he tilted it to his mouth, and he could taste the coppery tang underneath the bite of the raw spirit. But the eye-watering glow steadied him. He looked at his lacerated palms and sighed deeply. Oh, bravo. Well done, that man. What better way to prove you're not loopy?

'Arsehole,' he said savagely. He felt that some internal barometer was swinging wildly awry, his emotions see-sawing like a manic rocking horse. The feeling angered him further. He wrenched off his apron and threw it to the carpet, flumped down in an armchair.

Dishes is it? Who the fuck does she think I am — Fanny bloody Craddock?

That damned girl's face again, looking at him as he moved inside her. Christ, she had been pretty. Fine-boned, like Jo in the beginning, and dark as well. He remembered the firm grip of her thighs about his waist . . .

'Ah, shit.' He downed more of the whisky, ignoring the blood that oozed from his palms.

Where was she now? In a castle somewhere with her ladies about her? No, it had not been a castle. It had for all the world been like a . . . tent, a leather tent lit by candles, and the floor had been beaten earth.

He paused, struggling to remember. They had lain on furs — he remembered the soft prickle under his forearms — and she had called him *Tallimon*.

A method in my madness, then? This name — it keeps coming up.

'What in the name of God do you want with me?' he murmured aloud. He closed his eyes, tired of frowning.

'*To kill.*'

'Yeah, right. Make a murderer out of me, why don't you?'

'*The deed is greater than murder. You are to kill a king.*'

You've whacked out this time, Willoby. They're in the living room now. But he did not open his eyes.

'Why?'

'*To preserve the life of my liege lord, and to render him his rightful inheritance.*'

'Of course; should have known – how ignorant of me.' Enough of this crap. He opened his eyes.

The old man was there. He seemed ancient, but stood as straight as an arrow, and though he carried a stick he did not lean on it. A thick white beard jutted out from his chin like a chalk cliff facing the sea, and a shock of white hair sprang up on his head. His face was ruddy, youthful despite the white hairs, and his eyes were as grey as storm cloud under thick brows. The mouth was smiling under a harsh beak of a nose, the upper lip hidden by the snowy moustache. The old man wore shapeless robes of wool, but a long knife hung from a leather belt at his hip. He raised one white brow quizzically.

'Fuck me pink,' said Willoby, and dropped his glass.

'I am Aimon, mage at the court of King Courberall and vassal of Prince Tallimon, his eldest son. Greetings and good health.'

Willoby remained seated, his mouth wide open.

More hallucinations. But the man seemed so *real*, his feet in their scuffed boots planted fair and square on the carpet Jo had had him buy on their fifteenth wedding anniversary. He smelt of the rough wool – a greasy odour – and a hint of woodsmoke beneath it. There was even mud on his boots, damnit.

'What the hell is this?' Willoby asked. His voice rasped like a saw.

'I cannot stay long. It is hard labour, keeping the door open, but I cannot be sure of getting back if I let it shut behind me. Listen well, Turnkey. I come from a place that needs you. You are required to perform this service, and when we are ready you will be brought there, to the land beneath the mountains. My Prince' – his mouth was crooked with humour – 'demands it of me that I bring you there. Hitherto we have been able only to watch you and you us, for I have forged a link between your mind and that of my lord's. But now I have the ability to send living flesh from our world to yours and, with luck, in the

67

other direction also, else I am stuck here.' Again, the wry smile. 'Prepare yourself, my friend. Gird your mind against insanity. These things are real I speak of, not figments of your dreams.'

Willoby began to laugh.

'What is the joke, friend?'

'You. Jesus, you pop up in here like Gandalf's dad and start giving me this crap about other worlds and shit. Who in the hell put you up to this? Was it Jo, or is it some practical joke from those buggers at the prison?'

The old man seemed to stiffen. He was suddenly taller, and his eyes glinted. 'This is no joke. The lives of thousands are in the balance here. If I am successful then you will hold us all in the palm of your hand. Your own prowess could mean the difference between a bloodless exchange of power and civil war. Do not mock me, Turnkey. You have no idea of the enormity of the thing you are embroiled in. You are like my master in that, at least.'

Willoby stood up. Tall though the old man was, he was taller, topping him by half a head.

'I don't know who you are, mate, but I think you should go now. I have enough problems of my own without some ancient mariner offloading his fantasies on me. I'll see you politely to the door, and if you cause me any problem it'll be my toe that sends you through it. Savvy?'

'You have been warned, Turnkey. I have done my best to prepare you—'

'Out.' He took hold of the wool-wrapped arm.

– And found the point of the old man's knife under his chin, pushing against the skin with enough force to make his eyes water.

Oh shit, thought Willoby. A psycho.

'Remember my words, my friend, and prepare yourself for what is to come.' There was sweat on the old man's forehead, and his pupils were mere pinpoints. He looked almost feverish with strain, all his earlier composure evaporated.

But Willoby was not a prison warder for nothing. He had lost count of the number of times a blade had been pulled on him. His bulk moved with startling grace, and he flipped the knife from between his attacker's fingers.

'Now, you bugger— '

But there was a swirl of woollen robes – that sheepskin smell – and the old man had twisted out of his grasp –

– And disappeared. Willoby was alone in the room.

'What the— ?'

Muddy footprints on the carpet, and a bright-bladed knife with a worn handle lying there, abandoned.

'God Almighty!'

He rushed round the room, out into the hall, the kitchen. Nothing.

'Christ! Houdini isn't in it.' A fast mover. He had dodged away, sped through the door . . .

He *disappeared*, Willoby. He vanished into thin bloody air. Willoby bent and touched the mud on the carpet. Moist. What place had it come from, what weird world far away?

And the knife. He peered at it, saw the swirl of pattern-welding on the razor-like blade, the yellow bone of the grip. He picked it up. It was cold, heavy.

Real.

Six

It took them three days to fight their way back to the river and the city site. By that time there were less than a score of them still fit to lift lance. Most of them were on foot; the surviving horses bore the wounded. They were met by one of the outer patrols. Tallimon left his men in the care of the leech at the Outpost, commandeered a fresh horse and rode on with two companions to the tented city. Men looked at his face and did not dare ask him for tidings.

Tallimon would have liked to talk to Aimon, to simmer down, but he was not in his quarters so he went on to the hall where his father would be waiting for news of the patrol.

Had he known? That was the question. Tallimon's patrol had not been the first to go so far south, but no one else had sent back reports of murderous beasts in the hills. *Grypesh* his men were already calling them; wolfswine. They had seemed more like great rodents. Their hostility was unarguable, however. Tallimon had never encountered such implacable savagery, not even in the forests beyond the mountains. And the beasts had operated like a warband of intelligent foes.

Courberall the High King was surrounded by a coterie of his veterans when his bastard offspring entered the Great Hall. There was little ceremony among the Kristill. Tallimon bowed slightly to his father, as always, somewhat chilled by the unwavering stare of the King's one good eye. A flint spearpoint had taken out its fellow many years in the past. It had become a legend of sorts among the people, how the King saw more with his one remaining eye than most men did with two.

The flames of the firepit turned the lower portion of the hall into a vast red and yellow flicker, the walls looming into darkness high above. It was warm and close after the keen air of the hills, and sweat pricked out in the small of Tallimon's back. He was proudly conscious of the blood dried black on his tattered clothing. Soon the weariness would hit him, but for now he felt as poised as a bent bow.

'We've heard,' Courberall said curtly. 'Take a seat.' And he clapped his huge hands and called for heather beer and bread.

'News travels fast,' Tallimon responded, sinking on to a bench below the dais. Some of the tensions left him.

'Bad news, yes. What were your casualties?'

'Twenty-eight slain, and four others not likely to last longer than this moon.'

'And the enemy?' Courberall spoke as though they were rational, organized.

'We slew maybe ten score of them – half their number almost – but it made no difference. They only gave up the pursuit when we came in sight of the Great River.'

'The Courbering,' one of the veterans corrected him.

Tallimon smiled.

The King stood up and jumped off the dais with the lithe energy of a younger man. Attendants brought in food and beer, and he poured a flagon for Tallimon himself, then stood staring into the firepit with his arms folded and his chin on his chest. The flames underlit his thick beard and craggy profile.

'Other patrols have encountered these things, but from afar only and the beasts did not approach. But this was a large pack that attacked your Rimon . . . Can it mean, I wonder, that they are marshalling themselves in defence, that they recognize our presence?'

'Sire, they are mere beasts,' a man protested.

'Intelligent beasts, it seems. Once we start establishing the outlying fiefs and estates they will have to be dealt with.'

'We know so little about this land, this green world,' Haubedec, the King's counsellor, said. 'We have been riding across it and building over it as though it were already ours.'

'Who shall gainsay us?' Fferidan, a friend of Madavar the King's son, asked angrily. Tallimon looked at him with irritation. What was such a stripling doing among the King's companions?

'Did you provoke them?' Courberall asked Tallimon.

'Only if riding across the hills is provocation. They did not attack us out of hunger. None of them was lean enough for it, and there is game aplenty in the hills. It was . . . hatred, mindless loathing.'

'New rules,' Haubedec said thoughtfully. He sounded like Aimon, only older. As he bent over the firepit rubbing his skeletal, liver-spotted hands, it was hard to believe that he had been a great general in his youth, the mentor and patron of Courberall himself.

'What are you mumbling about?' Fferidan demanded.

'Quiet, whelp!' the High King roared. 'Haubedec was leading armies when your father was a tottering brat and you not even a thought at the back of his mind.'

Fferidan went white, and subsided.

'We must live differently here, I'm thinking,' Haubedec went on as if used to such interruptions. 'It was said, back in the Wildwood, that the ruins which littered the forests were once cities, the proud citadels of a warrior race now long turned to dust. The trees swallowed them, the roots overturning the foundations of the mightiest walls, and the men within reverted to savagery, becoming the degenerates whom we conquered before the Great Trek.'

'Degenerate or not, they pushed us out of the Wildwood,' one of the veterans muttered. Courberall fixed him with a cyclopean stare.

'What I am saying,' Haubedec continued with a touch of petulance, 'is that they did not change. They stayed in their cities until the cities were no more, and the savages were pouring over the ruined walls. They were destroyed, or absorbed if you will, because they did not adapt.'

'Yes!' said Tallimon.

'What are you saying, Haubedec?' the King asked.

'That we also must adapt, my King. We are used to roaming free, to living in scattered settlements, pitching our tents where we will and moving on when we will. But it may be that in this land we must live differently.'

'It's a wide, rich land – room enough for all and to spare. Why should we not wander it at will?' Fferidan asked indignantly. This time the King did not silence him. He was watching Haubedec intently, his eye a small refracted inferno from the flames of the firepit.

'Ask Tallimon and the survivors of his Rimon why we should not,' said Haubedec.

'Are we to hide behind walls, then, like men under siege – merely because of one skirmish?' the King asked.

'Think, my lord – think of the things we have encountered since first we left the northern woods. Giants of rime and ice; stunted men who live in caves and are mightier than our greatest fighters. These *wolfswine* are deadlier than wolves or boars. And we have only just begun to explore this place. It may not be enough to trust in our sword arms alone any more, and our tented cities may not be a firm enough defence.'

'We have Courbisker, this great citadel that is a-building as we speak.'

'Aye, but not everyone will or can live in this one place. I'm thinking we need roads, walls, strong places all over the land.'

'You read a lot into this one incident, Haubedec,' the King told him quietly.

'He's right,' Tallimon burst out, flushed with beer and firelight.

'Be still!' Courberall barked.

'We cannot live here the way we lived in the Wildwood. Already families are splitting off from the Host and striking out into the hills by themselves. They think they can return to the nomad's life they lived before. The Host will scatter if we do not hold it together, and then there will be . . . there will be no ruling them.'

Courberall looked down at his son. With the fire behind him, he was nothing but a vast, flame-limned shadow.

'It was to hold them together that I began the building of Courbisker.'

73

'Aye, and look how grand you have made it. The Great Hall a timbered barn as crude as the longhouses of the forest tribes. The walls dry stone piled upon dry stone and the buildings within them naught but the leather roofs of our tents. Where are the streets, the squares, the straight walls that the Lost Race used in the ruined cities of the Wildwood?'

'Much good it did them,' Fferidan said. He was looking at Tallimon with fervent dislike.

'It is different here. We have open country, we have good stone from the guts of the hills, and we have the river. Why not build boats and follow it south? Why not fish from it – and why not grow crops here, in the river valley. The soil is thick and good.'

They drowned him out with laughter. 'Crops! Fishing!' Courberall spluttered. 'Would you turn us into farmers, hewers of wood and haulers of water? What's got into you, boy?'

'We cannot hunt the wild things for ever,' Tallimon said through gritted teeth. 'There is a host of us here greater than any people yet seen in the world. We will strip the land bare of game in months.'

'Which is why we must split up, the clans going their separate ways, each to seek out their own hunting grounds,' Fferidan said.

'No! That way we will cease to be a people. We will become like the savages in the Wildwood. And these new beasts that roam this land will decimate the scattered clans.'

'The boy speaks like one mazed,' a veteran said.

'It is the fight. His wits are awry.'

'A skirmish will do that upon a time. Turning your rump to the enemy is apt to addle your brains for a while afterward,' Fferidan said. There was another gale of laughter.

Tallimon leapt up and seized Fferidan by the throat. He sank his fingers into the other man's flesh and saw his eyes bulge. He had found the tube of the windpipe and was about to crush it when a tremendous buffet on the side of the head knocked him sprawling.

'Enough! Would you brawl in the very presence of your King?' Courberall's fist was still clenched from the blow and his thunderous brows were meeting in the middle.

'King!' Tallimon cried, getting up. 'King is it? What are you but the war chief of a bickering tribe of savages, and this city of yours nothing but the hill fort of a bandit leader. There is more to being a king.'

'And you would know, would you, boy?' Courberall asked with perilous softness. 'Would you care to know what it is like to be a king? Is that the prize you strive for?'

He had said too much. It was the beer, and the smouldering anger at the slaughter of his men; they had been mixed into a deadly cocktail of resentful fury.

Tallimon bent close to Fferidan's face, ignoring his father.

'I will see you about the camp, and we will settle this matter.'

Then he turned on his heel and started off down the shadowed length of the hall.

'Tallimon, you will come back here!' his father shouted. 'You will make peace with Fferidan in my presence or I'll see you rue it. There will be no feud in this city while I am King!'

'While you are King,' Tallimon whispered, and continued down the hall until the doormen swung open the gate-like portals at the end, and the night air was filling his lungs like brisk wine.

He strode down the steep slope of the citadel site to the camp proper where the soldiers and the builders had their tents. It was quieter here than usual; word of the disaster must have got round. What women that were here would begin their mourning soon – but there would be no bodies to wail over. The thought sickened him a little. In his own way, he loved his men – as another man might love a fine horse or a faithful hound, perhaps.

I have sped things up, he thought. It is wearing too thin too quickly. The pretence cannot be carried on much longer. And that puppy Fferidan is the shadow of my half-brother Madavar. I am picking my feuds perilously close to the Royal Clan.

It must be done soon, if it is to happen at all.

Knots of men were clustered over the billowing campfires, the flames casting their shadows hugely on the walls of the tents behind them. They spoke to him as he passed, nodded or saluted. All of them knew Courberall's bastard son; the best warleader in the Host. He talked to them now, acknowledging their greetings, thanking them for their support. Before he had gone half a mile toward the outer wall he had taken the forearms of half a hundred men in the warrior's grip, men of all the clans. Members of the Haubedai – Haubedec's own clan – the Quirinir, the Arbolai, the Ordachai. But not one member of his own clan – the Royal Clan of the Courberans, the King's clan. They knew which way the wind blew.

He found his own tent at last. The black mood had fallen from him like a discarded cloak, and he was elevated, exulting. He had the men. The soldiers loved him – always had. Courberall had been a great leader in his day, but he had lost the common touch. His son had inherited his skill with men, and more.

I can do it, Tallimon thought as his page lit the candles and turned back the furs on the low cot.

I can carry them with me. It is only the Courberans I will have to fight.

'Send the mage Aimon and the lady Merrin to me at once,' he told the page.

The boy hesitated. 'Sire, it is late—'

'At once, I said.' Seeing the boy's face, he smiled. 'Go to it. If they argue, I will take the blame.'

It was like offering a morsel to a starving dog. The boy scurried off on his errand.

'Thus are loyalties won,' Tallimon said, lying back on the cot. He laughed quietly at the leather roof of the tent.

Merrin found him lying and staring fixedly into space when she reached the tent a quarter-hour later. She stood watching him from just beyond the open entrance flap for a few minutes, while the candlelight spilled out into the blue spring night around her. There was a glitter in his eyes, a set to his jaw that she did not like. When he was loving, he was as kind and eager as a child, but there were other times when she would have as soon shared her bed with a beautifully patterned snake. He wanted love, affection, loyalty so much, and when it was given without stint he never failed to return it. But be niggardly in one's devotion just once and he never forgot it. Merrin loved him, or thought she did perhaps. It mattered little; he owned her, as she had always been owned since she had been a grubby savage child pawing at the body of her dead mother in the smoking ruins of her village. The Kristill had seemed like terrible gods then, iron-clad men on tall horses with the pennons whipping from their lances. They had speared and ridden down the men of the Boar-clan who had been her kin, and one black-bearded giant had swept her up from her mother's corpse so she could stare in horror at his empty eye socket. He had taken her that night, after she had been washed, and she had wanted only to die. But in time she had grown used to it, and even enjoyed it now and then. Then Courberall had given her to his son. Tallimon, the bastard prince. She had expected him to be rough, violent even – one heard things in the women's quarters. But he had been gentle, and had set her up as a lady with servants of her own. And none of the noblewomen dared say anything about the King's drab who now wore finer linen than they, and amber beads about her throat. It was rumoured that Courberall was hugely amused; certainly, he always greeted her with extravagant courtesy. He was a man easily moved to laughter, was Courberall. She found herself still with a corner of liking for him in her heart. Only his son never amused him. And Tallimon? She thought she had seen him laugh – truly laugh – perhaps thrice in her time with him.

She entered the tent, and his eyes swung to her at once. Tonight there was no softening in them at the sight of her. He looked like a man exhilarated. He sprang off the cot as smoothly as a mountain puma.

'Where is Aimon?'

'No one knows. He is not in his tent, and his servants have

not seen him all day. I pressed them, and they said he had been . . . conducting magic.'

Tallimon's face lit up further. He was as bright-eyed as a fever patient. She felt that if she touched him her fingers would be burnt by his heat.

'Magic? Well and good.' He stood in thought. 'He is trying to bring him across, perhaps. I wanted it done before the patrol but he dared not. Now he remedies it. Good!' He seemed to have forgotten her, and turned to pour himself barley spirit from a jug. She mastered the momentary irritation. He was with his other mistress at the moment: that old whore ambition. She would have to wait.

He sat on the cot cradling his cup, and stared at her, detached and appraising as a stranger. She moved to join him.

'No. Stay there. Stay standing.'

One eyebrow quirking upwards, she did as she was bidden, but her heart had given a lurch. He was too detached, too clinical. Whatever he had wanted her for tonight, it was not for loving. She pulled the long cloak tighter about her; the air from the open tent flap behind was raw with the cold from the mountains.

'Undress.'

She hesitated. There was no passion in him. He might be studying a horse at the fair.

'Tallimon—'

'Do as I say.'

She let the cloak slide to the ground like dark water, then undid the lacings of the robe at her throat. In moments she stood naked before him, the cold night at her back raising her skin into gooseflesh. She stifled a shiver.

He is going to sell me, or give me away, she thought. And the black bitterness began to well from some long-forgotten spring inside her.

'You are beautiful, Merrin. Perfect.' His voice had thickened. He sounded almost as though he were grieving.

He stood and approached her. She backed away in spite of herself but he grasped her by the upper arms.

'Cold. You're cold.' And he hugged her to him with sudden roughness. She did not melt into his arms, but remained tense, stiff. Something was wrong here.

He kissed her, hard, his teeth pressing against her lips. His fingers sank into her buttocks and pulled her closer.

'You're mine, Merrin. I can do anything I want with you.'

She tried to push him away. It was true, then. He was letting her go to some other master, and this was their final fling.

He swung her round so that her hair spun in a raven circle. She was tumbled to the cot and he was on top of her.

So it came to this. The dressing her up and making her a lady —it had meant nothing. He had given her pride knowing he could take it away whenever he wished.

He pushed into her, hurting her in his roughness, but she did not make a sound, only glared at him with wide, dry eyes.

When he had finished he rolled away and sat on the edge of the cot with his elbows on his knees, his head hanging down. She did not move.

'I have a thing for you to do, Merrin. There is a man — Aimon is to bring him to me soon. He will be a stranger to us, to our world, but he has seen you. And feels something for you, I think. You must . . . be good to him. You must make him believe you love him. It is important, Merrin.'

She found her voice, and fought to keep the pain and bewilderment out of it. 'Why should I?'

'I will free you, once it is done, and you will be a lady in truth. I will give you a household, and retainers.'

'Only the King can do such a thing.'

'I know.' And he looked at her at last. She had never seen Tallimon weep, but she knew he was close to it now.

'What are you doing, Tallimon? Why did you do this tonight?' Her voice, usually low, musical, sounded as harsh as a crow's in her ears.

He smiled then, and the expression sent a chill down her backbone.

'You must not love me. He must not suspect any of the dealings we have had with each other, else he will know just

79

how he is being used. If you hate me, then so much the better – he will believe you all the more. But you are still mine, Merrin, remember that. When this is over you will be either a lady or a whore for the soldiers. It depends on how well you play your part.'

'Who is this man? Why is he so important?'

Again, the smile. Merrin was wondering how she could ever have thought to have loved this monster.

'He is the man who will make me King.'

Aimon found him much later, sitting alone in the dark. He entered the tent with the moonlight turning his hair to silver, and fumbled for a spill to light the candles. Tallimon never moved or spoke in the time it took to search for the tinderbox and strike a spark with the flint and steel. When the yellow light was finally glowing in the tent some of Aimon's triumph faded. Tallimon had been weeping; his face seemed ten years older and his eyes were dull. But he looked up at the old mage and smiled.

'You have been on your travels, Aimon.'

Aimon nodded, suddenly afraid of the white face and the dead eyes. He wondered what could have happened.

'Well?'

'I have been there, my Prince. I have stood in his world, and breathed his air. I spoke to him, told him to prepare himself for what is to come.'

Tallimon bent his head. 'So he is resigned, then. He knows we are real – this land is real, and all in it.'

The old man hesitated. But he had no wish to be the bearer of bad tidings this night. He had heard rumours of a lost battle. Women were keening in the lower parts of the camp, though there were no pyres being laid. It was an unsettling night. But he did not think that a lost battle would have made Tallimon weep.

'He does. I can bring him across whenever you are ready for him.'

'It will not be long . . . Tell me, Aimon: what is their world like? Is it like ours? Are they real men that ride in those horseless wagons?'

Aimon touched his bruised arm. 'They are men – or he is, anyway . . . I spoke his tongue, when I crossed over. I thought I was speaking our own, but the words were odd in my mouth. It is frightening, the power of the dweomer.'

'Indeed . . .' Tallimon seemed almost to lose interest. 'I told the lady Merrin her role in the matter this evening.'

Ah, thought Aimon. So that is it. The beloved Merrin a whore once more. He wondered how she had taken it. No doubt Tallimon would have found a way to keep her bent to his will.

'Everything then depends on you and your magic.'

'I will need a rest before I attempt anything so draining again. It is not the opening of the door and the crossing that is hard, but the maintaining of the door while I am there. I did not know if my magic would work in that world, so I kept the door open all the time I was there. It was . . . tiring.'

'But you do not have to do that with this man. Just bring him across. Do not be worrying yourself about doors and such. Just get him here.'

'But we may not be able to get him back.'

Tallimon laughed, an ugly sound. 'That is the least of our worries, my friend.'

Seven

The psychiatrist's room was pretty plush, Willoby had to admit, and he actually had a leather upholstered couch. Not sure whether reclining on it would be taking the piss, Willoby sat on a chair by the window and watched the rain mizzle down outside. Bloody miserable time of year.

The shrink came in. He was younger than Willoby had expected, a lean young man with a tweed jacket and cufflinks. On his desk an unlit pipe reclined. He was the sort, Willoby thought, who reach middle age in their late teens. Had a flabby handshake, too.

'Ah, you've found yourself a seat. Good, good. I notice you didn't take the couch. Always a bad sign when someone lays themselves down on it right away. Ha, ha, ha!'

Willoby looked at him incredulously. His name was Franks. He wondered if any of the good Doctor's patients lengthened the name behind his back. '*Good morning, I am Herr Frankenstein. Ha, ha, ha!*'

The doctor settled himself behind his vast expanse of mahogany desk. It was bare, save for the pipe and its rest, an ashtray, a tobacco jar, a fountain pen and Willoby's file. No paper-clip bending in here, Willoby thought. He fidgeted as Franks sucked on the empty pipe and ruffled through the file. When the shrink lit up that damn thing – if he ever did – Willoby would get out the fags. They'd calm his nerves, and that was what he was here for, after all.

He dropped a hand to touch the cigarette packet in his pocket, and touched instead a cold hardness – the blade of the knife the old man had left in his living room. It was wickedly sharp, well-used and starkly elegant. He looked up at the psychiatrist, bent over the papers.

Tell me *this* isn't real, you bastard.

'Ahhh . . . mmmm,' the psychiatrist said.

Willoby sat on. He felt like a schoolboy summoned before the headmaster.

Jo had insisted that he go private. He had been paying for private health insurance for years and never used it once, she said. So Willoby was paying good money to sit here like a melon whilst this snotty-nosed little prick sucked on his empty pipe and made odd noises. There was more than one motive behind Jo's idea, Willoby thought. It seemed so respectable – classy even – for him to be coming for a *consultation* at the Hathersage Clinic, which of course saw people by appointment only. And there was less chance of him running into anyone he knew.

'*Will, how are you? What are you doing here?*'

'*In the pink, mate. Just here to have the old slice of bread put to rights. A couple of electric shocks, and I'll be as right as rain. And what are* you *doing?*'

'You're a prison officer, Mr Willoby.'

'Right first time, Doc.'

Franks smiled thinly. 'I see here' – a ruffle of papers – 'that you were also a sergeant in the army, and you served in both Aden and Borneo.'

Willoby nodded absently. He could see it coming.

'Mind if I smoke?' Willoby shook his head, relieved.

At last the pipe was lit, gouting impressive clouds of grey, aromatic smoke. Willoby fumbled for his fags, nicked his thumb on the knife blade in his pocket, and hissed in pain. Franks regarded him gravely.

'Mr Willoby – may I call you John? John – I want you to think of me as an ear, someone who's always ready to listen. You can tell me anything, and I will never laugh at you or condemn you. I will always listen, John. In here you will always get the time of day.' He blinked as Willoby lit up in his turn, which spoiled the benevolent effect somewhat. Willoby knew why he smoked the pipe – he wanted to be everybody's father-figure. Christ, this was going to be a pain. How long had he left? But Franks was watching him closely, and he could not sneak a glance at his watch. There was no clock in the room.

'Have you any questions you would like to ask me before we begin? Any queries or things you would like settled?'

'Can you put me away?'

'I beg your pardon?'

'Can you have me locked up, stuck in the funny farm?'

Franks smiled. 'I don't think my staff would appreciate it if you went round calling our splendid facilities the funny farm, John. We prefer to call it a place of recuperation, somewhere where people can take a time out from the world and reassess themselves. We are here to help.'

The unctuous tone made Willoby want to punch him. But that, he thought, is exactly what he may be expecting.

'You haven't answered my question,' he said levelly.

The smile faltered a little. Franks waved his pipe in the air.

'I can, under the Mental Health Act, seek your spouse's permission to have you committed here; that is, if I feel that your presence in the community is a danger both to the public and yourself. And I could, if necessary, have you kept here for up to seventy-two hours on my own authority.'

There we have it, Willoby. The nitty-gritty. Now watch your fucking step, old son, and play the game.

'Of course,' Franks went on, 'the ideal scenario, and the most common one here in the Hathersage Clinic, is where you decide to admit yourself, of your own free will, and undergo treatment. This is 1985, not the nineteenth century, John. Bedlam is a thing of the past.' The smile was back in place.

'Now' – he was all briskness again – 'I mentioned your army service. It was – what? – fourteen years ago. Why did you leave, John? Let's start there. I think it may be an important juncture.'

'You mean you're not going to ask me if I fancied my mother and wanted to top my father?' Willoby asked, trying not to sneer.

Franks laughed. 'Later, perhaps. For now, I want to get a bit

84

of an overview, look at some of the major events of adulthood. So reminisce with me if you like. Tell me how it happened.'

How it happened. Jo had been pregnant with Maria and had complained endlessly about the married quarters, the other wives, the army. Always the fucking army. It was the root of all evil in her eyes. Willoby had been trying to make colour sergeant, keeping his nose clean for once, and it had not seemed impossible. He had had visions of Company Sergeant Major Willoby. It should have happened years before, the Company Commander had told him, except that he could not keep out of trouble. He had been busted twice. Fighting mostly – once for smacking a young officer in the eye. That had been hushed up. They had been a tight bunch in those days, the men who had sweated in the jungle and been scorched in the desert. Not major wars or anything, not like the Second, or even Korea. But men had died and others had survived, and they had seen it together. It had welded them into a daft, gossiping brotherhood, a clique jealous of its memories. It was the same with any unit that had seen combat. Others who arrived in time of peace always found it hard to fit in. And Willoby had been good when the bullets were flying. That was something he was still proud of, a thing untainted by any later absurdities, something pure in the rocky muddle of his life.

And he had left it for Jo, for the unborn child. He had let her browbeat him into leaving, as the battalion was leaving for Ireland. He had let them down. Because he had loved her he supposed, even then. But that had soon changed. Guilt and blame had been the crossfire they had both withered under ever since.

'Fascinating,' said Franks. And Willoby realized that he had been remembering aloud. He had been telling it all, and now his throat was thick and hard with the memories. Damn!

'Have you ever killed anyone, John?'

Willoby stared at him, and smiled his unpleasant smile. The same old question. For a moment Franks was not the good doctor, the patronizing professional – he was simply a man who had never experienced the ultimate, had never looked annihilation in the face. Willoby had seen it before, the prying, shameful curiosity. *What does it feel like?* Of course here it was called therapy.

'Oh, I've killed dozens.'

Franks seemed to recollect himself. His pipe had gone out, and he spent a few seconds relighting it. Willoby stubbed out his cigarette in the doctor's immaculate ashtray, and had himself another.

'How did you feel when you killed people, John?'

Willoby shrugged. Stupid question. 'When some bugger is trying to kill you and you get him instead, you feel pleased – happy you're alive. Happy that you've done the job, you're earning your money. It's what I was paid for anyway. And it means saving your friends, too.'

'Of course, of course . . . You enjoyed it then.'

'Enjoyed it? Yeah, sure. I got a buzz out of it – afterwards, at the bar. At the time I was shitting myself stupid.' But that was not true either. There had been a keenness, a simplicity about those times under fire that he had never known again, not even in the most violent of prison disturbances. And he had been aware of it even at the time. Even when the shit was hitting the fan and all about him were losing their noggins, Willoby had kept his. The prospect of violent death had not fazed him. The guys had thought him a lucky bastard, and had looked to him for leadership. Luck counts for a lot in the minds of men who are suddenly faced with mortality in its most brutal form. Willoby sometimes felt that he had used up his quota of luck in a few manic, bloody episodes, and he had been dry of it ever since.

Still not afraid of dying though. Even now.

The shrink was looking at him thoughtfully. All about the wood-panelled and book-lined room reams of pale smoke floated like a morning mist. Willoby's hand dropped into his coat pocket again. That knife. There was something terrifying about its presence here, in a place where his mind was being searched out and put to rights. Like carrying a gun at the airport.

86

What is it – all in my mind?

His hand clenched on the hilt of the knife. Explain this, then. How is this here? Who *was* that old bugger?

And if he was real, might not the raven-haired girl be also?

The doctor was making notes, the pipe jutting out from the corner of his mouth. What would *this* little turd say if I told him everything – the crazy memories that aren't mine, the hallucinations? It would probably make his day. I'd be his star fucking patient.

But the need was there, the desire to tell someone who would listen. What had he said? *In here you will always get the time of day.*

And besides, it was what he was here for – what he was paying good money for – to get this thing out of his head, to get back to normal.

Back to normal. Christ, there was a depressing thought.

'Doc?'

'Ah . . . mmm?' He was relighting his pipe yet again. 'What?'

'What is crazy? What sort of things rate as madness in your book?' *What sort of things could you have me put away for?*

'Yes . . . Well. I've spoken to your wife, John, and heard her side of the story. I know you have exchanged blows, and she has told me something of your behaviour.' He smiled. 'Nobody is crazy. That's an inadequate word for the things that go on in the mind, a blanket term that no right-thinking person should use. You have problems, yes, but they're not insuperable, and you're by no means the worst case I've dealt with. We won't need the straitjacket, I think.'

'What do you call these hallucinations then, seeing and hearing things that aren't there, hearing voices, thinking I'm someone else?' He gripped the cold knife in his pocket.

'Well, I'd hesitate to jump in with both feet at this early stage. It's not as if you have a bodily injury that I can look at and diagnose immediately . . .'

'Live dangerously. Take a wild guess.'

Franks met his eyes. The professional veneer seemed to melt away for a moment, and Willoby almost liked him.

'Some kind of schizophrenia, possibly paranoid – not severe as yet. It's good that you've come to us at this stage. I have every hope—'

'Will it get worse?'

'Maybe. We can help check that, with drugs and therapy. But it is entirely possible that the hallucinations will indeed get worse, that you will come to believe in them more truly than you believe that you are sitting here in my office talking to me. I have spoken to patients who have entire worlds in their heads, and a host of different personalities vying for their attention. It is a complicated disease, and no one has yet plumbed its depths. To be blunt, John, we don't know what makes people like you tick, what causes it, what cures it. But we can alleviate the symptoms.'

'So there's no cure.'

'If by that you mean we can't give you a prescription that will make it go away, then yes, there is no cure. But the condition can be treated, with some success. And it is not up to me alone. You have to fight it yourself, and your family must help. The family background is very important in these matters, the support you get at home. That is usually more crucial than any pills I prescribe, or any amount of sessions on my couch.'

Willoby almost laughed. So there you have it. You're on your own, Will. I can't see Maria bringing you breakfast in bed somehow.

He met Franks's eyes again.

And was no longer looking at him.

It is her again, the dark girl called Merrin. She is standing as straight and tall as a spear with a yawning gap of night behind her, her skin kindled to cream and shadow by the shimmering light of a candle. She is naked, and stands as though on display, with her head up and her fists clenched by her sides. Her eyes are locked with his, daring him to look elsewhere, and they are full of pain and baffled fury. She looks like a captive queen. He feels as though his heart has stopped, as though he and she were trapped in some drop of imperishable

88

*amber, and the wild night howling beyond them. But the look in
her eyes grieves him. He knows somehow he is casting away the
most precious thing he has ever known. And it must be done.
There is no other way. He must be sure.*

Sure of what? Why must he do this?

'*Merrin*,' he groaned.

Franks's face was six inches from his own, the eyes boring
into his. They were brown eyes, flecked with grey. 'Mr Willoby.
John!'

He drew in a deep breath. The shrink's hands were fastened
on his shoulders. The foppishness had gone from him and he
was alert, professional, clinical.

Oh, shit, Willoby thought. Right on cue. I've done it again.

'Back with us?' Franks asked. The grip on Willoby's
shoulders eased.

'Yes – yes, I am.'

'Where were you, John? Where did you go?'

If it was an odd question, it did not seem so at the time.

'I was away, in that other place. With – with other people.
Someone else.'

Franks nodded. 'This has happened before.'

It was a statement, not a question. It was Willoby's turn to
nod.

'You said something as you came out of it. Can you
remember?'

'Merrin. That's her name.' His mind was too confused for
subterfuge. Nothing but the truth would come out.

'Who is she?'

'I – I don't know. She's a woman. She's lovely, like a princess.'

She's in trouble, some deep part of him said.

Franks sat back on the desk. 'What did she say to you?'

'She . . . nothing. She just looked at me. She hasn't said
anything.'

'Who is she?'

'I don't know, I tell you!'

'Do you know where she is from, where you are when you are
with her?' The questions came like missiles.

'That other place – another world, damn it. It's all mountains and hills there, open country, and they're trying, trying to colonize it, I think. They came from over the mountains and they're settling down now . . .'

'Who are? Who are they?'

'The people! Men and women, old and young. I don't know. They have horses, and tents. They're building something. A city, perhaps. But there's trouble, fighting. Monsters.'

'Monsters . . .' Franks held his neatly shaven chin in one long-fingered hand. Willoby longed to strike him.

'Do you go there often, John?'

'Where? *There?* How the hell should I know? It's some crazy thing in my head, some kind of dream that hits me even when I'm awake. I'm a loony. Go on, tell me. Get the guys in the white coats and lock me up. That'll please everyone.'

Rage and self-pity were choking him, but they were not the worst things. It was that lingering grief, the feeling that he had lost her: worse, that he had thrown her away. Why had he done that? What was it for?

She didn't fucking *exist*!

The Hathersage Clinic was on the outskirts of a picturesque little stone-built village, but rising beyond it on all sides were the first green swells of the Peak District, whilst on the horizon were the dark lines of stone plateaux and tors. There was open country up there, heath and moorland broken with scattered stone, and ravens turned lazy somersaults in the low cloud above.

He left the car at a pub car park, not even tempted to go inside, and started up the steep slope to the hills beyond. He was not dressed for it; Jo had insisted he wear a jacket and tie for the *consultation*, and good, city-pavement shoes. And the short afternoon was drawing to a close. But he felt that his head had too much crammed into it, too many things, and he wanted the freer air around his face. He wanted to take long strides without shuffling round other people.

His fingers curled about the hilt of the knife as he walked.

He thought of her standing there with her head held high, the dark hair like a hood and the green eyes blazing. My God, she had been lovely. The memory made him groan aloud as he trudged on and up through the gathering dusk, the mud sticking to his soles.

But she had been in trouble, also. The look in the eyes had been a furious despair. Something was wrong over there, wherever there might be. That younger man whose body Willoby had once owned – was he her lover? She had said his name once, the night of the fight with Jo. Was it something to do with him?

He slipped in the slick mud and fell to one knee, plastering himself with the stuff. The knife skittered off a rock and disappeared.

'Shit!'

He scrabbled for it, squinting in the gathering gloom. He was frantic, on hands and knees.

Found it. He wiped mud off the keen blade and felt the chill slice of his own flesh as it broke his skin, cut deep.

'God-damn!' He hopped around in the mud holding his injured hand by the wrist. It had hardly healed since the last injury.

'You bastard!' And he flung the knife away into the darkness with all his strength. There was a far-off click as it bounded off a rock, and vanished. He sobered at once.

Nice one. Nice one, Willoby. That was the evidence, the only proof you had. And now it's gone.

He sat down on a boulder and held his head in his hands, smearing his face with mud and blood. The hot ache of tears was at the back of his throat and he clenched his teeth desperately.

I'd slash my fucking wrists with it, if I had it still.

When he looked up again it was dark. In a gap of cloud he could see Orion's belt twinkling away. Down in the valley the village had its lamps lit, yellow light spilling out from almost every window.

Mad; I'm mad as a hatter. Look at the state of me. He was

91

covered with mud. It had clung to his shoes, giving him another inch of sole, and he could feel it stiffening on his cheeks. Peering at his hands, he could see only the dark stuff that smeared them. The cut the knife had made stung abominably. There was mud in it, too.

What'll Jo say when I come back like this?

That croaked a laugh out of him. A few short months ago he would have come home in any state he pleased, and she'd have been as quiet as a mouse – Maria too. But now—

Maria. He held her face in his mind, momentarily puzzled. It reminded him of someone.

Nothing. It had begun to rain. Time to get back.

But he did not move at once. It was peaceful, up here in the dark. There was no sound but the soughing of the wind through the stones, the heavy rasp of his own breathing. Way down in the valley, the cars were disembodied and silent pairs of eyes hunting out each other. Their noise did not reach here.

He was tired. The consultation had gone more like an interrogation after his little episode. Franks had apologized, saying he was fact-finding, that the pace would ease in subsequent meetings.

Subsequent meetings. How many does the bugger think I need?

Time to go home. He stood, feeling like an old man. Could she love me, that girl? Someone that beautiful? It was crazy. She was a dream, part of his madness – part of his *disability* as Franks had called it. But he still wanted to know.

There's no such person, Willoby.

He started down towards the valley, stumbling in the rain-filled night.

Wish there were, though. I really do.

The predictable wail when he got home. *Look at the state of you!* Quack quack, water off a duck's back. He was too weary to care. He dumped his clothes, careless of the muck, and sank himself into the bath Jo ran for him. His daughter had helped him off with his shoes, not looking at him. For a moment, as her dark head had been bent over his feet, he had had the urge to stroke her hair, try and make her meet his eyes. But the urge had gone. There was yet a niggling thought that she reminded him of someone else. Still, the shaky truce seemed to be holding. Jo must have given her a talking to. Willoby could imagine.

'*Your dad isn't quite right in the head, so you have to be nice to him, OK?*'

He lay back, wallowing in the hot water and the bubbles. His hand pained him, a reminder of his own stupidity.

Jo came in with more towels, admitting a draught of cold air. Willoby sank farther into the water until only his face was showing.

She gazed at him without speaking, then plumped herself down on the edge of the bath.

'What happened? How did it go?'

He stared at her, crocodile eyes blinking above the soapy water. They had shared this bath more than once, but that was years ago. He wondered if she even remembered.

'Lots of questions. He's young, he smokes a pipe. He probably earns more in a month than I do in a year. Cocky bastard. Knows his stuff though, I think.'

'What did he ask you?'

'What did he ask *you?*'

He saw with satisfaction that he had seized the initiative.

'Things. Our marriage – he asked about that. Your drinking. My black eye.'

He felt that the ball had been socked right back at him and sat up.

'Come on in beside me,' he said, reaching for her with dripping arms.

She stood and moved away, folding her arms about her breasts. He had always hated that. It was the defensive posture of an adolescent.

'How did you get in such a state? Your clothes are ruined, and you've cut yourself.' She nodded at his palm. It was leaking magenta in the water.

'Walked about a bit afterwards, then I tripped up – cut it on a stone.'

'Have you been drinking?'

He smiled his dangerous smile. 'Come and smell my breath.'

She remained where she was.

'Are you a loony, then? Did he tell you?'

'Oh, yes. I'm a paranoid schizophrenic with catatonic episodes. I'm a real star.' He smiled again, hating her because she was afraid of him.

'You don't care,' she said with sudden bitterness. 'You don't give a shit, do you? It's all a big game to you.'

He stared at her silently.

'Maria and I are worried sick, and you come back looking like a tramp with that stupid grin on your face and tell us you're mad. It's all right for you— '

He laughed, throwing his head back in the water with a splash. 'It's all right for me, is it? I'm so sorry, love, I had forgotten about the real victims here – St Jo and St Maria! How self-fucking-centred of me. Strange, though: I was under the impression that I was the one with the disability. I'll have a word with the shrink next time I see him, and tell him he's barking up the wrong tree. You're the one with the problem, Jo.'

Her eyes glittered. 'You hate me. You hate us both.'

He sat up in the bath, a monster rising from the deep. 'No. No, I don't, love. Of course I don't. But damn it – don't you think we're almost strangers these days? When do we ever talk but to argue? And Maria . . . Jesus, she won't even give me the time of day.' He paused. 'There's hatred, if you like. In her.'

'Oh, don't be so stupid. She's only a child!'

'No. Not any more she's not. She's a young woman at the hardest part of her life.' And we've no time for her at the moment with all this, he thought to himself. No wonder she hates me.

Jo looked at him, lost. 'What are we going to do?' As she spoke he pitied her, and extended one water-wrinkled hand from the bath. She clasped it gratefully.

It's still me, he thought. Mad or not, the buck stops with Willoby in the end. And he realized with a dull kind of surprise that he had reached out his hand in compassion only. There was no love left there that he could find. He would have done the same for a stranger.

'We'll struggle on,' he managed lamely. 'We always do.'

Eight

The tent city buzzed with news. Prince Tallimon's Rimon had been cut to ribbons by an army of twisted beasts the likes of which had never been seen before, and the King blamed his bastard son for the massacre. The Courberan clan had ostracized him. Madavar and Idramon, Courberall's legitimate sons by his queen, Hiera, sat at his right hand with arm-rings of river gold, the massive heirlooms of the Courberan house, clasped on their forearms. Madavar had been named First Prince, and it was treason to acknowledge any other by that title.

Columns of the Kristillic heavy cavalry were going out to do a reconnaisance-in-force of the surrounding lands. Over fifty-score warriors – an entire Amon under the newly appointed Amarch Fferidan – rode out with the dawn, their task to scour the region for other bands of beasts such as that which had defeated Tallimon. Heavy escorts now accompanied the quarrying and timber trains, cavalry riding the hills above the slow convoys of wagons; and a palisade was being built around the huge main camp of the Kristillic people, which stretched for miles along the Great River north of the Courbisker city site.

Prince Tallimon remained in his tent.

'It's true, then. He has gone?' he asked.

'Aye, sire. He was promoted last night – a somewhat hasty appointment – and he and his new command rode out at dawn. They will be away at least two weeks, it is said in the barracks.'

Tallimon studied his informant closely. Ordachar was a good man, shorter and darker than the average Kristill, but that was the Primitive blood in him. His mother, like Tallimon's, had been a trophy of war, a member of a defeated race. But where in Tallimon the Kristillic blood predominated, with Ordachar his savage mother's race was plain to see. It had kept promotion out of his grasp until Tallimon had met him and gauged his worth. He was a Decarch now, a commander of a hundred, one of the five squadrons which made up Tallimon's Penton. The mauled Rimon had come from Ordachar's command. He felt their defeat keenly, though it had been Tallimon who had led them out, accepting a command beneath his station at the express orders of the King. Tallimon wondered if Ordachar thought he could have done any better. But no – the man's loyalty was unquestionable. He owed everything to his patron, the Bastard Prince.

'This Amon of Fferidan's – what is its composition?'

'All but two of the ten squadrons within it come from the Royal Clan, sire. Since some were detached to guard the main camp, Prince Madavar lent Fferidan three of his own squadrons to bring it up to strength.'

'It is a composite then, a mish-mash of units. No one was demoted to make way for the illustrious Fferidan?'

'Oh yes, sire. Old Quirinan goes as second-in-command. To keep an eye on things, he put it.'

Tallimon smiled. 'In other words, he commands the Amon in fact whilst Fferidan is tacked on as a figurehead to get him out of the city for a while.'

'It seems that way to me, sire.'

'My father does not want me duelling with his son's favourite. It is his way of defusing things. I wonder that he had to go so far as to give Fferidan a thousand men to do it, though. Maybe he is taking my advice seriously after all.'

'Fferidan sits high in the favour of Madavar, and Madavar is the heir apparent.' Ordachar halted. 'I am sorry, sire, but it is how things are seen since your altercation with your father. Madavar and Idramon bear the Royal insignia now.'

Tallimon clapped him on the shoulder.

'It's all right, man. I've seen which way the wind blows.

Have some wine. The women have found vines growing wild on the southern slopes. It's insipid stuff, but it does its work well enough and it beats our foul beer.'

Ordachar poured himself some of the pale drink from a flask of real glass that had somehow survived the passage through the mountains. Tallimon watched him drink for a moment and then asked:

'Who can I count on, Ordachar, which of the clans?'

The man blinked under his black thatch of hair.

'If it were left to the rank and file you would be King tomorrow. There are many in the upper ranks, too, who think the King's treatment of you has been unfair – the King's son leading out a fifty-man patrol in person like some common war chief! Some say you were not meant to come back from the patrol, that Courberall knew all along what sort of things you would run into.'

Tallimon nodded. He did not believe it himself – his father was not duplicitous enough for such a plan – but there was no harm in fostering the rumour.

'If it is officers we are considering – the clan chiefs and such – then it is harder to say. Many are not happy with how things have been turning out since we crossed the mountains. They do not like the way the people are kept together like this, all in a body. It undermines their own authority: they want to be on their own, carving fiefs out of the wilderness for themselves. And there are difficulties at the main camp. The foraging parties are finding game more and more scarce and the middens grow higher daily. If the people are kept huddled together like this much longer they say there will be disease in the camp, and hunger. It is spring, they say. They want to get the horse herds down on the lower plains and replenish their numbers. As it is, over half the warriors are still afoot, and they feel it keenly.'

Tallimon nodded. The mountains had been hard on the horses, though they had been as well looked after as the children. Barely half of the great herds had made it alive through the peaks, and the survivors were not yet up to their former strength. He had heard it said among his own men that Courberall had been the first king to accustom the people to the taste of horse flesh. Until the mountains it had been taboo, but the King had been the first man to try it, and after that his household. Horsemeat had kept them alive in the bare mountain passes, though Tallimon was almost sure that some of the older men had practised cannibalism rather than eat their mounts. It was a touchy subject, and therefore one to be exploited.

'Names, Ordachar,' he said harshly. 'Who among the lords can I count on?'

'Garrian and Arbolast, of course—'

Tallimon nodded. They were next in seniority to the Royal House. The kingship was a whisker away from them were the Royal Clan to falter.

'And Armishan and Pollogar.'

'Indeed?' That was good news. Both men were young, their fathers having died in the mountains. They would be easy to lead, and were no doubt chafing under the High King's restrictions.

'Any more?'

'None that I can be sure of, sire.'

'So. I have my own Penton that I know I can count on, and possibly the support of four of the other clans. That leaves seven against me, not including the Royal House. I believe it can be done. If I am swift, then all the men I will need will be those of my own Penton. Five hundred determined men can achieve much when the enemy is leaderless.'

'Leaderless, sire?'

Tallimon fixed him with a cold stare. 'Do you think my father is about to hand me the crown on a platter?'

'But, sire – you cannot kill a king. It is the last taboo. The hand of a kingslayer will wither. No man among the entire Kristillic Host would do such a thing. Courberall is inviolate.'

'But what if I found a man who would kill the King for me?'

'Then he would be accursed ever after. The clans would

99

shun him. He would be an outcast. And the clan he belonged to would be outcast with him.'

'And if he is an outcast already?'

Ordachar shook his head, evidently shaken. 'You cannot kill the King,' he repeated stupidly.

Tallimon gripped him by the shoulders. 'But if I could . . . if I found someone to do it who belongs to no clan, who is not one of us — if he sprouted out of the ground in our midst — would then these clan lords follow me?'

'If the deed was not done by you or any of your vassals, why then I suppose so. But we are the sole men in this land. There are no others. Where would this man come from?'

Tallimon smiled, and released him. 'You let me worry about that, Ordachar. All you have to do is prepare your men. When the time comes they must be swift and sure. They must know their minds in the midst of confusion and fear. They must know where their loyalties lie.'

Ordachar fell to one knee. 'Sire, I was nothing before you took me on. My men and I are with you to the death. You know that.'

'Good. Get up, Ordachar. The Kristill do not kneel to any man.' He raised his dark-haired subordinate gently to his feet, and then clasped him in a rough embrace, a grimace that Ordachar did not see crossing his face as he did so.

'Good! So that is settled. Ordachar, I want you to set aside a half-Rimon of your best men at my personal disposal. They must be discreet, and without wives. Men have a tendency to prattle in the marriage bed. And you may now consider yourself commander of Cardillac's Decon also. Send him to me at once. Tell him he is not being demoted. I have another task for him. And have both the mage Aimon and the lady Merrin ready themselves for travelling. They are to have their things packed by the evening, but they are to leave their tents standing. Is that clear?'

Obviously it was not, but Ordachar bowed and left, pushing out the tent flap to the bright morning beyond.

Tallimon remained standing. It was close in the leather tent, and the place was beginning to smell of mildew and mould. He wrinkled his nose. When the city was built he would gather the tents of the people together and make a bonfire of them. Their nomadic days would be done. With luck, those who supported him would realize too late that they had crowned a king with a harder hand even than Courberall.

'I will civilize you yet,' he said, only the empty tent to hear him.

Aimon burst in a scant ten minutes later, as Tallimon had known he would.

'Prince, what is this? I am to pack, to make ready for a journey. Do you know the delicacy of the work I am engaged in?'

Tallimon held up a hand.

'I know. I value its delicacy so much that I will take you from these distractions, Aimon. You are going into the wilderness.'

The old man paled. 'Why? What game is this you are playing? I am at a critical juncture in my theurgies—'

'Oh, spare me the details, Aimon! This man of ours must be brought across within the week, whilst Fferidan and his Amon are out on patrol. The time is ripe at last, so I will hear no more of your havering. You will have Cardillac and half a Rimon as escort. Not enough, I know, but any more will attract undue attention. I want this thing conducted away from the city site and its prying eyes, and out of the ears of my father.'

'Do you think I can set up my things in a howling wilderness, with the beasts ranging in on me?'

'It will at least teach you the value of haste! But I intend to send a group of artisans with you, and Cardillac. They will build you a palisade, a hut – whatever you require. You leave after dark.'

Aimon was silent.

'You can do it? You are ready?'

'I believe so . . . Is the good lady whore to accompany us?'

Tallimon flushed, and his glare made Aimon retreat a step.

'The lady Merrin accompanies you,' he said in a voice of frost. 'She is to be on hand when this man comes across. It is you and her who must ease his transition. I will come to you when I feel it is safe to bring him to the city, but tell him nothing of his mission until I arrive.'

'The King will note your absence, and ours perhaps. All hunting parties that leave the gates must now have his sanction.'

'He will be glad to be quit of me. If I go I will take only a few retainers, or I may summon you here if things are difficult. You he should not even notice. You are too small a fish. But it is time, Aimon. The planning and the twilit conferences have led to this moment. Now is the time for action.'

'I am not one of your troops, that need a pep talk before battle, Tallimon,' the old man said. He sounded tired. Sitting down on the fur-laden couch, he poured himself some of the thin wine.

'I wonder sometimes if you are as wholeheartedly behind my cause as you would have me believe.' Tallimon smiled.

'I would see another who is more wholeheartedly behind you! I have broken every law of dweomer I ever learned to do your bidding—'

'And to satisfy your own curiosity. Do not try to deceive me, Aimon. Mages were ever a prying and a proud folk. You do this thing for your own satisfaction as much as mine.'

'If it were wholly for my own ends I'd not be running headlong at it as I am now. Magic does not wait on politics, Tallimon.'

'Nor will the turn of events slow to suit the rate of your experimentations ... You had best start packing, old man. But be careful. You may take along a servant, but leave at least one behind to carry on the pretence that you are still in camp.'

'I hold no truck with servants. I do my own work,' Aimon said brusquely. 'It is Cardillac, then, who comes with us, to preserve our skins?'

'Indeed.'

'Aye well, it could be worse. Better him than that half-wit Ordachar.' Aimon drained his wine and bowed with a flourish. 'Good day, sweet Prince, and may your schemes come to the fruition they deserve.' He left.

Tallimon was still musing over Aimon's words when his page – attentive to his duty for once, it seemed – announced that the Decarch Cardillac was waiting outside.

'Bring him in.'

Cardillac was a young man, though older than Tallimon. He was another who, like Ordachar, owed everything to his patron. Men often wondered why Tallimon had promoted no one of noble blood to command in his squadrons, bringing forward always men of undistinguished lineage, unrelated to the more illustrious of the clan lords. At one time – when he had been in favour with the King – there had been a score of stripling nobles vying for his attention, but always he had brought his commanders up through the ranks. It seemed as plain as day to Tallimon himself: his officers relied on him alone for their advancement, and owed no allegiances to powerful families or the nobility. And besides, the King's bastard son had never wished to surround himself with men whose lineage was undisputed. An illegitimate is ever careful of his honour, Tallimon thought wryly. He takes a slight more seriously than the haughtiest grandee.

Cardillac had been with him since the tribal raiding days on the other side of the mountains. They had saved each other's lives more times than they could count. Cardillac was a fine leader, but more important, he knew how to keep his mouth shut, which was a rarity among the warriors.

He stood before Tallimon now, a stocky young man with a russet beard, dressed in worn leather and smelling of horse. A streak of white, legacy of an old wound, ran like a flash of rime through his thick hair. Tallimon clapped his hands, and the page poked a pale face through the tent flap.

'Bring beer, and another stool for the Decarch.'

Cardillac was not a wine drinker. When they had sat, and supped, he wiped his mouth with his forearm and said:

'It is Decarch Cardillac still? From what I hear Ordachar has been given my command.'

'You heard correctly. He is even now selecting a half-Rimon of the best men from his squadrons, and they will be yours. I have a job for you, my friend, one that requires tact and discretion.'

Cardillac chuckled. 'The latter I can guarantee, the former I am not so sure about.'

They grinned at each other. Cardillac was one of the few people whom Tallimon regarded as a friend. Aimon, oddly enough, was another. Merrin had been the third. There were no others.

'You will escort Aimon and the lady Merrin from the city tonight, and you will do it . . .'

'Discreetly?'

'Just so. The King has taken it upon himself to regulate all parties leaving the city site and the main camp, but you can by-pass the sentries easily by one of the gaps in the wall. With you will go also a party of artificers whom Ordachar will recommend. The whole party should number not more than forty. You will set up camp at least two days' journey from the city, and the artificers will there erect fortifications.'

'Is this to be an extended sojourn?' Cardillac asked in surprise.

'The mage Aimon needs peace and quiet for his work. He is engaged in experiments of the greatest importance. The greatest importance, Cardillac.'

They looked at one another without a word, and Cardillac nodded soberly. 'I see. And when will we know to come back?'

'Upon my order only. Once the camp is established you will send a rider to me and keep me informed. When Aimon is happy with progress I am to be notified immediately, and I will come out to you if I can.'

'And if these beasts which attacked you attack us?'

'Hold them off and send for help. Pray they do not attack wooden walls. I cannot give you more men, Cardillac. You must cope as best you can.'

'That reassures me mightily.'

'We live in troubled times.'

'We will soon, that's plain.' They both laughed, clinking wooden mugs together before drinking deep.

'Sire, what of Fferidan and his Amon? They will be patrolling the hills round about for the next sennight.'

'I know. Pick some inaccessible place for your camp. Go higher into the hills if you have to, even into the last of the snows. You must not be disturbed . . . The kingship depends on you and your mission, Cardillac. If you do well, you shall have more than a Decon to command.'

'And if I fail I'll be cleaning out the horse lines, no doubt. I will do what is proper, Tallimon, but I say this to you: *be careful*. The Royal Clan has ostracized you, but that does not mean that they are not still fascinated by your every move. Madavar's spies are everywhere.'

'I know. He is a capable man, my half-brother.'

'Your father, also, is suspicious that you are taking your . . . disgrace so easily.'

'My father's mind is not the most subtle in the world. If he was suspicious enough he'd summon me to him and ask me what I was at. That is his version of intelligence gathering.'

'He made himself King, all the same.'

'He was the greatest warleader we had ever known, and he made the warriors of the Royal Clan into a fighting force the like of which had never been seen before. If I were charging at him lance in hand, then he would be a man to beware of. But with our present kind of war it is his son, his beloved son, who worries me. He has his minion, Fferidan, wandering the hills even now with a thousand men. A good way to get him out of my way and the threat of a duel, but also a good way to have a full Amon in hand against emergencies. For all we know they could be out of sight beyond the next hill, awaiting Madavar's signal.'

'Signal to do what?'

'To do whatever is necessary to secure the King's bastard son, for one thing. To cut off the routes to and from the main camp for another. I have almost a full Penton here – five hundred men – but I have more supporters among the disaffected clans in the main camp. Now I cannot get to them without being watched, perhaps even intercepted.'

Cardillac shook his head. 'A murky business. But I am just a soldier. I do as I am told.'

'You are lucky in that, I think sometimes.'

'Do you remember the campaign against the Boar-people, back in the Wildwood? That winter . . . it was the longest I'd known before the passage of the Greshorns. We had that ford to hold at the bend in the forest river, and old Quirinan was our commander. You weren't much more than a boy then.'

'Aye. I remember. We watched the entire army ride off through the trees to do battle, and had to stay put, two hundred evil-tempered warriors left to guard the King's rear.'

'And then the river froze over, and the tribesmen swarmed across it in retreat wherever they had a mind to, your father and the clans galloping at their rear and hallooing like fiends, and we of Quirinan's squadrons seeing the tightest fighting of the lot.'

Tallimon remembered. It had been one of the proudest moments of his young life when in the midst of the battle the King had come thundering up on his wicked black gelding, the snow spraying about its hooves, and had looked down at him.

'You've done a man's work today, Tallimon.'

And then he had galloped off again. But from that moment Tallimon had worshipped his father. Until the death of his mother.

He drained his beer. 'How things change.'

Cardillac looked suddenly sombre. 'Aye. I never thought we'd end up fighting amongst ourselves again, once Courberall had united us.'

'Things change,' Tallimon repeated. 'Men change most of all . . . I'd have died for him, Cardillac. I'd have done anything at his word.'

'It isn't his doing, sire. He's a simple man. It's Madavar – he won't be satisfied with anything less than the High Kingship. He poisons the King's ear against you.'

'As I said, a capable man, my half-brother. But he does nothing that I would not have done in his place. We play for high stakes, we two: the lordship of the Kristill, and the ownership of an entire new world, no less.'

'You are your father's son, the best warleader in the Host.'

'I am his by-blow, the offspring of a savage tribeswoman whom he kept as a concubine and discarded like a spent horse.' As I am discarding Merrin, he thought, and the knowledge twisted cold and sharp within him.

They were silent for a few moments. Cardillac knew better than to argue when Tallimon had the closed look on his face. But it had not always been like this. When they had been younger he had been different. There had been no scheming then. He remembered accompanying Tallimon and Madavar on dawn hunting expeditions, he, the eldest, trying to keep their skins whole when the wolf or the boar – or the man – was cornered and came charging out at them. He remembered the shining wonderment on Tallimon's face the evening they came back to his tent and found Merrin waiting, a gift from his father. Tallimon had been the perfect gentleman, obviously terrified, whilst he and Madavar had nearly choked on their mirth.

'Why cannot the kingdom be partitioned, you and Madavar each taking your due? It is big enough. We have more good, open land here than I ever thought to see in my life.'

Tallimon stared into his empty flagon.

'It is too late for that now. The King would never consider it, and he would only be sowing the seeds for a civil war. In five years' time, perhaps ten, but it would come round in the end.'

'But why?'

'Because Madavar and I are too similar. Each believing the other to be fomenting dreams of single kingship, we would each try to strike first.'

'So it is about distrust then.'

'Power does such things. It makes truth into a cheap thing, and honour too.'

'Then what is it I have to do out in the hills that is so

important? I should be here with you, commanding my squadron.'

'Believe me, my friend, you will be doing me a greater service in the hills.'

'But what, Tallimon . . . what is Aimon up to? Is he conjuring some great magic in your defence?'

'You could say that.'

'And why send Merrin along? The hills are no place for a lady.'

'She is my slave; I will send her where I will,' Tallimon said in a sudden snarl.

Slave. That was a word Cardillac had never thought to hear applied to Merrin. Tallimon loved her, it was clear, and he had set her up as a great lady to rival those of the nobility. *Slave?* Something had occurred here. Once Cardillac would have bullied and cajoled the information out of the younger man, but this Tallimon he no longer dared to bait. He had changed since coming across the mountains – many men had. Perhaps it was the richness of the land. The whole host was chafing at the bit to be off, to carve it up, to possess it. Tallimon was right. Power, wealth – it did strange things to a man. Even Courberall. He was no longer as approachable as when he had been the Kristillic warleader. Now he was the High King, and a man had to go through half a dozen others to get to him. There was still no ceremony, and once a man was before the King he could speak his mind, but the distance was there.

'It will be cold yet, in the hills,' Tallimon said quietly. 'Make sure that Merrin and Aimon are . . . comfortable. Look after them, Cardillac.'

'Of course.'

Tallimon stood up. 'So there you are, then. That is your mission. Aimon will tell you more when it is necessary. Remember that you may be out there for some time. And, Cardillac, make sure your men are—'

'Discreet.'

'Yes. You are aiding me in treason. You know that.'

'I'm helping to keep you alive. For me that is no treason.'

They took each other's forearms in the warrior's grip. Tallimon looked pinched and worn.

I know now what he will look like when he is middle-aged, Cardillac thought. Like a well-worn knife, shining and lean. There was nothing left that he could see of the high-spirited boy he had taken hunting at dawn those years ago. Nothing at all.

Nine

In the dream it was very cold. The high moon glittered down on a landscape of shadow and grey, ice and rime gleaming diamond-like, the snow hard and brittle as glass. He could almost feel the chill settle into his own bones, the algid caress of the night breeze coming down from the drift-deep mountain passes. Stars spangled a vast black vault above.

There was a group of them behind the summit of a broken hill. The horses were standing patiently with their breath moonlit clouds of steam in the frigid air. Icicles hung from their muzzles.

Men were working silently. He could see the flare of flint being struck, others unpacking frozen rawhide bundles, hammering pegs into the hard snow and harder earth. They blew into their mittened hands, made and unmade fists to keep the blood flowing, but did all without a word.

There was no sound save for the faint sigh of the wind travelling over the peaks of the mountains. They were close up here, vast shapes darker than the black sky where the shadows lay, or bright and pale where the moon lit the snow and ice fields. They seemed to uphold the world's roof, their heights the very pillars of the heavens. They were awesome, frightening, beautiful.

Some of the people had climbed the summit of the hill that sheltered the camp. They stood there with weapons in their hands. Moonlight glittered cold and white on spear points and helmets, breastplates and chain-mail. They wore thick fur-edged cloaks with deep hoods over their armour.

But then a hood was thrown back and he saw a moon-pale face framed by raven hair, as perfect as a frozen lily. She was

looking along with the others out across the wide moonlit land
below, down from the snow-covered hills to a wide river plain
where the grass grew dark and dew-heavy, untouched by frost.
There was a glimmer of light there, near the horizon, and he
realized that it was not some far-off lamp, but the distant
flicker of campfires. A carpet of them burning in their
thousands, covering the land for miles but reduced by distance
to a faint glow.

But now there is a tenseness, an uneasiness in the air. He can
sense the woman's unhappiness and it grieves him. The men
are ill at ease also; and the old, bearded man who stands beside
the woman has his eyes shut. His face is familiar. He sways,
and the woman turns, alarmed, to support him.

Weird speech, foreign words in his mind chanted like a
nursery rhyme. He feels the cold more keenly. Suddenly there
are more sounds. The chink of harness, the click of rock and
crunch of feet in the frozen snow. He feels himself drawn into
the wintry night . . .

He made himself tea in the kitchen. Rain rattled at the window
in the black night beyond. He stared out at it, stirring sugar
after sugar into his cup.

Too real. The dreams were becoming too real. He could
almost feel the nip in his toes from that freezing night. Unless it
was just the chill kitchen floor under his bare feet.

At least Jo had not woken, so she wouldn't pester him to put
it in his log.

The log. It was something Captain Kirk dictated. Well, now
Willoby had one, in which he had to write down all the
dreams, hallucinations, voices etcetera that he experienced. It
was good therapy, Franks had said. He could look over it in his
lucid moments and see them for what they were – figments of
his own twisted imagination.

Lucid moments. Christ. He slurped the sickly sweet tea,
grimaced, and threw it in the sink.

There was a dim knowledge at the back of his mind that there was that crisis still approaching, some crux of events inevitably advancing towards him. The sense terrified him. It was like a dark cloud always in the corner of his eye. He had even tried to tell Franks about it, but the shrink had told him that he was not to worry; it was paranoia, and quite unwarranted. He must recognize that his emotions were responding to no rational stimuli. In other words, his strings were being pulled all right, but not by anything that made sense. Hence the mood swings, the catatonic episodes, the violent urges, *et cetera*.

Makes me feel a whole lot better, Willoby thought with a silent snarl. He shambled into the living room and got himself a Scotch. He had to tighten his dressing gown about him as he stood sniffing the heady stuff.

Losing weight. I can see my toes again. Well, every cloud has its lining. But he paused in mid-gulp. Maria was standing in the doorway with a pale robe about her, the dark hair awry. Willoby had a moment of déjà-vu which disappeared, maddeningly, before he could pin it down. He set down the whisky glass, feeling like a burglar caught in the act.

'You woke me up,' she said coolly, and came in with a rustle of cotton.

'Sorry.'

'Another nightmare?'

'Yes.' He could see the swell of her breasts, the imprint of the nipples through the flimsy robe. It was almost a shock. He realized he was looking at a young woman, and remembered her as the bright-eyed cherub whom he had bounced laughing on his shoulders. He remembered fixing the puncture on her bike – not so long ago, surely – and she kissing him and calling him daddy.

But it was an adult he faced tonight. He couldn't help but wonder if some pimply hormone-fuelled little bastard had already been pawing what was under the robe. The thought made his throat tighten with anger.

'I heard you shout out,' she said. 'Didn't it wake Mum?'

'Your mum could sleep through a cup final.'

'I'm a light sleeper. Like you.'

He nodded, faintly incredulous. His daughter was being civil to him.

'What's that? Whisky?'

Again the guilt, like a shamed boy. 'It helps me sleep, if you must know.'

'Cider does that to me,' she said.

'You're drinking, then?'

'Of course.' She sounded scornful. 'Everyone does.'

He sat down. 'I suppose they do, nowadays . . . Was there something you wanted, Maria?'

She tugged at her robe, not meeting his eyes.

'Samantha Cohen's dad works at the prison with you. She says you've had a nervous breakdown. You've gone potty, she says, and you've lost your job. They're going to put you away.'

He flushed. One of Howard's perfect daughters. The bitch.

'I'm not potty, Maria.'

'Then what's going on?' Her face was white, defiant. She didn't believe him. 'You're seeing a psychiatrist, aren't you? You go to the asylum every week for electric shocks and stuff.'

He laughed at that.

'Who told you about the electric shocks?'

'I saw it in a film. That's what they do in there. And afterwards you're a vegetable.'

'I don't get electric shocks, kiddo. I just talk to this doctor bloke. I'm a mild case.'

'They're not going to put you away, then?'

'Not unless I run off the rails completely and do something like— ' He had been about to say 'like murder my family in their beds', but thought better of it.

'Like go shopping in your mother's dress with my underpants on my head.'

She giggled at that, and seemed much younger.

'I'm sorry, Maria.'

'It's all right. I always wake up in the night anyway.'

'No, I mean sorry for this, this trouble, and the things that have happened.'

'Oh.' Her face shut again, the look of the stranger coming on it.

'You shouldn't have hit Mum.'

'She hit me first', he almost said, but remained silent.

'She says you're seeing things, people who aren't there, voices. You haven't been taking any drugs, have you?'

He burst into laughter, and found, miraculously, that she was smiling back at him.

'Only this.' He flourished his glass. 'Only this.'

They looked at each other without speaking. Willoby could think of nothing more to say. He had forgotten how to talk to her, he realized. He didn't know if she had a boyfriend, or was going to be an artist or a scientist when she grew up. All these things, the events of her life, had passed him by. She was stuck in time in his mind, a perpetual eleven-year-old. But now he saw her again, and the change was there without him even noticing. Small wonder she had hated him.

'Do you hate me?' he asked her. The words were like stones in his mouth. He had to force himself to speak them.

She folded her arms about her breasts, the defensive posture her mother used. 'No, I don't think so. I do sometimes, like when you had that fight with Mum; but I think you're in trouble, and if you're not right in the head then I suppose it's not really your fault.'

He smiled weakly. It always came down to that. No matter what clinical terms the shrink might wrap around it, to his family and colleagues Willoby was a nutter, someone to make allowances for. The familiar anger rose in him but he fought it down. His daughter was talking to him, that was the main thing.

Jo regarded his cheerfulness in the morning with something akin to suspicion. There was a lack of tension in the air that was palpable, and when Maria kissed her father goodbye as she left for school Willoby had to hide his smile at his wife's astonishment behind his coffee cup.

'What have you two been up to?' she asked.

'I don't know what you mean, dear. Have a nice day.'

She paused to stare at him, and then with calculated coldness said:

'Don't forget you have an appointment with the psychiatrist this afternoon.'

His face darkened, the good humour flitting away. 'I won't, dear.'

She left. No doubt she would quiz her daughter on the way to school. Willoby stretched his arms far behind his head, the muscles cracking in protest. Was she jealous because Maria was speaking to him? Women were funny things.

Later he took a bus out of the city to one of the quiet villages which surrounded it like tiny satellites. Jo had the car today. Willoby was an infantryman again. It was a cold day, but clear: the omnipresent rain was holding off for a moment. He had his next meeting with Franks in the late afternoon. Was it the third or the fourth? It was getting to be a routine. As though it were his job now to go and see the shrink.

'How was your day, dear?'

'Not bad. We went through my childhood and talked about Oedipus.'

He would walk to the clinic, he told himself, get rid of some cobwebs and breathe some fresh air, have a look at the real world. No doubt the shrink would approve. He even had his log in a daysack that dangled from one shoulder. I'm playing the game at last, he thought as his feet led him out of the sedate streets to the open country beyond. Maybe if I'd done that a long time ago things would have been better earlier.

But he was in a good mood. Maria was talking to him again. He'd buy her a present. What would she like? He didn't know. Jo did all the present-buying in the house, all the Christmas-card writing and the other happy horseshit.

But it can change, he thought. I can be different. As soon as I have this thing licked we'll go on a holiday, the three of us. And I'll get Jo some new dresses, and ask Maria what she wants to be when she grows up.

The scenes filed through his head like those in a rosy soap opera. He could see it: Willoby Reformed, the model husband and father. Maria laughing with her dad. Jo making soft noises in his arms in the dark. It was possible, by God. It was still possible.

'No, Cardillac, let him be!'

'But he's in convulsions!'

'It is the way the dweomer takes him. Do not touch him, or there is no telling the harm you could do.'

'He told you this, lady?'

'He told me. We are to leave him alone, but observe what occurs.'

'This is madness, Merrin. It is evil! We must get him in out of the storm at least.'

'It is the Prince's bidding. Would you thwart his plans? Aimon knows what he is doing.'

The scream went through him like a sliver of glass and he staggered in mid-stride.

'Jesus!'

Nothing here but the heather and the slopes of the fells. Open moorland, and far below the village he had left behind.

Nothing.

He groaned. It was starting again.

A blast of wind came from nowhere and slammed into him. He went to his knees, cursing wildly, and the air about him became suddenly arctic. Snow and sleet blinded him. He was in the middle of a blizzard, his palms scored by shards of ice. It was black as pitch except for the pale flakes of snow whirling before his face, thick as a curtain.

It's not real. This isn't happening!

He stumbled across a body in the snow, swathed in wool. It was a man, limp as a dish rag. His beard was thick with snow and his eyes were rolled up so that the whites were visible.

The old man – the one who had been in his living room. Willoby bent to feel for a pulse but someone cannoned into him and knocked him aside. There was a scrape of steel. A woman's voice was shouting but he could not understand the words. He glimpsed her face though, white as ivory with the black hair flying wild about it. A muffled shape lunged at him through the snow. He saw the sword blade coming at him and knocked it aside instinctively, the edge slicing open his forearm. The pain seemed to clear his head.

The woman shouted again. She grabbed the arm of the swordsman. But he shrugged her off. Willoby stood amazed. He knew her, too. She was the girl who haunted his dreams.

'Wait!' he yelled, but his words were torn away by the wind.

The swordsman lunged again and this time Willoby was too frozen by astonishment and confusion to move. He saw the old man's eyes snap into life at the same second as the sword came spearing at his stomach. Too late to dodge. It passed straight through him.

And came away harmlessly. The swordsman, off-balance, toppled forward, slipping on the ice underfoot. He fell clear through Willoby.

The snowstorm faded. Willoby saw the woman help the old man up. The swordsman was casting about with his blade in front of him. He looked like a blind man feeling with his stick. But they were disappearing, retreating from him. Willoby gripped his middle where the sword had gone in but there was no injury there, no wound, no blood. At the same time he could feel the cold sting of the cut on his forearm.

A curlew called, wheeling high above him. He blinked, feeling the weak sun on his face. He could hear cars moving in the valley below, and a pair of anorak-clad walkers climbed a hill less than half a mile away.

There was snow in his hair, half melted already. Blood trickled down to his wrist and dripped to the ground. Willoby took a deep breath.

Hallucinations. Imagination. *Madness.*

He peeled aside his tattered sleeve to look at his arm. The cut was shallow, clean-edged. The blade must have been as keen as a razor.

What had she been shouting? Who the hell were these people?

Hallucinations. Imagination. My arse.

He could still feel the nip of cold in his fingers and toes. He grasped at the last shards of ice clinging to his knees, but they melted between his fingers. He laughed bitterly.

Here's another one for the Captain's log. Franks will have a field day with it.

He felt the cut in his arm again. It had stopped bleeding.

A knife did that, or a sword. I didn't fall on a stone or cut it on a root.

This shit truly is *real*.

He stood up with his daysack weighing down one shoulder. They were in trouble over there – wherever *there* was. That old man really had been in the living room, and he had carried a knife – the one which Willoby had, stupidly, thrown away. What had he said to him? *Turnkey*. Charming. What the hell did these people want with him?

He shook his head like a horse beset by flies. Am I really going mad? Could it all be real? Real people, a real place?

And if so, then the girl was real too, that raven beauty whose face was branded in his memory.

Could I – could we . . . ?

He cursed himself. Franks was right. He convinced himself these things were real, but to everyone else they were fantasies, illusions. Jo and Maria – they were real. That was reality: the fact that his daughter had decided to call a truce. That was more important than any fantasy woman.

He ignored the ache in his forearm, the sliced-open sleeve that the wind flapped, and made his way on up the hill. He couldn't be late for his appointment.

'Let me see this arm of yours,' Franks said as they sat in the comfort of his office. Willoby had always thought the place was like the study of an Edwardian gentleman, and this was reinforced by the bright fire burning in the hearth, flame-light reflecting off polished wood and the gold leaf on the spines of books. It had grown dark; a squall had come blustering in over the fells and was hammering on the roof, battering the windows. For once, Willoby was lying on the couch. He felt that he needed it, and the walk had tired him.

He reached out his arm and the good doctor studied it intently, nodding to himself.

'Classic self-injury. Did you hear voices telling you to hurt yourself, telling you to kill yourself maybe?'

Willoby raised his eyebrows. 'No, I told you: this bloke came at me with a sword and I knocked it aside. The edge of it gave me this.'

Franks let the arm drop and retreated to the fire. He stood there with his back to the flames, looking like a turn-of-the-century father about to lecture his son on the facts of life. Willoby sat up, irritated.

'You don't carry anything edged in that rucksack of yours, do you? A penknife, a razor, even a sharp flint?'

'No. Nothing.'

'Interesting. Maybe you got rid of it. Do you remember throwing anything away afterwards?'

'No.' A vision of himself hurling the strange knife across the moor in a fit of rage. 'No.'

'You must realize, John, that these hallucinations of yours have the ability to convince you of their reality. They hurt you – they injure you, or so it seems, but in reality you are hurting yourself. I have seen it many, many times, though to be honest your case is quite unusual. Schizophrenics hear voices telling them that they are worthless or even evil. They have demons inside them that to an extent possess them, make them injure themselves because they think that way they are able to punish themselves for their own shortcomings, what they regard as the dark side of themselves. But there are no demons any more. Everything that is inside your head belongs to you and you alone, John. We know less about the human brain than we know about the far side of the moon. Most of it is unused, and houses the deepest instincts and impulses of mankind.' He smiled easily. 'Somewhere in your brain, John, is a caveman sitting before a fire waiting for night to fall.'

You're not kidding. Willoby was weary with the day's events; the walk, the episode in the snowstorm that had not actually happened apparently, and now Franks standing there and pontificating. He was tired of it all.

What I'd give to be coming off an early shift with Howard, and the two of us popping into the local for a few pints. Normal life, for God's sake. Normality.

'This girl – the dark-haired one – she seems to me an avenue worth exploring. She is a recurring feature.'

Willoby groaned inwardly. How much was he paying for this?

'What about her?'

'Does she remind you of anyone, anyone you know?'

That brought him up short. 'Yes, she does.' That pale face, the black locks framing it. He faintly recalled a sense of seeing them before, somewhere else. 'I don't know who, though. Can't pin it down.'

'Your wife?'

'When she was a young woman, maybe a little. Same colouring. But it's not quite right.' What the hell is the point? he asked himself, and lit a cigarette. He had been smoking less lately for some reason, and the taste was rather sour. Franks was looking at him closely. Had any other man done that Willoby would have asked him if he had a problem and then gone on to punch his lights out.

Ah, the good old days.

'Would you rather be there, John? There with this girl and the others? Would you rather be there than here?'

Cigarette smoke stung his eyes, watering them.

'Maybe. They seem like real people to me. That world of theirs, that other place, it seems so . . .' He struggled with the words. 'So open, so free. It's a wilderness, like the wild west.'

'And you would like to go there, to live a life in that kind of place?'

Willoby stared at Franks suspiciously. Was the man making

fun of him? But no – that was not in a shrink's job description. I could be telling him about bug-eyed aliens, he thought, and he'd still sit there looking saintly and understanding. Bastard. He doesn't know, can't know; and he doesn't care, but he's getting paid by the hour to listen and spin his own pet theories.

Anger began to flicker and flare deep within him. It burned hotter and blacker by the second.

'You see, John, the fact that this fantasy place of yours is attractive to you – an unusual twist in the normal course of this disorder, I'm intrigued to note – means it is that much harder for you to admit that it is not real. It is harder for you to reject it. If a man's dream life fascinates and attracts him more than the real life out there on the streets, then he has a tendency to withdraw into it. It becomes a barrier between him and recovery, though he in fact sees it more as a refuge. Therein lies the problem. Do you understand me, John?'

Willoby nodded, not trusting his voice. The fury was toiling inside him, heady as wine. *John*. Only his wife called him that. He hated the sound of it in this man's mouth.

Bottled violence quivered in his frame. He felt like a wild thing stung once too often with the corrective rod.

'What we have to do is to convince you of the worthlessness, the *fictional* quality of your hallucinations. We have to show you that this world which the rest of humanity shares has its own attractions, its bright sparks, its joys.'

This man, thought Willoby, truly loves the sound of his own voice.

But he would not give in to the rage, the quivering need for violence. He forced out a strangled admission.

'My daughter is talking to me.'

'Hmm? What?'

'I said my daughter is talking to me.' He was infuriated with himself for telling this pillock, but he wanted to tell someone and he was paying for this, after all.

'I see. How splendid. Well there you are, John. Your daughter has shown that she loves you, that you are still a family. There's something to encourage you, something to pull you out of this other place you feel you're drifting into.'

'I'm not drifting into it, I'm being pulled in there! Don't you understand? I think they're trying to bring me into that world for some reason, to haul me across. God knows why.'

Franks nodded sagely. 'That is what it must feel like, but it is in your brain alone, John. You have the strength in you to fight them. They are merely symptoms of your own disorder. They have no power over you. As soon as you recognize that the battle is as good as won.'

Willoby looked at him through narrowed eyes. The anger was simmering in him still, but it had cooled somewhat. Maybe that's what it was – his madness. Perhaps that was where the urge for violence, the raging helplessness, the aching feeling that he was not where he was meant to be came from. Out of his madness.

A tepid wave of exhaustion washed over him. He felt old, worn out.

'Too old,' he whispered. Too old. He should be beginning to think of rose-covered cottages and all that crap.

So why was it when he thought of that girl's face he felt younger, more alive? That vast, empty land of hills and forests thrilled him – the fact that it could be real, as real as the slice in his forearm. This damned shrink didn't know what he was talking about.

My mind's like a fucking rocking horse, he thought. Up and down . . .

'They're *not* real, John,' Franks said sharply, startling him into attention. 'No matter how solid they may appear, they are all in here.' He tapped his temple.

'So you keep saying.'

'Your family – Jo and . . . and Maria. They are what is important. Let them help you. They'll keep you here, with us. Don't let yourself be seduced into staying in that other place. You will only harm yourself . . .'

Harm yourself . . . No, I won't be going again to that far country. I have things to keep me here.

He walked the whole dark way home with the rain striking his face and his feet slipping in the newborn mud. In his mind a vision flickered, despite all he could do to keep it out. A chequered landscape of sunshine and shadow on hillsides, the sky above a blue ocean and the clouds stately galleons sailing across it to the New World.

But he found his way back to the city at last and his weary feet quickened their step as he scanned brightly lit shop windows. Presents. He would buy something for Jo and Maria. Franks was right: they were what was important in this life of his — nothing else. If one good thing came out of this, he wanted it to be for them. It was not yet too late.

He hardly noticed the scurrying crowds, the fact that he was soaked through or that mud caked his legs to the knee. It was not important. People shuffling past him, nudging him, jostling him aside. They did not infuriate him any more. He was stared at by shop assistants, but even their disdain did not fracture his new intent. He bought a scarf, perfume — something he had never bought before — earrings. A coat (was that the right size? Jo had been a size ten once but that was years ago). He bought another scarf, a bracelet, and because he could not find a florist he bought a display of dried flowers. Then he staggered out of the warmth of the lit shops to the rainswept pavement. He was bubbling with good humour, feeling like Father Christmas hefting his sack. I come bearing gifts, he thought. He could not remember the last time he had bought something without a reason.

But this is where it changes. This is where I start to get better.

Then he saw the old man standing in a shop doorway, watching him.

There was rime in his beard, and he was swathed in wool and furs. His eyes glittered like two frostbitten flints. He was beckoning to Willoby with one claw-like finger . . .

And all Willoby's happiness turned to ash.

No, it's not real. He's not real, never has been.

He watched the old man mouth a single word, and knew what it was.

Turnkey.

Then the world changed.

PART TWO

The Kristill

Ten

The old mage had gone, truly gone this time. The pallet he had been lying on was empty, though when Merrin placed her hand there she could feel the warmth he had left behind, the indent his body had made.

'I thought mages needed powders, spells, talismans,' said Cardillac, the shock thickening his voice. 'But he had nothing. I believe he used his mind alone.'

'Yes.' Merrin wondered what world Aimon walked now. She remembered his earlier attempt, the hulking man who had materialized out of the snowstorm, Cardillac's violence. He had sworn that his sword had passed straight through the man, harmlessly, and Aimon had been enraged when he had come back to his senses. He was a demon, Cardillac had said. They were summoning fiends from hell.

Merrin did not think so. She believed she had met his eyes for a moment in the storm, and they had been tortured, bewildered, wholly human. What was this man in his own world? Was he happy there? She thought not. There had been an odd yearning in his stare. He had shouted something she could not understand – and then that fool Cardillac had blundered in with a drawn blade, thinking she was threatened.

A big man, he had been. Not young. Would it be hard to share his bed? she wondered. The bitterness came back to sour her mouth. She would let this man bed her so Tallimon would be King. It was that, or be thrown to the mercy of his soldiers. She would not have believed it once, that he would do such a thing to her. There had been a time when she had thought him in the palm of her hand – but she had been wrong. She was a whore, a slave. Best to remember that.

The worst thing was the knowledge that she would not betray him, would not go to the King with her story. She raged at herself for that. Not that it mattered, now they were out here in the wilderness. Another reason for bringing them so far from the city site; to nip short the buds of treachery. Her beloved Tallimon had considered everything.

Yes, the worst thing, the fact that she loved him still. Outside the tent, the storm raged on. Down in the plains they were having rain, a strong wind perhaps, but here in the lower passes of the mountains it was snow, whipped into a shrieking white maelstrom by the gales that hurtled down through the Greshorn massif. The warriors had set up what tents they had and brought the horses in with them for mutual warmth. Buried under the snow lay piles of logs, felled in the preceding days. But the weather was too savage to allow any building of huts, so they huddled in the leather tents surrounded by the sweet smell of horse and the damp reek of mould, drawing lots every so often to go out and tighten the guy ropes as the shelters sagged under the deepening snow.

'It is almost as though the land knows what we are about,' Cardillac said, ear cocked to the blizzard.

'What do you mean?' she asked him sharply.

The look he threw back told her he knew of her loss of status, but he answered civilly enough.

'This land, it is as if it is trying to bury us here, knowing the unnatural forces we are playing with. I think the very mountains sense the forces at work here. I think Aimon has hurt the land with his magicks.'

She did not scoff. It was too easy to believe, here in the shadow of those terrible heights which had claimed so many of their people. She remembered the awful nights – worse than this – when they had no wood to light fires, and men had slit their horses' bellies and placed the children in among the warm entrails. Without Tallimon she would have died.

And so her mind came round in its inevitable circle. She cursed herself.

The lamp was burning low and Cardillac poured in more of

their precious oil for the wick to float on. They had charcoal glowing in a bronze brazier but it would not last much longer. Merrin hoped that she would not become so cold that she would have to share warmth with Cardillac. They had been rivals for Tallimon's affection, Cardillac jealous of the hold she had had over him, she resentful of the claims Cardillac had on his time.

Well, he has him now, all to himself. May they both grow fat on it, conspirators together.

'How long will he be, do you think?' Cardillac asked. He was plainly uneasy.

'I do not know. I am no mage.' Only a whore, she added to herself.

'What if he does not return?'

'Don't you have orders to cover such a contingency?'

He shook his head. His brows met over his nose as he frowned. His blunt features were not displeasing, she had to admit, the grey in his hair like a pale stripe. She had been haughty with him in her time as the lady Merrin. He must be laughing if he knows my present errand, she thought.

The tent flap was thrown back and a blast of snow whirled inside. A fur-clad, snow-thick shape peered in and a muffled voice shouted over the roar of the storm:

'Cardillac!'

'What? What is it?'

'Something is moving out in the snow, outside the perimeter. The horses are going wild. It is big, taller than the drifts.'

'I'll come at once.' Cardillac began tugging on his heavy furs. 'Keep watch for him. Send word to me if he comes back,' he ordered Merrin. She nodded, nose buried in her cloak. Snow was already settling on her hair, powdering the ground inside the tent. Then Cardillac left. He and his sentry tied the flap thongs after them, shutting out the shrieking night. Merrin huddled close to the glowing brazier, shivering. The lamp had been blown out and the red charcoal glow was the only light in the tent. Snow fell from her head and hissed on the hot coals. Cardillac had probably been relieved to have gone. He would rather face a beast of flesh and blood in the snows than sit here and wait for whatever Aimon was dragging back with him from some other, alien world.

It grew late. There was shouting outside, faint over the scream of the wind. She dozed. The coals sank low, settling in on themselves with tinselly rustles. It was almost dark in the tent. She wondered wearily how many hours were left to the dawn, if any dawn could lighten the blizzard.

She opened her eyes from a doze. Something had changed in the tent. The storm still battled outside and she could hear the warriors calling to one another. But she knew she was no longer alone in the coal-lit dimness. There was something in here with her.

She spun round, searching the shadows. Something was breathing harshly beyond the dying glow of the brazier, the sound carrying even above the noise of the frantic wind. Her throat seized upon a scream and strangled it. At last she gritted out, 'Aimon?' But the presence in the shadows did not answer.

'Speak to me, Aimon.' Her hands fumbled with flint and steel. She should never have let the lamp go out.

A low groan from the darkness, deep as the growl of a beast.

She nicked her cold fingers on the flint. 'Cardillac,' she whispered. 'Help me.'

Something moved. She heard a heaviness shuffling across the packed earth and stone that was the floor. She flattened herself against Aimon's empty cot—

And met the body that lay within. She turned and stared. The old man lay as if asleep, blood smearing his lips and nose. His chest moved rhythmically, his breath a tiny whistle lost in the roar of the wind outside. She shook him.

'*Aimon! Wake up!*'

Something shambled into the hellish light of the coals. It was a man, huge and broad as a troll. His hair was plastered over his face. His legs were mud to the knees, and he grasped a forgotten bunch of dead flowers in one knotted fist.

His eyes were red with the coal-glow, pinpoints of mad fire in a twisted face.

'You bastards,' he snarled, his voice as deep as a drum. 'You took me away, and it was going to be all right.'

'No,' she breathed.

He was on her with impossible speed, his bulk moving as swift as a deer. The fists fastened on her upper arms, pulled her upright until the bones quaked and her spine was taut as a bow. She stared into the mad face. The looming shadows made it into a wasteland of light and dark. Heavy jowls hung from the jaw and thickened the neck, and deep lines scored it like scars, but even in that moment she could see plainly the despair that lay under the rage, the bewilderment beneath the anger. This is him, she realized. This is the man Tallimon needs – a madman who does not care if he lives or dies. He will kill me.

She thought he was going to fling her across the tent. She felt the muscles bunch and saw the cords leap into relief in his bull-like neck. She fought her fear, strove to remember what she had to do.

She pushed gently against his grasp and, tilting her head up, kissed him lightly on the lips.

He jerked like a startled horse and to her surprise she saw tears glitter in his eyes. His grip relaxed, and she breathed out deeply.

'You're hurting me.'

He let her go at once. He looked confused now, a lost child. But she was too afraid to feel any pity. She was aware of her own sour triumph. Tallimon had been right, once again.

'I am Merrin.'

A long silence as his eyes drank her in. 'I know.'

That halted her. But he seemed less menacing now, less like a wild beast. Reaching backwards she found Aimon's wrist with one hand. The old man moaned.

'What did you do to him?'

'Nothing. He – I hit him. He was kidnapping me. He's mad. He had a knife, once.'

She turned her back on him deliberately and bent over the old mage. He was breathing freely, and his eyes were moving under the closed lids. He would come round soon. Some of the hardness that knotted her belly eased.

'This isn't – I'm not here. You're all in my head.'

She turned to face the big man again. 'What did you say?'

'I'm mad,' he said unhappily. His eyes were still devouring her as he spoke. His great frame shook.

'This is in my mind. Catatonic schizophrenia. None of this is real.' He was almost pleading. '*I'm losing my mind.*'

More shouting out in the blizzard. A man screamed, a high note of agony cut off. The pair of them stopped short, listening.

An animal roar bellowed above the wind.

'What the hell was that?' The man's confusion had vanished in an instant. He seemed unaware that he had fallen into a fighting crouch.

'I don't know. Some beast that is prowling the snows. It has been stalking us since the early night, but the warriors will take care of it.'

'Warriors?' His eyes widened. 'So it's all here, then – you're all here, Tallimon too. But why the snow? It's supposed to be spring.'

She could only gape at him, wordless. He knew Tallimon? He talked as though he had been here before, and not merely as a shadow in the blizzard either.

'Who *are* you?' she asked, baffled.

'John Willoby. I know who you are. I – we . . .' He trailed off. She realized he was embarrassed.

'I've seen you before, in dreams and things.'

'Indeed?'

'That old man – he tried to get me before. He cut me. He ought to be locked up.'

That made her mouth twitch. It was not the first time someone had suggested imprisoning Aimon.

'He brought you here. He is a mage.'

'A what?'

'A wizard, a sorcerer. He can open doors between worlds.'

The man digested this for a moment. His flowers lay

132

abandoned on the ground beside him. Merrin was no longer afraid. She reckoned she was getting the measure of him. This had been a shock to him. Even though he knew about the existence of her world, he did not truly believe in it. And now he breathed its air, whilst one of its monsters stalked the snows close by.

She remembered Cardillac's conjecture – that Aimon had hurt the land with his magicking. Could the land then seek revenge? Maybe the creature outside had been drawn here. But best to leave such speculation until later. Their quarry had been caught, and her task had begun.

A not unattractive man. He had been handsome in his youth, she thought, but the years had bruised and bent him, and now a paunch hung over his strange breeches. But he had the look of a fighter nonetheless. It was the battered but wary face, the brooding ferocity she had seen in the eyes. He had killed before. He might even be good at it. She found herself momentarily wondering how it would be with him; rough, gentle, swift or slow, and her face hardened. She must not lose sight of her mission to make this man love her.

The way he had looked at her at the beginning had been propitious. That was something, at least.

'I'll wake up soon, and you'll be gone. That's the way it happens,' the man said. 'You always go, and there I am back where I started with the shrink dissecting my brain.'

She wondered what he was talking about, but his tone was gentle. She forced herself not to recoil when his great hand came up to caress her cheek with surprising gentleness. But he must have seen something, because he smiled wryly.

'Ugly big bastard, aren't I?'

His hand dropped but the smile remained, self-mocking, slightly bitter. She found herself liking him a little. He reminded her of someone she had known: something about his build, the way he carried himself, and that smile.

Where was Cardillac? What was going on outside?

There was a grunt of pain behind her and she turned at once. Aimon struggled to sit up, holding his mouth.

133

'Did he come?' he demanded thickly. One thin hand bit into Merrin's forearm. She pulled it free, tired of being manhandled.

'Yes, he's here.'

'And his mind – the intellect is intact. Have you restrained him?'

Merrin helped the mage upright. As he caught sight of the tall shape in the dying glede light he shrank back against her.

'Fools!' he hissed. 'Have you no guards to set about him? He is half mad. He would have killed me.'

The man smiled, this one a smile Merrin did not like. It reminded her somehow of Tallimon.

'I'm sorry, granddad, but you gave me a bit of a shock. I don't usually make a habit of socking pensioners.'

Merrin and Aimon looked at one another, baffled.

'You shouldn't pull knives on people, though. Where I come from that could get you in real trouble.' He stepped further into the dim light. Merrin could see that he was soaked and his legs mud-caked. He was swaying where he stood.

'The man is exhausted, Aimon,' she said in a low voice.

The old mage clawed his way to his feet impatiently. 'We all are, lady. Where is Cardillac? I must inform him the attempt has been successful. There are things which must be done— '

Again, the deep-throated roar of a large beast out in the storm. The men's voices were faint, now. Aimon's eyes narrowed. 'Are we being stalked by something? That sound, I know it.'

'It sounds as if it's drawing them away, making them follow it beyond the perimeter,' Merrin said.

'What the hell is it?' the man asked for the second time.

Aimon sank down on the cot. He wiped absently at his bloody mouth with the back of his hand.

'That sound, the roar in the wind. I recall it now. Remember the high passes, Merrin, the blizzards there?'

She nodded, suddenly afraid.

'The warriors kept the women and children in the centre

134

whilst they took to the flanks. That was before we straggled and so many perished.'

Again, she nodded. An entire clan, the Fullnir, had been lost. Upwards of three thousand people cut off from the rest of the Host by a blocked pass. And when the storms eased, and the warriors had forged back to link up again, they had been found lying dead in the drifts. Not with cold. They had been torn apart. Their bodies lay there still, no doubt, perfect with the arid cold of the Greshorns.

'Beasts harried us, probably the same which destroyed the Fullnir. They were man-like, but huge – giants of rime and snow with white fur that hid in the drifts.'

Another bellow, farther away.

'*Rime Giants* the men called them. I believe one stalks us now.'

'Terrific,' the big man said. He strode forward to the brazier and hit it a kick that sent the sparks flying like birds. A little flame started up, and his shoulders cast a huge winged shadow on the walls of the tent. He cocked his head to listen whilst Aimon and Merrin watched him silently.

'Wind's easing,' he said.

'Turnkey— ' Aimon began, but he was cut off.

'The name's Willoby, not Turnkey or Warder or Governor. Willoby. Close friends call me Will, but that doesn't mean you. Savvy?'

'Willoby.' The name was so awkward in Aimon's mouth that the man smiled. Merrin, catching his eye, forced herself to smile back.

'How do you feel? Is your mind at peace with itself? Have you suffered any ill effects from the transition?'

Willoby roared with laughter. 'You people are a scream. *I'm not right in the head.* If I were, none of you would be here. I'm lying on the pavement drooling like an imbecile, and the early Christmas shoppers are staring down at me.'

His tone grew hard, ugly. The abrupt descent into coldness made Merrin flinch.

'At home my wife and daughter are waiting for me,

wondering where I am. They're worried about me. And my daughter cares about me now. *She talks to me.* So I want out of this bullshit, pronto. I haven't the time for it any more.'

So he had a wife, a child. Merrin glared at Aimon but the old mage was refusing to meet anybody's eyes.

'You brought him here, even though he had a family in that other place? I thought he was to have no ties.'

Aimon said nothing. She spun away from the cot and her foot caught on something. It was the battered bouquet of flowers the man Willoby had been clutching. They must have come through with him. Dried flowers, they smelled of lavender. She handed them to him and he curled his fist around them, looking puzzled as if he had never seen them before. And now she did pity him in truth. She reached up and stroked his shoulder.

'I'm sorry.'

'I know. You remind me of my daughter,' he said quietly. 'That's what's been bothering me all this time.' His face gnarled into a grimace of grief.

'The blizzard is dying,' Aimon said unexpectedly. 'Perhaps the beast has drawn off.'

Willoby sat on the cot and warmed his hands at the brazier. Aimon regarded him warily.

'I shall go and find Cardillac,' the old mage decided. 'It is about time he knew what has happened. Keep an eye on your guest, Merrin.' He gave her a fierce, knowing look, and then fumbled his way outside, fighting the door flap against the declining wind. The big man gazed at the snow Aimon's exit had admitted.

'Where are we? We're not near that big hill where they're building, are we? It's too cold.'

Merrin took a seat beside him. There was a half-formed thought in her head. If this man was so important, then by controlling him she, too, could become a force to be reckoned with amid Tallimon's machinations. But she had to tread on eggshells.

'We're two days' ride from the city site that men call

Courbisker, up in the foothills of the Greshorn Mountains, the highest peaks of the world. It is colder here in the hills. Winter is a long time going, this high.' Tentatively, she set her hand on the back of his thick neck and caressed the soft skin there.

'Nice place, this,' the man said. 'I've seen bits of it. Open country. No towns to speak of. No crowds or cars or concrete.' He rubbed the lines on his forehead.

'I'm tired.'

She pulled him close without protest, made him nestle his head in her shoulder.

'My daughter's talking to me again,' he said, muffled, then his weight slowly came to bear on her. She manhandled him with difficulty until he was lying on the cot with his feet still on the floor, then got up with relief. He was asleep.

'You poor fat fool,' she said, not without compassion, and pulled the furs round his shoulders.

'Fat yes, a fool, no,' he said.

She gaped, one hand going to her mouth in horror.

His eyes opened. He smiled that perilous smile of his. 'I'm a light sleeper.' The eyes closed again. 'It's only a dream anyway, just a fit I'm having . . .' His breathing slowed.

Merrin smacked one slender fist into her palm. Fool! What damage had she done? Would he trust her? Damnation!

She bent and kissed his cheek, his eye, the corner of his mouth, but he did not respond. Was he truly asleep, or faking?

She felt a moment of panic. She had seen the soldiers' whores, worn women thrown from one to another in the barrack tents, used and discarded like old shoes. That would be her, if she failed in this. How they would enjoy taking the lady Merrin.

No, she must not fail, could not. This man would love her or she would kill herself.

Momentarily she considered putting her plight to Cardillac, using her wiles on him instead. Perhaps she could get him to turn against Tallimon.

No. Impossible. He was Tallimon's hound. He would die for his Prince without a second thought. It was this man, this alien – or no one.

Voices outside. The wind had died to a stiff breeze but the snow was still falling, muffling sound. Rime Giants ... if Aimon were right then perhaps none of them had any cause to worry. They would never live to see Tallimon's plan come to fruition.

Aimon came in, blue with cold, and after him Cardillac. Merrin caught her breath in shock at his appearance. The Decarch was livid with ice, his beard frost-grey and stiff. Snow had frozen into every crevice of his clothing; he was as pale as flour except for a bar of black, crystallized blood that stuck down the hair at one temple.

'What happened?' she asked.

Neither of them answered her. They stared at the motionless man in the cot.

'You got him, then,' Cardillac mumbled through blue lips. 'Good. The Prince will be pleased.'

'Wine,' Aimon barked. 'Stoke up the brazier and get us furs. And light a lamp! Moon and stars, it's as dark as a badger's sett in here.'

Merrin hurried to do their bidding. Cardillac seemed near to collapse. He did not protest as Aimon peeled off his cracking garments. They were as hard as armour.

'Your nose is frostbitten,' a strange, deep voice said, and the three of them paused. It was Willoby looking at them.

'Rub some alcohol on it or you'll lose it.'

'We have some knowledge of these things,' Aimon retorted. 'We were taught in a hard school.'

Willoby sat up, rubbing his eyes. 'Suit yourself. Bit rough out, is it?'

Cardillac glared at him like a pallid and angry ghost. 'He speaks our tongue.'

'It is the dweomer. I have found the same in his world. Be still.' Cardillac jerked as the strong alcohol was gently rubbed into his face by the old man, but he did not take his watering eyes off the big figure on the cot.

'Do you have a name?' he asked, hissing with pain.

'Willoby. What's yours?'

138

'Cardillac. I am Decarch – or was – of the third squadron of Prince Tallimon's Penton.'

'Good for you. That makes you the head man around here, does it?'

'Until the Prince returns to us.'

'You picked a hell of an unpleasant spot for a campsite.'

Cardillac did not reply.

'The beast,' Merrin asked him. 'What was it? Have you slain it?'

'It was a Rime Giant, like the ones we glimpsed in the Passage of the Mountains. It slew one of the sentries. We drove it off with javelins, but I fear it will return.' He brushed Aimon away impatiently and staggered to his feet.

'Let me drink some of this stuff instead of throwing it in my eyes.' He snatched the wooden flask from Merrin and swallowed deeply, then, after a pause, he offered it to Willoby.

The big man grinned, and his face became almost handsome. 'Thanks. Your health.' And he tilted the flask to his mouth—

– Then choked and spluttered, 'Jesus Christ! I thought you said it was wine.'

'Barley wine,' Cardillac told him. 'Good for the cold.'

'It has a kick like a horse, but by God it warms the vitals.' Willoby took a more cautious sip.

'You have been well entertained, I hope,' Cardillac said, drawing a cloak round his bare shoulders.

'Oh, admirably.' The big man winked at Merrin and she felt herself colouring. But he seemed to harbour her no ill-will. Was it her imagination, or did it seem that he and Cardillac had taken a liking to each other?

'What kind of man are you in your own place, then?' Cardillac asked. Blood was melting and dripping down the side of his neck. Aimon blotted it with a cloth, but he waved the old man aside. 'It's nothing – not a wound. I fell in the snow and hit a stone.'

The man Willoby seemed to pause, as if sizing Cardillac up. 'I used to be a soldier,' he said.

Cardillac nodded. 'I am not surprised. But you are one no longer.'

'No. I gave that up a long time ago.'

'Well, *Willoby*, I hope you are important enough to warrant our little expedition, and the life of one of my men.'

'You had your orders, Cardillac,' Aimon said in a raven-harsh voice. 'They did not include questioning the intent of your master.'

'Rest easy, wizard. I am curious merely. It is not every day that a man stands face to face with a being from another world. He looks normal enough to me, though – too normal, perhaps. I hope he is worth the trouble.' Cardillac stretched his tired muscles. 'The blizzard is easing, at least. We may be able to begin building tomorrow. A palisade first. I'm thinking we'll need it.'

'Word must be sent to Tallimon of the happenings here. Someone must get through,' the mage said.

The Decarch nodded wearily. 'It's not a mission I'll entrust lightly. It will be done.' Then, in a burst of exasperation, 'If I had my way we'd ride like fiends for the city site now, while the storm has eased. I don't like it here, Aimon. I have this feeling we have become a beacon for all the misshapen beasts of the mountains, and your magicking the flame that draws them.'

'You may be right, but we have our orders. I have carried out mine. It is your turn now, Cardillac.'

And mine, Merrin thought. My role also has begun tonight.

'I had not forgotten,' Cardillac said tetchily.

'It has been a long night,' Merrin said. She went to Willoby's side and stroked his arm. The big man was tense, alert. He seemed to be absorbing the detail of everything and everyone around him. He did not react to her caress and alarm shivered through her once again.

'We should get some sleep,' she said as steadily as she could. She could not meet Aimon or Cardillac's eyes. They knew what she was about, what her task in this was. Their knowledge made her face burn with shame, but she held her head up.

A whore I may be, but I was a lady once. I'll not let them forget that.

She retained her grip on Willoby's arm defiantly as Aimon and Cardillac left for the other tents.

'Leave the booze,' the big man said, gesturing towards the flask. 'Another nip will keep out the cold.' They nodded in unison, like a pair of sages. As they exited Merrin could see that it had stopped snowing. The wind had dropped and the night was as still and silent as milk.

Eleven

It was warm in the tent with the brazier glowing, and the dips smoking brightly. Willoby drank in the scene, savouring the smells of leather and wet earth, burning wood and oil, feeling the velvety fleece of the furs under his palms, the warm sear of the spirit in his gullet. Real medieval stuff.

And the girl. What was she up to? This tactile business. She gave him goosebumps. Too beautiful, too perfect to be truly interested in him, and yet here she was pawing him all over the place. And where was she going to sleep? With him? He shook his head over the flask of liquid they called wine. He would have called it moonshine himself. It was strong enough. No, there was something else going on here, some agenda hidden to him. Beauties did not go pie-eyed over John Willoby without a reason. And then there was her comment as she thought him asleep. Why had she called him a fool?

Hell Willoby, he thought. Lie back and enjoy it. It's only a hallucination. What an entry in the log this'll make! Franks will wet himself.

Jesus, I hope I'm not just lying on some wet pavement somewhere. I could catch my death.

So *real*, though. God, I love it. Monsters out in the snow, wizards and princes. That frostbitten bloke – what had his name been? *Kardalak* it had sounded like. That had been a real sword at his hip. Willoby would have liked to have examined it. Still, he had seemed a decent bloke, a real soldier type. More straightforward than the other two.

He wondered if it were possible for him to stay here long enough to see the sun come up over the snows, to see dawn in another world. That would be a hell of a thing. Worth catching a cold for.

He watched the girl as she moved about the tent, taking simple joy in her movements. God, she was lovely, like some long-limbed animal. She was small-breasted, lithe, slim-fingered. Her hair fell forward over her face and she tucked it behind one ear. He would have liked to kiss that ear.

Like Maria, yes, but yet unlike.

Yep, Franks would get an infinite amount of mileage out of this one; fancying his daughter's doppelgänger.

What was she doing, kneeling before that chest? He could smell something gamey, meat near to going off overlaid with a sharp herbal pungency. And bread – she was heating bread over the brazier. The wholesome scent filled the tent and brought the water springing into his mouth.

Oh, don't let me wake up, he thought. Not just yet. I want to taste everything, to guzzle it down and remember it, hold it in my head.

Inexplicably, he found tears burning in his eyes, and blinked them away.

'Are you hungry?' she asked, and he nodded. Easy, Willoby. Dreams can become nightmares. Tread softly.

She brought him warm bread with a hard, stale crust. It was full of husks and tiny pieces of grit that crunched between his teeth like sand, but it had a solid taste to it, as though it had been baked from the very soil of the earth. And tangy meat seasoned with rosemary and thyme. A dark taste, rich on the tongue. They washed it down with more of the potent spirit until he felt light-headed. He had so many questions to ask her, but was afraid to speak, to burst the bubble.

'Merrin,' he said, experimenting with the sound. Everything was new here, even the sound of the words he spoke. It was as though he had suddenly regained a voice after years of dumbness.

'Yes?'

'I like your name, the way it sounds.'

She seemed confused. 'Thank you.'

There had been tension in the air before, with the other two here. He sensed that there was a lot of water under the bridge with this trio. Now with just himself and the girl in the womb-like warmth of the tent there was a different, delicious tension Willoby had not known in years. He felt like a youngster, a young soldier sure of his own invincibility, convinced of the world's infinite variety.

And yet at the back of his mind the warning bells were insistently ringing. Take it easy, Willoby, test the water. Dreams fade, even if they are the product of madness.

'How old are you?' he asked her. She brushed crumbs from her shapely lips. 'I'm not sure. I was captured fourteen winters after Courberall made himself High King in the Battle of the Clans, and I was maybe twelve winters old at the time. The tribes do not keep much track of the years. Courberall has been King for more than twenty years—'

'So that makes you eighteen, nineteen maybe.'

She shrugged, then smiled at the look on his face. 'Did you think me older?'

'I'm old enough to be your – your father. What do you mean, *captured*?'

She bent her head and delicately picked her bread to pieces.

'The Kristill – Courberall and Cardillac's people – they are great warriors. They conquered many of the tribes in the forests beyond the mountains, and took them captive. At first they were treated little better than slaves, but with time the tribespeople grew as one with the Horse-folk and the differences between them were lost. But a great confederation of the Tribes finally drove the Kristill out of the Wildwood, and Courberall led them across the Greshorn Mountains that men said marked the rim of the world. And we found this wide place beyond them, this empty land.'

'You were captured too then, your tribe?'

Her hands were stilled in her lap. 'Yes.'

Willoby wondered if he had hit a nerve. He seemed to have subdued her. He bent forward and lifted up her chin. She smiled at him again but he thought it forced. Again, that sense of unease, the feeling there were currents here below the surface.

Or maybe I'm just being paranoid.

The drink was beginning to loosen his brain, and the dips seemed to burn very bright. He heard, faint and far off, the sounds of men and horses, the crunch of hardened snow, but otherwise the night was silent.

She pulled a rug from the cot and sat on the ground, leaning against his knee. All he could see was the head of dark, shining hair. He plunged his fingers into it and she tilted her head back. The flame-light made her skin a golden bloom and writhed in her eyes, as though they were windows on some far-off conflagration.

She was too perfect. It was too good. Willoby reached for the wine flask and drank. The fire in the stuff seemed to clear his mind.

Merrin had turned. She was kneeling between his knees now, her palms resting on his thighs.

'Don't you want me?' she asked.

For a second time the question stunned him. Something boyish in him whooped with delight – but the old Willoby, the battered middle-aged man, held back. He sensed intrigue in the air. It was the same sixth sense that in the army had saved his life more than once. All the same he laughed aloud, and for a second saw irritation – and something like fear – on her face before the mask came down again.

'Of course I do. Bloody hell, you're one of the loveliest girls I've ever seen.' But that's just it: you're only a girl, and I don't know if you really want to do this. 'I'm tired. I don't think I'm up to anything tonight.'

He felt she was assessing his veracity. There was a formidable woman in there behind the simple-minded caresses. He liked what he detected of it, and wondered what it would take to bring it out into the open. But now was not the time. Maybe there would never be the time – he might wake up first. The thought grieved him. Do it with her now. You might never get another chance. And that made him laugh again. He bent and kissed her forehead.

'I'm whacked, kiddo. I'm going to grab some shut-eye.'

To her puzzled look he said: 'Sleep. I'm going to sleep,' and added deliberately: 'Where will you sleep?'

That threw her. He saw again that edge of panic in her face, and wondered what the hell was going on in her mind, what wheels were turning. But then she lifted her head like a queen, and he saw the pride there.

'I would like to sleep here, if you have no objection,' she said stiffly.

'Suit yourself.' He yawned and began removing his filthy clothes. She helped him, and when he was naked laid the warm furs about him in the cot. When he saw her unfasten her own robe he turned his face to the wall of the tent, quietly amused at himself. Perhaps he was turning over a new leaf.

She blew out the dips and he turned at last to see her a scarlet shadow as she climbed in beside him. The touch of her skin sent his mind racing. She smelled of lavender and her flesh was firm and young, taut as an athlete's.

But he truly was tired, and the wine had blunted the edge of his desire. He did not object when she pushed close and laid her head on his shoulder, but kissed her hair and hugged her. He had the strangest feeling that she was seeking refuge in his arms, looking for oblivion in sleep. The notion disturbed him, and he found himself being sorry for her. But he drifted off into sleep somehow at peace, knowing that when he woke she and everything else would have gone. He nuzzled her hair, his last thought being that the pavement would seem damn hard after this.

When he woke he was for a moment totally bewildered. Everything was dark except for chinks of sharp snow-bright light. He wondered how he had got home and what time it was. But then he felt the prickle of the furs instead of the duvet, and remembered.

She was in his arms, asleep. He chuckled with the happiness of it.

Mad as a hatter I am, but Christ, what an imagination! He

146

could hear the knock of wood on wood outside, the sounds of men encouraging horses. It occurred to him that perhaps, in his madness, this tent was all that existed of this world, like a tiny film set with nothing but sound effects and blankness beyond.

He eased out of the warm cot. It was freezing cold in the tent. He touched the girl's hair as she lay sleeping, then hopped, cursing and hissing under his breath, to where chinks of light indicated the door flap. He pulled aside the thick hide and squinted out into the brightness.

Blue-white light, almost unbearably sharp, the sky a cerulean vault supported by pristine mountains. Snow everywhere, sparkling, the shadowed parts almost indigo. Tents, great shapeless affairs of dun hide weighed down with snow, the stuff drifting feet deep against their windward sides. Guy ropes were doubled in thickness by ice. Men were crunching through the morning with their breath snowy pennons in the air about them, men in high boots and cloaks with the glint of bronze brooches at their shoulders. Men hauling ice-heavy logs, hammering and chopping. The horse smell everywhere, men clicking with their tongues to urge the animals on. Woodsmoke, roasting meat, dung and the eye-watering winter smell of ice and clean snow, the hint of pine from the snow-deep woods on the lower slopes of the mountains.

'Bloody hell,' Willoby breathed. 'It's here. It's still here.'

He heard movement behind him and turned in time to see Merrin sliding her robe down over her shoulders. He felt a twinge of regret at his high-mindedness of the night before, and then remembered his own nudity. He bounded over to where his clothes lay on the floor, but Merrin stopped him.

'Wait. I have other things for you, more suitable for the season. Get back in under the furs. I won't be long.'

She darted outside. Willoby gave the brazier a nudge but the charcoals were as cold as gravel.

'Jesus, it's arctic in this place.'

Merrin was not gone long, and when she returned men came with her bearing kindling, food and furniture. The tent flap was pinned back, the dazzle hurting Willoby's eyes. It was like the fading of a dream. He had his first doubts about the hallucinatory nature of this. Surely delusions could not be this cold?

Another brazier was brought in, and a rough-hewn table that looked as though it had been pegged together that morning. Suddenly the tent was full of people coming and going. Willoby felt halfway between spectator and spectacle as he struggled into the strange clothes that Merrin had brought him. She was ordering about the ruddy-cheeked young men peremptorily, and Willoby realized dimly that she must be a person of some consequence.

Leather and wool, rough on the skin, and boots of thick, fur-lined hide with wooden soles. The cloak and brooch pin baffled him completely and he left them to one side. He stamped his feet in the new boots. They were clumsy, but warm; everything fitted perfectly.

'For the winter.' Merrin pointed at them. 'The Kristill prefer thin-soled footwear as a rule. It gives them a better feel of the stirrup.'

Flame started up in the new brazier. The food was laid on the table – apples and a strong-smelling cheese, more of the grainy bread and joints of meat as well as the inevitable wine. But there were flagons of dark, yeasty brew also, and Willoby sipped one cautiously.

'Beer! Good beer, too. Well I'm damned!'

'The King's favourite drink,' Merrin told him.

'Mine also.'

The men left, and he was alone with her again, but she hitched up almost one entire wall of the tent so that they sat and looked down-slope at a series of white hills broken with outcrops of wind-scoured stone and low trees. Beyond them the land levelled out and it was possible to see a green plain, vast in extent, and far off the glint of a river shining in the thin sunlight.

Spring down there, Willoby thought.

In the near distance men and horses were erecting tall posts in the snow, a line of them. They looked like a stockade. Willoby recognized Cardillac there, obviously directing things. He had a linen bandage about his head and his face seemed grey and pinched above the russet bloom of his beard.

Willoby picked at the food on the table, stifling a momentary craving for coffee and a cigarette. Thin needles of unease were pricking him. This was one hell of a catatonic episode. Could everything seem this real, this solid?

What if the shrink were wrong? What if he was not mad at all?

The alternative was so ridiculous though. No, more than that: it was terrifying.

But he did not feel very afraid, with his morning beer warming his stomach and his toes flexing in the furry warmth of his new boots.

Merrin was less clinging this morning, more business-like. He wondered if she could have been a little drunk the night before and was regretting it, but she had seemed as clear-headed as any of them. Women were odd at the best of times, he consoled himself, and he remembered the taut firmness of her body as she had slept in his arms, relishing the memory as a man might roll a good wine around his tongue. He had a lot of questions to ask her, but was somehow sure he would receive few answers.

'It's nice here. I like this,' he said tentatively.

'Had you seen the weather of the last few days you'd think less of it,' Merrin retorted.

'I did see it – or part of it. That guy' – he pointed at Cardillac – 'he tried to run me through.'

She was all ears. 'You remember that, then?'

'Of course I do.' He marvelled at the internal logic of his own delusions, the continuity. It was like picking up a book at the page he had left off every time. Was that usual? Franks would tell him, once he woke up.

'Aimon collapsed. He did not have the strength to keep you here on that attempt. He said you were not ready yourself – your mind was not at peace. You broke away from him. We thought he was going to die.'

'I was thinking something similar about myself,' Willoby said drily. 'It's no joke, having this thrown at you.'

She became coy. It did not suit her.

'You know then why you are here? Aimon told you?'

'He visited me once in my own bloody living room. Went at me with a knife. He said something about killing a king.'

Her eyes were wide. 'He told you that – that's what you're here for?'

'It's what he said. Doesn't make much sense. Personally, I think he has a screw loose; and I should know.'

But Merrin was not listening. 'To kill Courberall – of course! No Kristill could ever do it. It would consign his own clan to exile, oblivion.' When she looked at him again he was alarmed to see pity in her eyes.

'You are to be the royal assassin, then. No wonder Tallimon thinks you are so important. More important than anything or anyone else.' She was suddenly bitter. Willoby sensed deep waters, and had no idea how to approach her. He sipped his beer.

This is getting a bit much. Hallucinations ought to be more surreal.

The unease fluttered like a black bat at the edge of his vision.

Bollocks. I'll wake up soon and have some explaining to do. I bet I look a sight, lying twitching on the ground, those presents scattered about me.

'But how is it to be done?' Merrin mused aloud. 'And afterwards, how will— ' She stopped and gazed at him for a long moment before stroking his flabby cheek with one hand. 'I see,' she murmured. 'How stupid of me.'

'What?' He was irritated, and felt he was being humoured like a child.

But she kissed him on the mouth, hard. It was not affectionate, more like a blessing, as though she were sending him on a quest.

'You must look out for yourself in this world, Willoby. There are people in it who do not mean you well. Nothing is what it seems.' She hesitated, and smiled sadly. 'Trust no one. Do you hear me? No one. Not if you want to live.'

He stared at her, wondering what she was trying to say.

'I wasn't born yesterday, you know. I can look after myself.'
'Good.'

She left him after that, told him to amuse himself for a while but not to leave the confines of the camp. He had a feeling she was reporting to someone – Aimon maybe. He wondered who was really in charge here. That Cardillac bloke had seemed straightforward enough, not the type for intrigue.

He wrestled fruitlessly with his cloak for a while, finally draping it round his shoulders in a graceless fashion that kept out the worst of the cold. Then he ventured outside, the beer of the morning warming his belly.

It was sharp, clear, bright and white, blazingly snow-covered with those savage, magnificent mountains rearing up on three sides. The air was so cold it hurt his throat, and he muffled his mouth in the folds of his cloak.

Men were working everywhere. Some had discarded furs and jerkins and were working bare-chested, hammering in palisade posts with their sweat a small fog in the air about them. He could see others on nearby hills, mounted and armoured. Watchful. He wondered if there were any of those giants around that they talked about, and if he might see one.

The blare of heat from a smithy. A blacksmith was reshoeing a horse with studded horseshoes for the ice. His forge was a red, shouting glow and around it the snow had melted into brown mud.

The horse lines themselves, surrounded by a waist-high wall of snow. Men were rearing up crude shelters here while the horses nosed pale green hay that had been tossed on the ground.

And here, a wooden tower some eight feet high with two men guarding it. Willoby studied it, perplexed, until he saw the corpse lying peacefully at its summit. It was a funeral pyre.

Everyone was busy, and none of them paid him any more attention than if he were the corpse at the top of the pyre; a ghost wandering invisibly. It was unsettling, but not surprising. More like a dream, he thought.

There were maybe fifty men in the camp, all of them lean, hard-faced, ruddy types. Their rude health made him feel fat and old. He observed with satisfaction that he was taller than most of them, though.

He ventured down towards the work party that Cardillac was directing. The Decarch laughed as he approached.

'You've found a new way of wearing cloaks then, Willoby?'

'Damn thing. I can't get it right.'

'Let me help you.'

Cardillac twisted the folds round until they came down over Willoby's left arm, leaving the right arm uncovered. 'That's your sword arm, you can't encumber it,' he said, and stabbed home the big bronze pin. 'There – now you look a little more like one of us.'

The men were watching covertly, Willoby noticed. They did not seem unfriendly, merely curious and wary. He wondered what they knew of him, if anything.

'What are you doing – building a fort?'

'Indeed. Since last night I'm thinking we'll feel more secure to have a stout wooden wall between us and the local fauna.'

'How long are you staying here?'

Willoby thought the men working pricked up their ears at this, but Cardillac did not deign to notice. His answer was slightly curt.

'I only do as ordered. We stay here until we are recalled to the city.'

'Why were you ordered out here in the first place? Isn't it more dangerous than lower down in the plains?'

Cardillac took Willoby's arm in an iron grip, though he was smiling pleasantly. He edged the big man away from the working warriors.

'Perhaps it would be better to discuss such things over a flagon of beer. It is cold out here. We would not want you to come down with a mountain chill.'

Willoby wrenched his arm away. 'I'll bet you wouldn't.'

Tension sizzled in the air between them. Willoby felt the eyes of the warriors on their backs.

'What would you do if I said I'd had enough of this place – that I'd like to start off for the lower lands on my own, perhaps walk to that city they're building by the river and have a word with a king.'

He did not know if it was fear or murder in Cardillac's eyes, but the man's fingers bit into his arm again until it seemed they were driving into the bone.

'Regrettably, it is not safe to go wandering the hills alone. I would be forced to restrain you if you decided to hazard yourself in such a venture.'

'I get the message,' Willoby admitted. 'You have your orders.'

Cardillac relaxed and released Willoby's arm.

'You say you have been a soldier. You know, then, the importance of obeying them.'

They both smiled at the same instant, understanding each other. 'Fair enough,' Willoby said.

A man came leaping through the snow towards them.

'Decarch – '

'What?' Cardillac turned irritably.

The man looked at Willoby, hesitated, then said, 'The mage Aimon and the lady Merrin would like to have words with you. They are in the mage's tent. Also – also you are to see that the newcomer remains within the camp confines.'

Cardillac roared with laughter. 'There – you see, Willoby? I am not my own man. I must run the errands of a sorcerer and a — ' He faltered. 'A noble lady. I trust you will do as I ask and will not stray into the snows.'

Willoby nodded. 'You'd best go and join the conflab. Give my love to Merrin.'

Cardillac stared at him. For a moment Willoby had the feeling he was about to be told something, let into some confidence. But then the Decarch shouted out to one of his men: 'Ho! Caridan! Look after our guest here. I have an errand to run.' And he hurried off in the wake of the messenger.

Willoby watched him go. When he turned back the man Caridan, a big, beefy fellow with sweat on his forehead, was standing before him with an outstretched hand.

'Caridan son of Ferahin of the Surbadan clan. How may I call you?'

Willoby shook his hand, grinning.

'Call me a mushroom. They keep me in the dark and feed me bullshit.'

Twelve

Cardillac found Aimon and Merrin crouched over a shallow firepit in Aimon's tent. It was dark and stuffy inside, and the smoke stung his eyes. They had closed all the flaps.

We are a trio of conspirators, he thought with distaste, huddled in the dark.

Aimon was cradling a birchwood goblet of wine – real wine, the thin stuff that Tallimon liked to drink. His mouth was still swollen where Willoby had struck him. Cardillac stood warming his hands.

'I trust my men make capable errand boys for you, my lady?'

Merrin regarded him coolly.

'Enough, Cardillac,' the mage said. 'You pair can leave your bickering till later. We have things to discuss.'

'I am all ears, Aimon.'

The old man drained his drink, wincing.

'The messenger has been sent, has he?'

'He left at dawn.'

'When can we hope for a response?'

'It will be two, maybe three days to the city site. He should be clear of the hills by tomorrow, or the next day if the weather thickens again.'

'And the Rime Giants do not take him,' Merrin said.

'Indeed. We can expect a response within a week, if all goes well. I'm hoping to leave then. Our supplies will do well to last that long, and the snow has sent the game to ground.'

'What of the noble Fferidan's men?'

'No word. I have a few scouts out. They are to report back by this evening. But I doubt if Fferidan's column will venture this high. It is hard enough keeping forty alive up here – with a thousand the risks would be multiplied. What I believe he will do – if he is set on finding us – is send out small parties of Rimon strength. Half a dozen of those could cover a lot of ground very quickly. Last night's blizzard may have been a blessing in disguise. It will allow us to remain undetected a little longer at least.'

'I know.' Aimon poured himself more of the yellow wine. Cardillac began to sweat under his heavy cloak. He could feel the sticky throb of blood where the dressing bound his temple, but he scorned sitting down. He studied Merrin, wondering how the big man had found her last night, how she had taken it. For a moment pure envy twisted in his heart, until he lashed it away. Perhaps the lady would not be so high and mighty now. Perhaps she would even admit the lowly Cardillac to her bed.

Merrin looked at him with an unfriendly eye, as though she had read his thoughts. He smiled back.

'What do you think of him, Cardillac?' Aimon asked. 'This assassin of ours, is he fit for the task ahead of him?'

Cardillac considered. He had taken a liking to the man Willoby for some reason – perhaps because he was not stupid, nor did he have any airs and graces about him. He was a warrior gone to seed, but a warrior nonetheless.

'I think he will fulfil your expectations, Aimon, but . . . '

'But?'

'But I would be careful how you handle him. He is percep-tive. He has an inkling of the forces at work here. Only just now he threatened to leave the camp and march down to the city, to see the King.'

'What?'

'The threat was not made seriously, but it was not a jest either. I think he is letting us know that he is aware of some of the currents abroad. As I said, he is perceptive. He can smell treason, perhaps.'

'That is a strange word for the Prince's trusted lieutenant to use.'

'Do not play games with me, Aimon. We are all traitors.

Tallimon's plans threaten thousands of lives. The King would be justified in impaling every one of us. But I for one – and most of Tallimon's command – do not share the popular belief in the semi-divinity of kings. Courberall is a man. I have seen him drunk and frostbitten and exhausted, as have most of the warriors.'

'Nevertheless, the common people think of him as their saviour, the man who brought them out of the dark forests of the north, who united them against the tribes. Hence the exaggerated respect for the King's person these days. And hence our current dilemma. The man who kills a king is accursed, and his clan with him. That is why we have had our assassin brought here from the Iron World— '

'To do Tallimon's murdering for him,' Merrin put in. The other two glanced at her, surprised by the mordant tone of her voice.

'To do Tallimon's murdering for him,' Aimon repeated drily. 'I think sometimes that even if we are successful, Tallimon will never be King. I think that Courberall is the first and last king of the Kristill.'

'Tallimon will rule after his father is gone,' Cardillac said.

'Rule, yes – but not as a king.'

The Decarch threw up his hands. 'Why could we not have sent someone back over the mountains, kidnapped some tribesman and forced him to do the deed, instead of this magicking and sorcery?'

'Think, Cardillac. Think how long such a journey would take. Think how uncertain he would be of surviving it. And think how much better off the tribesman would be if he simply denounced the conspiracy at the moment of truth, instead of carrying out his orders.'

'Why shouldn't this Willoby fellow do the same?'

'Two reasons. First, he has no vested interest in seeing either side win. He does not care. All he wants is to be returned to his own world. We hold that power over him. Secondly— ' And Aimon gestured mutely at Merrin. She glowered but said nothing.

Cardillac laughed, throwing his head back. 'What? Has he fallen head over heels in love with the lady already? Merrin, you must have surpassed yourself last night.'

She sprang up, swift as a panther, and slapped him full across the face.

He did not move, though he could feel the trickle of the reopened wound down his cheek.

'A sore point? Have you not accustomed yourself to your newfound role, lady?'

Aimon flapped a hand, his eyes glowing like two coals in the firelight. 'Stop it, both of you. This absurd fencing only hurts our own cause.'

Cardillac bowed deeply, and wiped the blood from his cheek.

'Has Tallimon entrusted you with the training of our novice killer?' he asked Aimon calmly.

'In part. I am to paint him a picture, and show him his place in it. After that we will await the course of events and the will of our liege lord. You, Cardillac, are to give him tuition in the . . . finer points of his education.'

'I am to be the teacher of butchery, then. I have had small experience of covert killing, Aimon.'

'He should be taught the way of the long knife, the poniard, the rapier – and the longsword,' Aimon went on, ignoring him.

'So? How many months will my pupil have to digest this? With most men we would have to set aside years.'

'Teach him the dagger,' Aimon said waspishly. 'It is all Tallimon wants him to be able to use.'

'That will be no heavy task . . . I take it, Aimon, that the assassin will no more survive the assassination than the King will.'

Aimon looked up. 'That is for the Prince to decide.'

'He has a family in his world. A wife, a child,' Merrin said.

'He will never return to them,' the old mage said heavily. 'Even if he survives, he is not going back. And he will not survive. We will need a body to show the mob so they can impale it as the corpse of a king-killer.'

The three were silent. Momentarily, Cardillac wondered why he was here, plotting murder. For Tallimon, of course. He owed everything to his Prince. But he wondered if he were not still serving the youth he had hunted with long ago rather than the hard-faced man Tallimon had become. No matter. It was too late for all of them now, and especially too late for the man Willoby.

He was already buried.

The good weather held throughout the day. Some men hunted out their wooden eyepieces against the glare of the snow – the Greshorns had taught the Kristill much about surviving in high places. The palisade was finished by the artisans in the early evening, and they began laying out the walls of the huts that were to replace the tents. It kept the men busy, and stopped them from thinking. A dozen had been sent off to the woods with most of the horses, to fell more timber. Cardillac had watched them go with some misgivings. Nearly half his command was outside the stockade, either on scouting missions or on the timber party. He stood the rest to as the first stars began to glitter, and the men stamped paths through the snow as they kept watch. It reminded him of the mountains; the endless cold nights, the wind in the peaks; the waiting.

Willoby asked to accompany him on his rounds. The big man had wandered about the camp all day, fascinated by everything – the horses, the smithy, the weapons, the armour – even the frugal meals of the warriors. He had listened to Caridan's tales of battle and brigandage, drank the sour beer of the pack train and handled the Kristillic longswords with something like relish.

He's enjoying himself, Cardillac thought incredulously. He likes this. But Willoby's references to waking up from the dream puzzled him. Did the man truly believe that none of this was real?

They stood by the fire at the rough gate and watched the timber party come toiling back up the slope towards them in the gathering dusk. The men were at the horses' heads, and the animals were toiling hard through the deep snow, trailing new-cut logs behind them.

Willoby stamped his feet and held his huge hands to the wind-whipped flame of the fire. He looked healthier, Cardillac thought, than he had that morning. The cold had put colour in his cheeks. He had too much meat on his bones, though.

Willoby saw one of the horses go down. Its forefeet had plunged into a crevice beneath the snow and it was on its side. Men were shouting, stick-figures moving in the gloom.

'Take charge here, Caridan,' Cardillac ordered, and leapt off down the slope with one hand steadying his sword hilt. On impulse, Willoby followed him.

It was hard work, slogging through the snow. The horse was a big, grunting blackness against it. They were clustered around, struggling to move it. Cardillac swept his arm at them. 'Get on up to the fort – get the rest of the horses in. Gamran, Neyr, you stay and help.'

They pushed and hauled like maniacs at the heavy beast, and half rolled it out of the hole. Cardillac slashed free the log harness with his sword, but the animal refused to regain its feet.

Willoby pushed and hauled with the rest, his breath a dim cloud in front of his face. The horse moaned like a human being, warm under his hands.

A thin, wailing cry out in the rocks. They paused to listen.

'Rime Giant,' the older man, Gamran, grunted.

'Where?'

'There, on the nearer hill – no, it's gone to ground. Hard to see it when it stops moving.'

Cardillac cursed. He beat the horse with the flat of his sword. The animal whinnied pathetically but remained on its side. Willoby peered out into the darkening distance but could see nothing moving.

'A break in the leg,' Neyr told them. He was feeling down the animal's limbs in the failing light. It thrashed and moaned beneath them.

'Kill it.'

Willoby saw the knife flash, and heard Neyr mutter something soothing, a horseman's prayer. Then there was the gurgle and steam, the reek of gushing blood. Neyr had cut the animal's throat.

'It's moving again,' Gamran said hoarsely. The ice from his breath had settled in his beard.

'It's coming this way. The blood will draw it.'

Cardillac backed away, bumping into Willoby.

'I can't see anything,' Willoby said irritably.

'It's there, believe me. And you should not be here. Neyr, get him to the fort. Gamran, come on, quickly, or it will be upon us.'

They left the steaming corpse in the snow, and heard a clatter of rocks in the twilight. The watchfire at the gate was bright and yellow in the darkness. It seemed a long way off.

'The bastard is well-nigh invisible.' Gamran spat.

'Get to the fort, I tell you. It'll be on us in a trice.'

They fought their way upslope, the breath rattling in their throats. Willoby fell behind, gasping for air. His legs were burning with effort, the breath a harsh rasp in his throat.

'I'm not fit for this,' he panted. Neyr and Gamran grabbed his arms and half dragged him along. Men were clustered in the gateway with torches burning in their hands. Then someone shouted.

There was a great crunch and swish of snow behind them. Willoby turned in time to see a vast darkness rear up out of the drifts. Two icy blue lights burned where the eyes were. His nose was filled with a musky potency, a gagging reek of carrion.

Jesus Christ!

'Run for it!'

An arm swept out, thick as a tree trunk. Willoby saw Cardillac throw himself aside and it hissed over his head. He jumped up and stabbed with the longsword. The blade entered under the hollow of the arm. Transfixed, Willoby watched the iron slide easily into flesh for half a handspan. There was an

161

enormous howl that seemed to stun his ears. The blade was almost ripped from Cardillac's grasp as the beast recoiled. The Decarch staggered, went to his knees in the snow.

Missiles landed around them. Javelins. Men had come down from the gate and were hurling them at the monster. Cardillac scrabbled away on hands and knees as the beast clamoured and batted the raining missiles aside.

Torchlight brightening the night, sparkling yellow and saffron off the broken snow. Shadows capered madly. Willoby was dragged upslope by the others, then dumped like an unwanted sack as they turned back to help Cardillac fight the whatever-it-was. He struggled to his feet, some irrational part of him hugely reluctant to be left out of it all. And he wanted a closer look at the thing which had attacked them. It was something to marvel at, not to be afraid of. And he hated taking a back seat in any fight.

'Give me a sword,' he said, as they retreated upslope towards him. 'Let me do something.'

But someone grabbed his arm and propelled him back up to the flame-filled gateway. 'Keep him here!'

Aimon was there, and Merrin. Willoby was scarcely aware of them. His whole being cried out to be in the thick of things down below.

But the fight was finishing. The giant was retreating down the hill, shrieking as it went. The snow was black with blood. Cardillac was calling his men in across the javelin-littered slope. The dead horse lay forgotten.

I missed it, damn it.

Aimon was saying something in a shrill voice: 'You were told not to leave the stockade, you damned fool! You could have been killed!'

'So sue me,' Willoby quipped, and he saw Cardillac's tired smile at the exchange.

Next time, he thought. Next time I'm going to get right in the middle of it.

Cardillac had them work through the night by the light of

watchfires, strengthening the stockade and rearing up the huts. He had the feeling that their luck would not last. The weather was being too kind, and they had been fortunate in seeing off the Rime Giant with no loss. He wanted the fort – they had all begun calling it that – secure as soon as possible.

He had the dead horse jointed and roasted over the fires despite the sullen looks of the warriors. They could hold out for ten days or so now. After that they would be on half rations, and he would have to send out hunting parties – a thing he was loathe to do. He thought of Ordachar, as faithful as a hound and with about as much brains, commanding his Decon down in the city. Cardillac had indeed been given the harder task up here, but he wondered what was going on in Courbisker, what intrigues were being hatched. If Fferidan's command intercepted the messenger then they were as good as dead.

He joined Aimon for a jug of barley wine in the middle of the night. The mage's tent was warm and close after the keen night air. There were herbs and unguents scattered around the place, tiny glass phials full of multi-coloured powders, a tang of spice hazing the glow of the tallow candles. And yet Cardillac was convinced that it was all for show – that the real magic was in the power of Aimon's mind. The fripperies of sorcery were merely to convince the credulous. They were props, laid on to impress.

He told Aimon this, and the old man laughed.

'Maybe you are right. But have you ever thought that I myself might need some encouragment too? That these things might be something of a comfort to my own mind? Men can convince themselves of anything if they try hard enough.'

'Is that how you do it? Is that how you make the magic happen?'

'Partly. It is my task to bring into being a space in which anything is possible, then to let the dweomer within it and bend it to my will. I can draw a pentangle or a circle in the ground if the area is small, but it is not necessary – it just helps sometimes to see it. And as you have said, it impresses the credulous.'

'Where does such power come from?'

'From the same place that gave birth to us all and will receive us when we are no more. The earth, the rocks, the trees. The world under our feet. There is power in the land for men to harness if they are able. It can be as simple as planting a seed and watching it grow – that too is magic, if you like. Or it can be used for other ends, if focused properly. The wolf-woods that we went through before the Greshorns – they were strong in magic. I could have learned much, had I stayed there.'

'You could have learned to die,' Cardillac told him. 'Those woods were as dark and savage a place as I've ever seen. And the beasts!'

'A man can be a reed or an oak: he can bend with the wind or break under it. Mages must be reeds, sometimes mere channels for the dweomer. They can try to direct it to suit themselves, but in the end nature prevails. The balance is rectified.'

'What do you mean?' Cardillac asked, mystified. The old man was speaking gibberish. Had he not seen evidence of his powers it would have been tempting to regard him as an eccentric. But even if Aimon had not been a mage, Cardillac knew he would still be a formidable man. There was a flint-sharp mind in there, behind the whiskers and the old-man's mannerisms.

'I am an instrument of the land,' Aimon explained patiently. 'As are the Rime Giants, the grypesh, the wolves of the northern forests. We are buds on the same branch – the same sap runs in us all.'

'You have lost me, Aimon.'

'Maybe. I am trying to explain the dweomer to you, Cardillac. If a man understands its nature, then truly he is a wizard of power. Myself, I am little more than a meddler on the edge of great mystery. But this man, this Willoby— '

'What about him?'

'He worries me, Cardillac. He does not belong here. When I stood in his world, however fleetingly, I felt a great emptiness. There may have been magic in that Iron World once, but it is dead now, or dying. The heart of that place is hollow. The men there have burrowed through it like blind moles. But now one of those men is here, in our world, and the land knows it. It is not my magic that draws the creatures in on us, Cardillac, it is the man Willoby. The land knows he does not belong.'

'Are you saying that the land itself is trying to kill Willoby?' Cardillac was astonished.

'I believe so.'

'That's absurd, Aimon. I don't know what woolly-headed notions your studies have stuffed into your head, but I'll tell you this: earth and stone, wood and water – they are not *alive*. They cannot think and feel. The world is made for men to walk it, because they can do these things. They can alter it as they see fit. It cannot fight back.'

'That is what the men of the Iron World think,' Aimon said sombrely. 'And they are killing their world. You lack a certain vision, Cardillac, a certain willingness to believe. It is strange in someone who survived the passage of the mountains.'

Cardillac threw up his hands and laughed. 'We have worries enough, old man, without your vapourings adding to them. You must spare me your magical theories. I have much else on my mind.'

'So be it,' the mage said, and he drained the last of his wine.

'We must talk of realities,' Cardillac went on briskly, hoping to jog Aimon into a more practical frame of mind. 'I must know if there is anything you can do, should we run into Fferidan's men.'

'Fferidan's men may not even know we have left the city. Our exit was discreet enough.'

Cardillac shook his head. 'Madavar gets to hear everything. He will have informed Fferidan of my absence – and yours. He

165

may even know of Ordachar's promotion. In any case, there are trackers among the Kristill who could follow our trail with their eyes shut. The blizzards will have baulked them somewhat, but I think they will continue quartering the hills until they find us.'

'What do you intend to do?'

'There are more than forty of us here – too large a party to make it back down to the city unnoticed. I do not believe that Tallimon will come out to meet us in person, whatever he said. He is being too closely watched. So we are on our own. Once the time comes to go I intend to leave most of the men here, as bait to distract our pursuers. Fferidan's men have no quarrel with mine so long as I am not present. But we will journey to the plains with no more than half a dozen.'

'And you want to know if my magic can aid our journey.'

'I've heard it said you raised a fog out of the river at the Battle of the Clans to hide Courberall's reserve wing, and that you beat off the tribes with creatures you had created out of loam and dead leaves.'

'So you want the dweomer to conceal us, or to harry our pursuers?'

'Yes – of course.'

Aimon looked irritated. 'Have you not listened to a thing I've said? This man Willoby, he disrupts the balance of our world. He is alien here – and you want me to summon up the dweomer in his presence, to unleash it around him?'

'Well, I— ' Cardillac felt angry, shamefaced at his own lack of comprehension.

'I cannot do it. I will not. There is no telling what might happen. I might blast him back to his own world, or even send him to some empty, in-between place. Did I not tell you that I am a *channel* for the power? I can bend it to my will, but only if it allows me. The power in the land, were I to let it loose near Willoby, might destroy him, could destroy all of us.'

'I understand, Aimon,' Cardillac said wearily. Things were too complex. He was not the right man for this. To accomplish this mission it seemed a man had to be a diplomat and a wizard as well as a soldier.

'Let us hope so. No, Cardillac, there will be no fogs called up, no homunculi. We must depend on our own ingenuity to make it to the city.'

'And luck, if we are to survive the Grypesh packs. But say we do, Aimon, then . . .'

'Then . . . what?'

'The – the assassination. When do you think it will take place?' Cardillac despised himself for the way his voice had turned into a whisper.

'When do you think? Use your head, Decarch. Is it best to kill a king in a secret place when no one can see who did the impious deed? Or in public, where all and sundry can point their fingers at the killer?'

'And no doubt tear him apart, in their rage and despair.'

'You begin to see. We have that rare commodity, a faceless man, an expendable man. He shall be given to the mob. They will kill him before he can talk. Tallimon will make sure of that.'

'The city founding!' Cardillac cried.

'Indeed. A ceremony at which all the clan heads and nobles will be present.'

'It must be – that must be it.'

'Yes.'

'But then what?'

Aimon sighed, making Cardillac feel like a slow-witted child.

'For a start, no one will carry arms to the founding. Except, no doubt, Tallimon's household warriors.'

'The founding is two weeks away. Can Willoby be kept secret for that long?'

'He can if he is kept here. We are in for a protracted stay I think, Cardillac.' He yawned, showing yellow canines.

'Indeed? Then I had best set about the problems of food

and timber.' Cardillac was happier now, with a concrete problem to solve. Aimon grinned at him.

'You do not make a great conspirator, Cardillac.'

'I know. I'm nothing but a soldier.'

Thirteen

Tallimon was surveying the rapidly rising wooden longhouse where his tent had been when Ordachar rode up with a dozen retainers behind him.

'Sire, I must speak with you urgently – in private.'

Tallimon's heart lurched. It could only be one thing: bad news from Cardillac. He motioned Ordachar into the end hut of the longhouse where he was now living. It was the only section yet roofed. The gales of the past few days had flattened other tents besides his. He shut the ill-fitting door behind them.

It was dark after the bright blue day, and the hubbub of the building city was cut off somewhat. Tallimon struck a light, forcing himself not to rush. When the lovely beeswax smell and lambent glow of the candle had kindled he looked his vassal in the eye, composed, emotionless.

'Well?'

'Garran, of your eighth Rimon – he has been taken by a clearance patrol on the way into the city. Cardillac must have sent him. They have him in a house next to the Great Hall, awaiting Madavar's attention.'

So it was news from Cardillac.

'Do they suspect— . Can you get anyone near him?' He fought down the shake that threatened to invade his voice.

Ordachar shook his head doubtfully. 'He is not the first to be detained for leaving the city without authorization, since Courberall's decree. But the others were soon released. Garran is well guarded. They mean to keep him, is my guess. They know something is afoot and will let no one see him. It is my view that Madavar knows of Cardillac's absence.'

'Of course he knows,' Tallimon snapped. 'He knew the

morning after Cardillac left. And he knows Garran comes from the high hills. He is good at arithmetic, my half-brother. He has put two and two together very swiftly. Damn him!'

'What shall I do, sire?' Ordachar sounded almost plaintive.

'Do? I am not sure . . . Garran knows not to talk. I shall make a protest when next I see the King, plead for the deliverance of one of my men, as is only right. I'll bet Courberall does not even know of his capture yet. Madavar will want to keep this one to himself for a while, until he is sure of events.' He paused. 'How have you come to know of Garran's capture? Is the knowledge widespread?'

'No, sire. One of my Decon happened to be down by the river when Garran was brought in. Few others know, or will know.'

'Do not let it stay that way, Ordachar. What clan is Garran?'

'The Serradai, sire.'

'Then let the clan head – it's Taurberad – know that one of his clansmen is being detained for no good reason. We must make a noise, Ordachar, before Madavar has any facts to act upon. We must get him released before my half-brother has had a chance to work on him.'

'Will I try to get near him?'

Tallimon considered. 'Yes – perhaps you should. Or you could get a wench from one of the barrack brothels near him. I want to know what has become of Cardillac, how Aimon has fared. Before we know that we can do nothing.'

'It will be done, sire.'

Tallimon fixed his subordinate with a cold stare. 'If you do use a whore, be sure to kill her afterwards. Be discreet, Ordachar, or we will play straight into Madavar's hands. He has been praying for an opportunity such as this. If Garran talks we are all dead men.'

'But sire, surely he does not know anything treasonable – only that Aimon went into the hills to carry out an experiment, and whether it was successful or not.'

'He knows Cardillac's location. If Madavar gets it from him then Fferidan's command will be sent to snap up the whole party. It will not be long before they discover what is in the wind.'

'Then we should send another messenger to Cardillac, tell him to move, to go higher up in the mountains.'

'Ordachar, Ordachar.' Tallimon placed one slim hand on his Decarch's shoulder, making the man flinch. He smiled reassuringly. '*We* do not know where Cardillac is either. Hence we are entirely helpless without Garran's information.' His face hardened in an instant.

'Get it for me.'

He wondered, after Ordachar had gone, about the wisdom of making a conspirator out of such a man. Ordachar's only virtue was his loyalty – Tallimon had saved his life in a forest battle when they were both youngsters. The man had stayed by his side like a hound ever since. A good warrior, and an excellent junior officer; but perhaps Tallimon had promoted Ordachar beyond his abilities, given him too many responsibilities – too much information.

He is an old comrade, he thought. He has always been there. And the hardened, logical side of him said: he is a liability, a weak link. Someone has to watch him lest he trip over his own feet and bring us all down with him.

Curiosity burned in him. He felt a fierce hunger to know whether Aimon had succeeded. Was the Turnkey even now walking the hills of this world?

And sharing Merrin's bed.

He shied away from the pain of that.

Time was slipping by. Less than two weeks to the city founding, the day when it was supposed to come together. He could not afford hitches at this late stage.

If I do go down, he thought, I will at least be sure to take Madavar with me.

High in the Greshorn foothills, Cardillac lay in the snow and shielded his eyes against the reflected sun glare. It was hard to see in the massive brightness, but he thought he could make something out moving on the lower slopes.

Caridan passed him his wooden slit goggles to ease the glare, and he held them against his eyes. The world instantly became a dimmer place. His eyes were able to focus.

'Horsemen. And foot also. I count . . . thirty-four of them. What about you Caridan?'

'Thirty-six, but then my eyes are better than yours. Eighteen only are mounted. It's my thinking that they lost their horses in the storms. They'll be a weary bunch by now.'

'What clan, do you think?'

'Fferidan took out most of Quirinan's men, with three squadrons from the Royal Clan. They could be Quirinir or Courberans. Unfriendly at any rate.'

'Aye,' Cardillac said heavily. He studied the tiny, distant figures intently. The cavalry were in an extended line, with the infantry clumped behind them. He could sense the men's weariness as he watched their legs pump up and down through the deep snow.

'They'll be here by mid-afternoon.'

'If they don't give up first.'

Cardillac grunted acknowledgement. Then he tensed as a terrible thought struck him. What if they had captured Garran, the messenger he had sent to Tallimon?

No – they would be sending more men than this single understrength Rimon. This was just one element in Fferidan's sweep of the hills.

But what to do about it?

He and Caridan lay on the reverse slope of a small hillock half a mile from the camp. In the hollow behind them three more warriors waited silently. The world was wide and white, the sun flashing from a flawless sky and refracting tenfold from snow and ice. It was early morning. They had a few hours, at most, to think about it.

Kill them? And then have more of the enemy out looking for them. Tracking would be child's play in these conditions.

Hope they would go by without noticing the camp? Too risky.

Cardillac looked at the blue vault of sky above. Not a cloud. A blizzard would be ideal, but the weather had settled down again. No hope of that.

There was a third option. He could decoy the pursuers away from the camp. He bent his head and tasted the cold snow. He hoped he would not have to choose that option.

'How well hidden do you think the fort is, Caridan?'

Caridan lay on his back in the snow, staring up at the sky. 'We have plastered everything we can with snow, even the stockade. It looks reasonable enough. It is movement that stands out at a distance, and the artificers are still moving around at their work. Also, once they start their hammering and chopping the sound carries for miles. They are champing at the bit back there to get started.'

'I know. Thank Neyr's eyesight that they did not. There would be no avoiding a fight otherwise.' Neyr had been the southernmost of the pickets Cardillac had sent out with the dawn. Work in the fort had halted as soon as he had come galloping in with the first light to tell them that there were men on the slopes below.

'You're going to try and avoid a confrontation then?' Caridan sounded distinctly disappointed.

'Of course. We cannot be glory hunters all the time, Caridan. For now we must be more like foxes. We must be cunning, wary— '

'And keep our tail between our legs.'

'Even so.'

'I don't like it, Cardillac, and neither do the men. This witchery and sneaking around, and then building ourselves a fort, no less, here in the middle of the wilderness. And this man, Willoby. He seems a normal enough fellow, but where did he come from? They are saying that Aimon's magic brought him here from another world. They are saying also that it was Aimon's magic that brought the Rime Giants flocking round us like summer flies round a honeycomb.'

'*They* say far too much,' Cardillac said testily.

Caridan fell silent. They lay side by side, oblivious to the

173

numbing chill of the snow beneath them. The sun was warm on their necks. The men in the distance plodded on relentlessly.

'And the lady Merrin – she is sharing his bed,' Caridan said in a whisper. 'What will Tallimon say when he finds out about that, eh Cardillac? He's sweet on her. There will be hell to pay.'

'No doubt,' Cardillac said wearily. He rubbed his smarting eyes. He would have to decide what to do soon, and he did not like it – he didn't like anything about this whole mission. He had thought that part at least of the world he had known had survived the Passage of the Greshorns, but Tallimon was going to tear down every shred of the life the Kristill had known before. For the first time, he wondered if his liege lord were in the right of it, if it would not be better to persuade him to drop this madness. Courberall was not an unreasonable man. He could be talked to, surely.

He sighed. Pipe dreams. Better to follow orders, to make the best of it. *You will have more than a Decon to command*, Tallimon had said. If they survived.

'Come,' he said to Caridan. 'Let's get back to the fort. We have preparations to make for our guests.'

It was less cold this morning, Willoby thought. His nose was not quite so chilled above the furs.

Furs – yes. Still here.

Panic beat frantic and far-off wings at the back of his mind, but he ignored it.

She was asleep in his arms. They lay entangled like two wrestling children caught by the Sandman. He smiled.

There had been barley wine, and candlelight, and the glow of the charcoal. Aimon had asked him questions about his own world – the Iron World they called it here. Not a bad old bloke, once you got to know him. Willoby could sense the dangerous side to him, though.

He had told them about cars and planes – that had astonished them especially. He had told them of men walking on the moon, sailing in submarines, making war on a scale more vast and appalling than any of them had ever imagined. Cardillac had appeared briefly, and Willoby had told him about weapons: rifles and grenades and machine guns and artillery, but the Decarch had merely looked incredulous and left again to do his rounds.

Merrin had wanted to know what the women in his world wore, and he had described things, some of them Jo's, to her intense interest.

And then Aimon had left, almost friendly at the last. Maybe it had just been the wine. And Willoby had been left alone with her again.

That same tenseness had immediately sprung into the air as the candles burned low. Willoby remembered the way words had dried up and died in his throat, despite the alcohol he poured down it.

She had combed her hair with a comb of ivory. It had shone like a raven wave in the flame-light. And she had hummed something, a dark, crooning sound that set the hairs up on his neck. Then she had let her robe slide down to her waist so that as she sat at the foot of the cot he could see the muscles in her back sliding under the pale skin while she combed that dark-shining hair. Willoby had been afraid to breathe.

It had been exquisitely slow. He wanted to relish her, to imprint every movement, every caress in his mind. He watched her face as they joined, and knew she did not dislike him, unless she were the most consummate actress he had ever seen.

She had been cool and calm at first, but all of a sudden she had kindled, like dry furze taking fire on a hot summer's day. He could still feel the tracks of her nails tingling in his back. They had finished panting and sweating, tight in each other's embrace, and Willoby had laughed aloud with the pure, unadulterated joy of it. He had seen her face flash with real humour for an instant, and felt that he had at last caught a glimpse of the real Merrin, the young woman behind the accomplished temptress. But the mask had come down again, and she had been dutifully tender, avoiding his questions by falling asleep.

Is it possible to love someone from a dream? he wondered, and kissed the top of her dark head as she lay breathing softly in his arms. He did not care. He didn't care if this was a dream, a hallucination or full-blown insanity, but he felt happier here, in this place, with this girl, than he had in more years than he liked to count.

I want to stay here, he admitted to himself. Even if it means what I'm really doing is drooling in a padded cell for the rest of my life, I want to stay. I'll do whatever they want me to, if it means I can remain.

Merrin stirred but did not open her eyes. He kissed her temple, wondering what she really saw when she looked at him. A paunchy, balding man with blurred tattoos on his forearms, one index finger nicotine-orange. A big, broken nose in a battered face with every one of those discontented years written across it in a network of lines as clear as Braille. Why was she here? What had he done to deserve her?

And yet he knew, deep down. She was the sweetener, the sugar on the pill. She probably hated every second that she lay here with him.

The pain at the thought allied with the buzzing panic so that for a second his stomach tightened and a chill spread through his gut.

I'm here to kill their king, whoever he is. Get real, Willoby. How do you think assassins are treated, in any culture? Think they'll give you Merrin, a pension and a rose-covered cottage?

It's a dream some last, rational part of his mind said, but he had lost patience with that line of reasoning. The world was as real as he cared to consider. This girl – she was real, the cold air in the tent that made his breath a barely visible steam, the smell of the tallow in the candles.

How could he find an argument to refute all this?

It was no good, Cardillac decided. They were not going to pass by. He could see them clearly, down to the rime that had frozen on their fur capes. They would keep going until they reached the head of the valley, and the camp was almost directly in their path.

It was nearly noon. If he was to decide it must be soon. He looked at the sky. Still bright and cloudless – no hint of snow there.

Caridan and his party sat on their horses in the hollow behind him. He could almost feel their taut impatience. They were fully armed but had left off the leather chamfrons and breastplates for the horses. They would need speed, for what they hoped to do.

At last he nodded to himself, and waved a hand to the riders behind him. He saw Caridan's face quicken. He gave a wide grin, then launched off through the snow closely followed by his four comrades. They kicked their horses into a lopsided canter, the snow flying in white clods. Cardillac withdrew behind the crest of the little bluff on his belly. Now was the sticking point. Would the enemy commander possess the guile to see this for what it was?

He chanced a look, squirming round the side of a frozen boulder. The shapes of the men and horses were blurred against the snow glare and he wiped his watering eyes, cursing.

The horsemen had taken the bait. Almost a score of cavalry were lumbering off to their right to intercept Caridan's riders. His party was moving faster – downhill for one thing, and their mounts were fresh. They were hallooing like fiends. Cardillac smiled. Caridan had always been an impetuous hothead. He loved being centre-stage.

But the infantry – what of them? They had come together in a huddle and seemed to be consulting with their officer. Cardillac saw fingers pointing upslope, to where Caridan's group had appeared.

There was fighting down there now. Caridan had halted his men to clash with the first elements of the pursuers. They were straggling, struggling uphill to meet him in ones and twos, the horses clearly exhausted. Their officer wants hanging, Cardillac thought. Caridan, clearly, intended to inflict casualties, to sting them into a definite pursuit.

The flash of iron in the cold sun. The horses were milling around. It was strangely unreal, soundless with distance. Cardillac saw one figure topple from his steed, another horse go to its knees after receiving a blow to the skull. A confused, ugly little skirmish. But more of the pursuers were closing in. Caridan must break off, or be overwhelmed.

And at last the infantry moved. They began bounding upslope with the unsteady stagger of tired men. Caridan had done well – he had decoyed the entire enemy command. If only he could get away!

The fight splintered. What had a moment before been a tight knot of struggling figures suddenly fell apart. Cardillac had seen it happen many times. Sometimes it seemed that the combatants came to some telepathic agreement and both withdrew at the same moment. Here he could see bodies on the snow, a horse kicking on its side. And then Caridan's men, only four of them now, turned and cantered off downhill. The pursuers were slower to follow – Cardillac reckoned that Caridan had accounted for at least three of them – and were waiting for the last stragglers. Fourteen, fifteen of them – they were off. The infantry were going through the corpses. Cardillac doubted if they would try working their way back up the valley without cavalry support.

He wondered if Caridan would make it. There were a thousand men scouring the hills. He hoped they would be led a merry dance.

He turned as someone joined him on the snow, and was surprised to see Aimon, his lined face ruddy with cold, ice caught in his beard.

'You should be in the fort, Aimon.'

'I came to see how things fared. Our friends have drawn off.'

'Caridan has bought us some time, at what price I do not know. He has orders to double back right up in the Greshorns if necessary, but to avoid capture at all costs. At all costs,' Cardillac repeated.

'What of our messenger? Do you think he has avoided capture?'

'Who knows? Garran is a good man. He will get through if anyone can.'

'But how will we know? What are we to do if he is unsuccessful – wait here for Fferidan to pick us up?'

'Give it a few days yet, Aimon. If I come to believe the worst then we will start off for the city, as I told you before.'

'And we will run the gauntlet of the hunting paths without magic to aid us. I remember, Cardillac.'

'I heard Merrin cry out in the night,' Cardillac said casually, watching the men off in the distance who had now begun skinning the dead horse.

'He's hurting her, is he?'

'It was not that sort of cry, Aimon.'

The old man chuckled. 'She plays her part well, does she not? I can hardly keep a straight face sometimes, when I see her leaning on him, looking at him with those great, beautiful eyes of hers.'

'He suspects, I think.'

'He is not stupid, though his appearance is deceptive. Yes, I think he does. But I get the feeling he means to enjoy himself while he can, the poor fool.'

'What kind of man is Tallimon, that he can cast her off like that – throw her away as though she meant nothing to him? And yet I know what he felt for her.'

'He seeks a grander love affair. He has power as a mistress, and he wants her as his wife. Everything else comes second to that.'

'Including us.'

'Including us. We are his foot soldiers, Cardillac. We also would be cast away, were it to shift him one jot nearer his goal. You would do well to remember it.'

'He is my friend,' Cardillac said stubbornly.

'Mine also – or he was. He threatened me with Carberran's fate when I was slow in getting the Turnkey here.'

Cardillac stared.

'Oh yes. He is not the disingenuous young man we once knew. Power, and the contemplation of power, have soured him. Had Courberall recognized him as he does Madavar, then perhaps things could have been different. But Tallimon's pride has grown in proportion with the number of slights his father has thrown upon it.'

They were both silent for a moment, looking down the great, blinding sweep of the hills under the palest of blue skies to where Fferidan's men were labouring down the way they had come. They were heavily burdened, bearing the bodies of their fallen comrades and the jointed remnants of the dead horse.

'More good men slain,' Cardillac murmured. 'Kristill killing Kristill. I thought Courberall ended that, but now it begins again.'

'It begins again. But hear this, Cardillac: the way Tallimon intends it to happen there will be less killing. The King must die, yes, but that way more lives will be saved. Tallimon owns the allegiance of at least four clans. He could lead eight thousand swords against Courberall.'

'But he is gambling it all on a knife in the dark.'

'Yes, because that way the resistance will be without a figurehead. Most will accept Tallimon as King to avoid civil war – as long as they are sure he did not spill Courberall's blood himself. The present skirmishing is of no account.'

'And Madavar?'

'He and his brother Idramon must die, obviously.'

Cardillac nodded. And then: 'They're going, Aimon, back down to the plains – and a long, weary walk it will be, carrying their dead with them until they find wood enough for a pyre. But they will link up with Fferidan again eventually. Caridan has bought us some time, nothing more. I wonder who it was he lost, which of his party.'

'It was Phelan.'

'How do you know?'

Aimon flashed him a look of irritation. 'I know.'

'Magic is good for some things, then. Well, he is not the first, I suppose, and he will definitely not be the last. Not by a chalk as long as your arm.'

*

Merrin did not stir as Willoby disengaged himself and clambered out of bed. Either she was a heavy sleeper or she preferred not to speak to him. He raised the furs for a moment to peer at her nakedness. Her beauty stirred him, and he felt an urge to climb back inside her and see if she would oblige him again. But he somehow knew it would be impolitic. It was one thing with wine and the dark of the night outside, quite another in the harsh chill of the morning.

He kissed her shoulder nonetheless, and covered her up.

It was definitely warmer this morning. There had been a hubbub earlier, horses moving about, the clash of metal, but the camp was as still as a grave now, without even the sound of the builders' axes and adzes. Maybe it was a holiday.

He dressed quickly, slugged down some wine, his eyes starting from his head, and ate a few scraps from the night before. Then he left the tent, wrestling with his new cloak as he went.

There was something odd about the camp. There was nobody about, not a man in sight. And everything was plastered with snow, even the new-built huts. He frowned against the insistent, omnipresent white glare. It was so clear the mountains seemed to be hanging in the sky, pennants of snow blowing off their summits like long flags. He could smell pine on the faint breeze, the resin of cut logs and the faint hint of woodsmoke. No fires burned, though. The camp seemed deserted. He felt a pang of alarm through his puzzlement, and wondered if he and Merrin had been abandoned for some reason.

He wandered out to the near-finished stockade and clambered over one of the few half-built portions that were left. He was outside the camp, and stretching out before him was an illimitable expanse of snow-deep hillside speckled with dark rocks. An eagle or some such bird circled overhead – there, two more. They looked disturbingly like vultures that had sighted carrion, wide-winged specks against the blue.

'They've gone,' he whispered. 'Merrin too, I'll bet.' He had a sudden conviction that his madness had taken a new turn. His imagination had jettisoned the characters it had conjured up and there was nothing left in his brain but snow and ice and stone. He felt a pang of loss that surprised him.

Get a grip, Willoby.

'I wish Franks was here,' he said aloud. 'The bastard might be able to make some sense out of it.'

But then he saw movement on a nearby hill. Black smudges moving against the snow. He squinted. Cardillac and Aimon, it looked like.

That prickling unease, what he liked to call his sixth sense. Something was not quite right. Surely these were odd tracks about him here in the snow. Did they have dogs in the camp?

That odd smell on the breeze.

Definitely Cardillac. He had seen Willoby and was waving. He broke into a run. There was no sound. It was like watching a film that lacked soundtrack.

Something was near him. Suddenly he felt absurdly exposed out here beyond the stockade. Cardillac was sprinting heavily through the drifts towards him. Aimon lagged behind.

Movement in the corner of his eye. He spun round in time to see the snow explode like a geyser. There was an impression of a huge rat-grey shape, yellow eyes – a naked snake that might have been a tail; and then the world became a heaving chaos. He was struck on the chest and a great weight sent him tumbling backwards into the snow. He threw his arms in front of his face as he went down, and felt the fleshy side of one forearm seared by agony – a bite that seemed to rip muscle from bone. He screamed.

Human voices, a storm of flying snow like a minor blizzard. His fists were gripping coarse fur and an unutterably foul breath was smoking in his nostrils. He was holding the thing back, his injured arm screaming at him, blood streaming down to fill his armpit. Yellow teeth, a wet maw – those eyes glaring a foot from his own and the harsh heather-like prickle of the fur as he gripped its neck to keep the teeth from his throat. It was squealing like a burnt pig. He felt its claws scrabble at his belly, rip his clothes and score his skin, and he brought his knee up savagely into its guts in the familiar reflex.

It lunged, collapsing his weakening arms. He jerked his head aside in a vain attempt to avoid the jaws, then felt a shudder go through it – another; the communicated jar of many impacts. The thing seemed to grow heavier on top of him, slumping on to his chest. There was a hot wetness on his legs, and he did not know if it was blood or if he had voided himself in his extremity. A series of blows quivered through the beast. He heaved the stinking, inert head off his face and sucked in the cold, clean air. Cardillac was there, flailing like a madman, and Aimon looking near to collapse. Other faces, other people. Was Merrin there?

He felt boneless, dizzy. They heaved the thing off him, dead, its spine hacked to bits. He lay in the sodden snow like a dead thing himself. They were shouting, men running about, Cardillac yelling orders. He was aware that there were more of the things. Monsters springing out of the snow everywhere. They were going to be torn to pieces. There were too many of them.

'Do something, Aimon!' he heard Cardillac scream. 'Use your power or we are lost!' Aimon shouted back a retort, angry, afraid. And Willoby became aware of a strange thrumming in his bones. The old mage was chanting something as the warriors fought for their lives around him. The words were alien, but they set the hair on Willoby's neck upright. He felt a spasm of nausea. There was an electrical-ozone smell in the air, like the premonition of a tempest.

But here was Merrin at last, kneeling beside him and feeling him.

'Are you all right? Are you all right? Where are you hurt? There's blood everywhere!' That was what the words meant, but they sounded odd. Not English.

There was a silent detonation, a flash of blue light as intense as a lightning bolt, and a sickening burnt-flesh smell.

The warriors cheered. But Willoby retched. He felt as though he had suddenly been thrown into a plummeting elevator.

Christ, he thought. I'm going to faint. Giant rats . . . there's no end to it.

And he did faint, his head falling back limply on to the broken snow.

Fourteen

White light, fluorescent tubes fizzing above his head. He hurt all over. His arm felt as though someone had bound a hot coal next to the skin. There were people coming and going, the clack of shoes on hard floors, the squeak of wheels. And that smell. He grimaced. Hospital.

So I woke up at last. They must have called an ambulance. I bet I looked a sight.

He tried to sit up. His head was splitting and down his belly he could feel the flare of pain, long lines of it. *Where that thing clawed me,* he thought.

But no – that was not possible. The hallucination was over. He made it into a sitting position, moving as gingerly as an arthritic old man. A nurse bustled past, halted as he caught her eye and came over to the bedside.

'Don't try to sit up. Lie down and relax.' She pushed him back. He tried to thrust her away but made the mistake of using his bad arm, and a groan was ripped from his lips.

'There, you see? You're not fit to do anything much yet. Hang on a second and I'll go and get Sister.'

'No, wait.' Willoby's head was swimming with images. 'Where was I – how did I get here?'

'Don't you remember? Do you remember anything?'

Plenty, he thought, but all the wrong things. He shook his head for her.

'Sister will tell you. She was on duty when they brought you in last night. Now lie at peace. You lost a lot of blood.'

She bustled off again, all starched and white and busy. Young enough to be his sodding daughter.

So it *was* a dream. Those people – that girl, the camp in the snow. Damnation. He was truly mad, then.

'What the hell happened?' he asked the ceiling.

A matriarch in blue accompanied by a young man in a white coat materialized at his bed.

'Good to see you awake, sir. Now if you'll bear with me a minute.' He was prodded, shifted, peered at and palpitated. The blue woman seemed satisfied; the young doctor made notes.

'There are a few questions we'd like to ask you, sir. There was no ID of any kind on your person when the crew picked you up, and you seemed to be in fancy dress.'

'Where was I found? What was I doing?'

The woman pursed her lips. 'Some shoppers tripped over you in an alleyway. You had been badly cut. There's a nasty gash in your forearm that might yet need plastic surgery, and then long . . . knife wounds' – she looked at the doctor, who shrugged – 'running down your abdomen. They could have been particularly nasty.'

The young doctor leaned forward. His nose shone under the overhead lights. 'They may be knife wounds, but they're a little ragged. They could almost be claw marks. And the wound in your forearm – I'd nearly swear it was a bite. Do you know what happened to you?'

'I was in fancy dress, you say?' Willoby asked.

'Yes, sort of medieval. Had you come from a party? There was alcohol in your bloodstream.'

'A party – yeah, right.'

'We have to ask you your name,' the ward sister said rather testily. 'We'll need to inform your family.'

'My clothes . . . where did you put them?'

'They were torn to shreds and covered with blood. I'm afraid they were incinerated. The police aren't too happy about that, either. One of my nurses was over-enthusiastic about cleaning up. Sir, I must know your name.'

'Willoby, John Willoby.' He reeled off his date of birth, address, next of kin, the whole spiel; but his mind was far away.

'How soon can I leave?'

'Someone will have to collect you, bring you some clean clothes. But we'd be happier' – she and the doctor nodded sagely at each other – 'if you'd stay another night. Those are nasty wounds. And the police are waiting to speak to you.'

Fancy dress. What did that mean?

'My God,' he said.

'Mr Willoby?'

'It was real. It's all real. That monster – it bit me. The bastard bit me. I fainted, and now I'm back again. My God!'

'Mr Willoby, calm down. Any sudden movement could burst your stitches.'

He sat up and twitched the blankets aside. 'I've got to get out of here.'

'No, Mr Willoby, you have to take it easy. Get into bed!'

They grabbed his arms, but he offered no resistance. As he had moved, a white wave of agony had coursed down his chest and stomach. His head reeled. They tucked him in.

'I told you not to move. You have to rest.'

He stared at the ceiling, breathing hard. Cobwebs in among the fluorescents. That hospital smell, an old odour somehow akin to the stink of the prison.

'Hold still.'

They were working on his good arm. He felt a needle-point of thin pain. *Bastards are sedating me.*

'Just rest, Mr Willoby. We'll get your wife here as soon as we can.'

Jo. Jesus, she'd be going up the walls by now. God, he was tired. Back in the real world, Will. Back to reality – and doesn't it suck?

'I'm mad,' he said, chuckling, but no one answered him.

'Merrin.'

And then his brain flipped over and did a long roll into velvet, sparkling darkness.

They were there, standing in the snow with their mouths hanging open. He could have laughed at the blank look on their faces. The beast was a bloody mess of fur and hacked

187

flesh. Men were pouring out of the camp with swords and spears in their hands. All was confusion, shouting.

Merrin. Hear me, can you? He knew she could.

You don't exist, any of you. You're in my mind, figments of my madness. But I love you, Merrin. I believe I do.

Nothing, of course. She could not hear him. He felt as though the stuff of which he was made had been atomized and was drifting across a billion light years of imagination. John Willoby no longer existed – there was only this presence, this awareness of an impossible variety of things.

Jo was at the side of his bed with red-bordered eyes and a bitter set to her mouth. A man in a raincoat stood behind her.

But she can't touch me. I'm not really here.

He heard Aimon's voice, shrill with fear. '*He's gone – he went back. Moon and stars! You made me use the dweomer, Cardillac, and it sent him back through the door! We've lost him.*'

You've all lost me, he thought contentedly. I am yours no longer.

Panic on Merrin's face, something akin to real terror. She was looking inward, one hand in a fist at her mouth. He didn't like that.

She needs me. Without me, she's lost.

Where the hell am I?

As the question occurred to him, so he felt himself slowly begin to coalesce. Willoby was coming together again. He could see them both – the hospital and the snow-covered hillside. Jo was talking to the doctor, the raincoat-man beside her. Cardillac was shouting out yet more orders, and they were all running, slogging through the snow. Willoby felt the distance of a god.

I'm on the threshold. I can go either way. It's up to me.

It doesn't matter. I'm insane anyway.

Merrin tripped and went sprawling in the snow. They were fighting great grey shapes that were springing out of the drifts like jack-in-the-boxes.

One of them pounced on her.

Here. Now. I'm going back – I want in *here*!

And he was there, on hands and knees in the snow, hospital pyjamas on his back and the bright pain of his wounds flooding his brain.

'Help her, Cardillac!' That was Aimon. What the hell was going on?

He heard the high-pitched *screes* of the monstrous beasts around him. They were all over the place. Men were fighting, grunting with effort, yelling. The hiss and crunch of blades impacting. Willoby fell to his side. The snow numbed his pain.

'Help Merrin,' he croaked, and thought; oh hell, I'm off again.

But though the world flickered and spun, he remained vaguely conscious.

The beasts were squealing so shrilly that it hurt his ears. Cardillac was swinging his sword like a man possessed, his men around him, hacking with grim ferocity. But Willoby could see more of the misshapen animals on the surrounding hillsides. Packs of them were gathering there, ready to rush the group of men outside the fort. He tried to groan a warning, lifting his good arm out of the snow; and Aimon appeared out of nowhere, yanking him to his feet. Through the red curtain of pain Willoby heard him shout: 'Get into the fort. They'll overwhelm us else!'

Willoby was dragged along with his legs trailing. They were all retreating now, fighting every step of the way to the gate. He saw Merrin flung over one man's shoulder, her back a bloody mess. Cardillac and a few others fighting a desperate rearguard action as the rest made it within the stockade. Then Willoby was dumped in the snow. Another wave of pain left him speechless.

'What happened to you? Where did you go? How did you get back?' It was Aimon. The old-man wattles on his neck shook with passion. Willoby could not speak. He was gasping for breath. His stitches, rows of black ants in procession down his torso, had opened and thin ribbons of blood were trailing over his belly, soaking his striped garments.

189

'No matter. Neyr, over here. Help me. Someone get Willoby and the lady inside. Ho — listen, damn you!'

But the warriors were lining the stockade, and the fighting was raging along it. Some had had the foresight to bring their lances and were stabbing down from the rough catwalk into the packed mass of the beasts below. They had slammed the gate and bolted it, but the raw timber shuddered as the animals threw themselves against it, striving to batter it down with brute strength and weight. The artificers were there, having come running from their quarters with tools to hand. They were pitching in also.

Aimon began dragging Willoby towards one of the stoutest of the huts. The man carrying Merrin paused beside them and together he and Aimon got the two of them inside. The warrior left at once to rejoin the fighting, but Aimon hovered a moment.

'I must go and see if I can help.' His fingers brushed the neat stitches in Willoby's wounds. Then he pulled furs from the nearby cot around him and Merrin.

'I'll need to talk to you later, if there is a later. Look after Merrin for me. Don't worry. I'll not be using the dweomer again with you around. We were lucky this time!'

All gobbledygook, Willoby thought as the mage left. I could have stayed in a warm hospital bed, and he talks of luck. Christ, it hurts.

But Merrin was stirring beside him. Her back had been ripped by one of those damn things before they had pulled it off her. Willoby groaned aloud to see the long tears in her flesh, the blood that soaked her robe.

'Aimon?' she whispered with her eyes still closed.

'He's gone. But it's all right. You're safe now, Merrin.'

The eyes snapped open. 'Willoby, you're here! I thought you had disappeared.'

'I came back. No, lie on your side. That's it. They're not deep, they just look spectacular. I don't think they even need stitches.'

When the colour had returned to her face she touched his

190

chest, much as Aimon had done. They were lying close together on the cot with the furs around their shoulders. Outside the fighting raged on, but it seemed faint and far away.

'What happened to you? Who did this?'

'I went to my own world for a while, and they fixed me up. But I wanted to come back. I saw you – I could see you all, and I wanted to come back.'

A spasm of pain shuddered through her. When it had passed she asked, 'Why?'

Why, indeed? He could not tell her. Because he thought he might love her? No way.

'I don't know. Just born stupid, I guess.'

They were too weak to do anything about each other's wounds, though Willoby managed to peel the shredded robe from Merrin's back. They lay close to each other, sharing their warmth, and listened to the fighting. It seemed unending but, strangely, not threatening. They even dozed for a while, though the insistent pain did not let them relax for long. Willoby was oddly content. He thought it conceivable that they might die here, swamped by these monsters from the mountains, but he did not greatly care. He wondered if the drugs from the hospital were working in him.

Merrin. That was the reason he had returned. And he mocked himself viciously for the schoolboy-like flutter he felt as he lay there with his face six inches from hers. He took her cold fingers in his own massive hand, and she did not protest, but smiled briefly at him. She was listening, still tense. Perhaps she expected them to be overwhelmed. It was too unreal for Willoby. He had been in hospital less than an hour before. Better not to think too much about that.

He slipped into a deeper sleep at last, a smile etched on his battered face. He did not feel Merrin gently disengage her hand from his.

She edged out of the cot, wincing at the pain. Her eyes filled with tears as she thought of the scars she would have. Tallimon would never want her; he hated a marred thing, no matter how small the flaw.

Stupid thought, hysteria from the battle. Tallimon was done with her and she had best remember it.

She looked down on the man Willoby as he lay there asleep. He seemed so very much younger when asleep, the lines easing out, the frown disappearing. She could see something of the man he had once been.

When he had disappeared like that, she had seen the whole of her life crumble. She would end up a soldier's drab in one of the brothels. Perhaps that was why she had almost welcomed the attack. Hadn't she been wondering how Tallimon would take the news of her death?

But he was here, this strange man. He had had a choice, she was sure – it was the way he had talked of it. He need not have returned. Why had he, to this place of murder and battle and intrigue where he was an alien, a mere pawn, expendable in a game of kings? For her? Had she done her job so well?

She listened. The fighting was petering out. She could hear Cardillac shouting. He was as hoarse as a crow. They had won then, they would not die after all.

She began to shudder and gasped at the smarting pain. Her wounds had tightened the skin of her back. The side of one breast was scored almost to the nipple. She gazed fearfully at the sleeping Willoby. How could she fulfil her mission like this – and, more importantly, how would Willoby?

Willoby was to be the King's assassin, but if his right arm were scarcely able to hold a knife, then what?

Her head swam. She groaned, hating what her life had become; hating Tallimon with a hopeless loathing for doing this to her.

Silence outside, or near silence. The squealing of the beasts had stopped, and there was only the low talk of men, the occasional bark of orders. Someone moaned in pain quite close by. It was over. She wondered how many of Cardillac's men had survived.

This was Aimon's hut, full of the sharp reek of herbs and

192

unnamed things in glass phials. She seized one of his old robes and drew it gingerly over her shoulders, unwilling to be bare-breasted when they came in. The fine-spun wool clung to her wounds and she gritted her teeth.

'Mad,' Willoby said clearly, and she stared at him. His eyes were still shut.

'Never, never going. Don't care.' He smiled. 'Love you.' Then his breathing became even again.

She touched his face. It was cold. The stubble on his cheeks was growing long; his beard would be dark. Once again, she thought he reminded her of someone she knew. It might be important to remember who . . .

The door creaked open and both Cardillac and Aimon stomped in, destroying the train of her thoughts.

It had been a trying morning for Cardillac. His men had almost been overwhelmed in the attack. They would have been, had not Aimon shrivelled up a score of the grypesh with a fireball of blue, crackling light. And Cardillac had almost needed to threaten the mage at sword point before he would use his magic.

But the mage had blamed him for Willoby's disappearance. The dweomer had been used too close to him. It had blasted him back to the Iron World. Cardillac remembered that moment, the awful sinking feeling as he realized the utter failure of his mission. When the rest of the pack had attacked he had thrown himself into the thick of the mêlée, had joined the rearguard. For a few, mad minutes he had been hoping to die there, at least ending like a soldier with a sword in his hand.

Except that Willoby was back again. There was too much to take in here at once, and he had lost a third of his men before the grypesh had been driven off, their bodies a rampart under the walls of the stockade. Too many things – but he knew this much: they had to abandon the fort at once, orders or no orders. The chance that the noise of the battle had carried down to Fferidan's Rimons was too great. They had to leave for Courbisker while they could.

That was as far as his weary mind was able to look ahead. He was not even curious about how Willoby had disappeared and then come back again.

As he stooped into the pine-scented dimness of Aimon's hut he saw Merrin sitting on the cot with an old robe about her shoulders. It was Aimon who struck a flame and lit dips. Cardillac slumped down by the wall. He smarted from a few scratches but could not care less. He could not stay long. Soon he would have to start organizing things. He wondered if they dare risk a pyre for their dead – no, of course not. The tiredness was blurring his thinking. He saw the smile on Willoby's sleeping face and shook his head.

'Here.' Aimon thrust a clay jug towards him. Barley spirit. He drank it gratefully. The stuff seemed to glow through his very muscles, easing his aches.

'Let me see, Merrin,' the mage said.

'No, they're all right. Nothing too bad.'

'I'll decide that. Let me see.'

Aimon peeled away the robe, making Merrin wince, but she did not move. Cardillac saw one pink-tipped breast before her arms covered it. Too tired even for desire, he thought sourly. Merrin was glaring – evidently she was not so sure.

'You will scar, my dear,' Aimon said sadly. 'Not badly, but you will scar.'

'It doesn't matter.' Cardillac knew she was lying. It was plain on her face.

Aimon was dabbing some kind of ointment on her as delicately as a bee nuzzling a flower.

'There are other wounded who need you, Aimon,' Cardillac said. He had seen one of his men with his guts spilling out of his belly.

'I know. Be patient, Cardillac. I've seen them. They'll keep for a moment, and those who will not are too far gone for me to help. Besides, old Gamran is attending to them.'

'A horse leech.'

'Aye, but it is mere butchery we have to patch up, and a horse leech is as good at that as anyone.'

Cardillac drank more of the spirit. He felt very much like getting drunk; it was the usual after-battle reaction. He had added respect for Tallimon now, getting the survivors of his Rimon home after fighting four hundred of those beasts.

'This is an awful place,' he said.

'There.' Aimon stepped back. Merrin pushed her hair from her face in a gesture that had always given Cardillac a pang. Her slim torso was a mass of dressings.

'What about him?' she asked, gesturing to the slumbering Willoby.

'Somebody else has already looked after him. He will do very well if no fever sets in. See the smallness of the stitches? Neat work.'

'What happened, Aimon?' Cardillac asked. 'What happened to him?'

'Willoby? I thought I told you, and I warned you days ago. When I used the dweomer close to him I think it sparked off some other thing that is in him, or in the land maybe, when he is present. He was sent back for a while. Back to his own place.'

'He had a choice,' Merrin said. 'He could have stayed. He said so, I think. But he chose to return.'

'I wonder why,' Aimon said drily. Something in his voice made her drape his robe over her shoulders again, though the bandages covered her as effectively as a tunic.

'Well, it is something to know, I suppose,' Cardillac said wearily. 'We must leave here. We cannot wait for Tallimon's messenger.'

'Are you so sure Fferidan's men will have learned of the fight?' Aimon asked.

'There is a good chance. Sound carries in these valleys. But there is also the fact that these beasts do not give up easily. Tallimon found that out. They will return, in greater numbers perhaps; and there are less than a score of us who are fit to fight. We must set out for Courbisker at once.'

'All of us? What of the wounded? Two at least I saw who cannot be moved.'

'Then we will leave them. I propose splitting the Rimon. We will take a small party, no more. The rest will follow on when they can. We cannot afford to wait for them.'

'You are learning the value of expediency, Cardillac. Tallimon has been a good teacher.'

'I am a soldier. I do what I think is best. My job now is to deliver Willoby alive to the city, no matter how many grypesh lie on the way.'

'So be it. Merrin, are you fit to ride, do you think?'

'I'll get by.' She did not look up. Cardillac wondered if she was thinking of her scars.

'And Willoby – what of him?' he asked Aimon. A cold thought struck him as it had Merrin earlier. His eyes widened.

'Moon and stars, Aimon – this arm. How bad is it? In two weeks— '

'I know. It had occurred to me also.'

'It may yet be for nothing.' All the intrigue, all those deaths.

'He may recover in time, Cardillac. One blow is all he has to strike. After that he has no more worries in this world.'

Merrin raised her head at that. 'It will be that way then? There is no way he— ' She stopped, and bent over Willoby as if to gauge his breathing. 'He cannot survive, can he?'

Aimon shook his head. 'We have been through this before. The people will want a scapegoat. Willoby will die.'

'It's wrong, Aimon. This whole thing is wrong,' Merrin said softly.

'What's the matter with you, lady? Have you begun to play your part too well?'

'He is a man, Aimon,' Cardillac said.

'Maybe, but it is too late for a crisis of conscience, Cardillac. The wheels have begun moving. There is no way to stop them. Do you think Tallimon is sitting on his hands back in the city? By now he will have sounded out the clans. The plot embraces more folk than us alone. If Willoby does not fulfil his task, there will be civil war in any case. So choose your option. One man's sacrifice will save the lives of many.'

Cardillac had seldom felt so . . . tainted. His men had lost

196

comrades and wanted to know why. He was taking an innocent man to an ugly death – and aiding the murder of another, he reminded himself. Neither of these men had ever done him any harm. And he was no longer sure if he much cared for the man to whom his life's loyalty had been given. He met Merrin's eyes, and for once understanding passed between them. She was the same. He realized in a flash of insight that she liked this man Willoby also.

'You are a heartless bastard, Aimon,' he said with low venom.

The old man did not bridle.

'I am a realist, and I have a vision you lack, Cardillac. It will be good for the Kristill if Tallimon achieves his goal. He will civilize them, whereas under Courberall they will always remain a collection of tribes, nomads in their hearts.'

'Is that so bad?'

'In this land, it could lead to their destruction. Tallimon knows the rules we must live by here to survive. Courberall does not. He is a king of the past, and has outlived his purpose.'

'And Madavar, and Idramon – what of them?'

'Together Tallimon and Madavar would have made fine kings in their own turn, but that cannot be. They would never allow it.'

Cardillac took a last slug of the spirit. 'I must go and see to my men. Start packing, you two. We leave once it is fully dark.'

'So soon?' Merrin asked.

'I'm sorry. Yes, tonight. We must be out of these hills by tomorrow's dawn if we are to have any chance of evading Fferidan's men. Get some rest before dark. You will need it.'

'What of the dead?' Aimon asked harshly.

'We cannot burn them. We will have to bury them – deep.'

Cardillac left the hut for the dazzling brightness outside, but despite the clean glare of the sunlight on the snow he felt as dirty and worn as an old bone.

Fifteen

Garran was dead; he had at least managed that. A smuggled jug of beer with some of Aimon's belladonna at the bottom. He had not talked to Madavar as far as Tallimon knew, and the head of Garran's clan, Taurberad, was raising heaven and hell trying to find out how one of his men had died in Madavar's keeping. The secret of Cardillac's location had remained just that. To everyone but Tallimon, that was. Garran had told everything to the girl who had smuggled the wine – and his death – into the cell. Fool, not to realize that his unique knowledge was all that safeguarded his life.

It was time to send for Cardillac; the city founding came nearer day by day.

Tallimon leaned back and smiled at the ceiling of his new hut. The girl beside him stirred, snuggled closer, and his face changed. A spasm of distaste crossed it, and something like despair, before it straightened again. Ordachar had bought her for him, the well-meaning fool. She passed the time, though he had had to box her ears a few times to teach her what he liked.

So Willoby was here. Aimon had succeeded. And they had thus far avoided Fferidan's patrols. It was going too well, too easily. At least Madavar would be busy now, fending off Taurberad's outraged accusations. It might tie him up long enough for Cardillac to re-enter the city.

The messenger was ready to go, a veteran of the grypesh battle so few had survived. He would leave tonight, slip beyond the sentries by way of the river, and ride like the wind for the hills.

Willoby was here. He remembered a picture, the image of a

big, burly man gone to seed with a dangerous look in his eye
and an unpleasant smile. Did Merrin enjoy his taking of her?

His stomach contracted into a cold ball, but he forced
himself to imagine it.

Gone, now. It would be as if he had never known her.

'I hope it's worth it,' he whispered aloud, and then, furious
at himself, he leapt from his cot. The girl beside him grumbled
and he tipped her on to the hard floor.

'Get your things!' he barked. 'Get out, damn you!'

She scurried out naked and tearful, clutching her pathetic
rags to her breasts. Tallimon poured himself wine and drank it,
swallow after swallow. Too late for regrets – they were only a
weakness. He had to think like a king.

She hates me. She's gone for ever. Who will be my queen
now?

He flung the jug against the wall of the hut and it shattered.
Then he shouted for his page in a voice of thunder.

It was good to be out, on a horse again with a column of men
behind him. They reined in on a hill overlooking the city and
surveyed the land around them. Courbisker hill was beginning
to look like a true settlement, with new houses and halls
springing up everywhere within the walls and smoke rising in a
score of places. A muddy road had been carved out of the turf
leading from the main gate through the hills to where the Host
was encamped. Another branched off from it to the woods and
quarries of the foothills, carved by the timber trains and
quarrying parties that trudged its weary length a hundred
times a day. He could see mounted pickets on the neighbouring
heights, and not far off the camp of a Rimon-sized patrol that
helped to secure the road. Now that the walls were almost
complete most of the warriors had been siphoned off to the
main camp to guard the non-combatants, or else they were
working in the forests and quarries. It was a fine thing to see,
the thin sun glittering on the wide sweep of the Great River,
the horse herds on the lower pastures, the city rising on its hill
like a citadel. This would be a wondrous place some day,

Tallimon promised himself. He would pave the roads, build jetties where the river widened, and rear up a palace of stone on the summit of the hill. He would have it renamed after its second, true founder.

'Sire.' Beside him Ordachar pointed.

A small cloud of horsemen was coming up the hillside towards them.

Tallimon nodded. 'Surbadan.'

The clan leader of the Surbadoi reined in ten feet away. Behind him were half a dozen of his personal retainers, lean-faced men on tall horses. He nodded curtly. 'Tallimon, Ordachar; well met.'

'Well met, Surbadan,' Tallimon replied easily, though his heart was thumping fast. Surbadan was the leader of the largest clan of the Kristill yet uncommitted to either Courberall or himself, as far as Tallimon knew. Hitherto he had been loyal to Courberall, but he had not shunned Tallimon as the other loyalist clan leaders had. And he was close to the aggrieved Taurberad.

This man is the weight that will tip the balance one way or the other, Tallimon thought. Without him the coup would be possible, but hellish difficult. With him its success would be well-nigh assured.

Tallimon dismounted first, as befitted the younger man.

'Let us talk.'

Surbadan grunted, then followed suit. He was a big, square man, built like a plough horse. His beard was striped with grey, and a livid pink scar ran from one temple down the line of his jaw, legacy of a long-ago skirmish in the Wildwood.

They walked away from the cluster of horsemen who had already begun exchanging banter. Surbadan's face was closed, admitting nothing. Tallimon was momentarily at a loss how to begin.

They stood and watched as a timber train rattled down the muddy stretch of what men had already begun to call the North Road.

'We'll have to fare farther afield for timber in a month or

two,' Surbadan growled. 'The lower hills will soon be plucked bare.'

'Game is scarce also,' Tallimon added wondering if the other man had deliberately given him an opening. 'If we don't range out in search of better hunting grounds before the autumn, it'll be a lean winter.'

'You look far ahead, Tallimon.' The older man's face was expressionless.

'I'm thinking of the folk in the main camp. They had a bad enough time of it in the Greshorns without adding to their troubles here . . . You know the King has begun the drawing up of the fief boundaries?'

'I do.'

'The land we are looking at is Haubedec's. And to the west is Quirinir's. Good land, with the river soil and the woods on the higher slopes. The woods that are not being felled, though they are nearest the city.'

He knew he had Surbadan's interest now. Very few people yet knew where the new fiefs were to be, but Tallimon had ears everywhere. He wanted to make Surbadan *ask*, though.

'I take it all the clan leaders have been allocated their appointed fiefs then?'

'Oh no, not all. Only a few have been outlined in detail. Haubedec and Quirinus, Oradan and Ffermius – and Madavar and Idramon, of course. Their fiefs are within a day's ride of the city. The King is leaving the outlying fiefs until the lands beyond are more fully explored.' He had him. Surbadan was to be given a fief far from the hub of power: the King had not numbered him among those close to him, though his clan was one of the largest of the Kristill and he had ridden with Courberall for thirty years. Tallimon saw his face darken.

'So the rest of the clans are to be *given* land out in the wilderness.'

'That would seem to be the way of it,' Tallimon said. 'He gives land he does not own, land he has never even seen. He will *allow* our people to carve their homes out of the wild. And he expects gratitude.'

Surbadan laid a spade-like hand on Tallimon's shoulder.

'Enough of the prattle Tallimon. I have an inkling as to why you wished to meet me. There are rumours flying around the city. Your mage and your second-in-command are both missing and it is said that Fferidan's Amon scours the hills for them. And it is no secret that Madavar and Idramon have superseded you.' Surbadan grinned, showing square, yellow teeth. 'Your fief has not yet been drawn up either. If the King's affection is measured in closeness to Courbisker, I'm thinking you'll find it somewhere on the other side of the mountains.'

Tallimon stiffened. 'That's as may be. But you are not so dear to him yourself, Surbadan. You are too powerful. And neither is Taurberad. He is making too much noise over the death of his clansman, Garran. Courberall is drawing up the lines that will shape our lives in this world – and the lives of our heirs. Will you let him consign you and yours to a fief in the undiscovered wilderness, far from the court, where you will be left to fend for yourself as best you can whilst other men have the King's ear close at hand?'

'Do I have an alternative?' Surbadan spoke lightly but his eyes were boring into Tallimon's face.

Tallimon hesitated for a fraction of a second. The speech he had meant to make, about Courberall's increasing paranoia, the rise of Madavar, the new way of life being forced on the Kristill, was shunted aside. He knew that a man like Surbadan would not appreciate it.

'You have an alternative,' he said simply. 'You can make me King.'

Surbadan stared at him, chewing the inside of his cheek, until Tallimon, cursing himself, was sure he had signed his own death warrant. But the older man smiled suddenly, a wry smile that might have had something like admiration in it.

'You take a risk saying such things, Tallimon.'

'You like the truth plain and unadorned, so I gave it to you.' Still Tallimon was unsure how things were falling out. He was as tense as a taut rope.

'Two points,' Surbadan said. He seemed unconscious that

his voice had lowered. 'One, we have a king already, and no man may touch him without bringing ruin on himself and his cause. That is what the people believe, and they will never follow a kingslayer.

'Two, how would it be to my benefit to turn traitor and throw in my lot with you, even supposng Courberall were out of the way?'

Tallimon breathed out slowly. There was an ache in the lower part of his back, as though he had been bearing a heavy weight all morning. He rubbed it with his fist but kept his face grave, assured.

'I have a man who will rid us of Courberall, a man who is not of the Kristill, who cannot be traced to any clan – in short, a man without a past who is not even a part of our world. He will take care of your first point.'

'Where— ?'

'Forgive me, Surbadan, but you must trust me as I trusted you a moment ago. Courberall is taken care of. As for your . . . benefits. I am sure the new King would give you the choicest of the fiefs, and a place at his right hand in the new court. He will need friends about him when he comes into his own.'

Surbadan looked perplexed, troubled. Tallimon's heart skipped a beat. He had not landed his catch yet.

'You said Courberall is taken care of. Let us assume that you are right for the moment. What then of the King's legitimate sons, Madavar and Idramon? Will they simply vanish as well?'

'I am hoping to rid us of all three in almost the same moment. That is why I need your help, Surbadan. I need your men. My own Penton is not enough.'

'You have the support of other clan leaders, Tallimon. You think I do not know that?'

'Yours is the strongest; also, many of my men have close ties with your clan.'

It was true. Tallimon's five hundred retainers came from many clans, including the Royal one, it being the practice for a Kristillic warrior to follow any leader he chose in war, if he had his clan leader's permission. Tallimon's men had been following him for so long that they were in effect a miniature clan. Madavar had the same kind of following, but originally many of Tallimon's men had been Surbadoi. Cardillac was one prime example. Tallimon's second-in-command was Surbadan's nephew.

'You speak rightly,' Surbadan admitted. 'When is this . . . transition of power going to take place?'

'Are you with me, then? I can count on you?'

'It would seem so – if for no other reason than you intrigue me. I would like to know who this man without a past, this rootless assassin might be.'

'You will find out, Surbadan. Indeed, it will be your job to kill him, in the end. But we have many other things to discuss first.'

He tried to restrain the triumph that he felt from breaking out on his face.

'And we must discuss also – in detail – your plans for the Surbadoi when you become King, *sire*,' Surbadan went on. The two men looked at each other unsmiling, gauging.

'Done,' Tallimon said, as though they had been haggling over the price of a horse rather than the fate of a king.

'When – tell me that. When is it to be done?'

'The city founding.'

Surbadan's eyebrows shot up his forehead. 'In front of the whole people?'

'Of course. Walk with me a little while, Surbadan, and I will tell you why. And I will tell you how many of your men I need.'

They strode off with the long grasses of the hills lapping at their knees like a placid green sea.

Tallimon's company was returning to the city when he saw the hunting party. A large one, with the King's horsetail standards floating above it. He cursed as it changed course towards him, and looked back over his shoulder. But Surbadan's group was out of sight, well on their way to the Camp of the Host.

'The King wishes to speak with us, it seems,' Tallimon said casually to Ordachar. The man was sweating, he noticed with annoyance. 'We had best go to him.'

They ambled easily down the hill and reined in as the King's party halted before them. Tallimon's eyes flicked over them. Courberall, his one eye bright and keen as two, Haubedec, too old and frail to be astride a horse. Idramon, as open-faced and vacant-looking as ever. He would have done better being born a common soldier. And Madavar, smiling slightly as their eyes met. They both nodded imperceptibly at the same moment.

'Tallimon! Here's a surprise,' the King boomed. A false note from the start, Tallimon thought. This was no hunting party, despite the boar spears in the stirrup sockets. Old Haubedec was not dragged from the firepit for nothing these days.

The King looked to be in a good humour. It was always the way. He was always either black as a thundercloud or as breezy and bright as a maid in springtime. Impossible to believe that this man held the fate of some eighty-odd thousand people in his hands.

'Are you on the same errand as we? There are boar big as ponies in the hanging woods to the north, I'm told.'

'It is late in the day for setting out on a hunt,' Tallimon said.

'We go overnight, to start on the beating at dawn,' Madavar said smoothly. Their eyes met again, and again there was the slight, shared smile. We both know the game must be played for the moment, Tallimon thought.

Courberall did not look quite so jovial.

'And yourself, Tallimon: if you are not hunting, then what brings you into the hills?'

Tallimon bit back an angry retort. Courberall was questioning him as if he were some witless junior officer, not the man many had until recently seen as the heir to the throne.

'The air of the hills clears the woodsmoke from my lungs, sire,' he said cheerfully. 'And besides, the horses need to be exercised every now and again.'

'Indeed,' Madavar put in. 'It is always best to be ready for the unexpected.'

There was a small pause. Then Courberall asked: 'Where's that wench I gave you? She was a comely lass. I never see her around camp these days. Used to be she stuck to you like pitch.'

Tallimon whitened. 'She is indisposed, sire. A chill. But she will no doubt be recovered soon.'

'Should have kept her myself. She—' Courberall stopped. 'No matter. How is Aimon, the old mage?'

'He is – well, sire.'

'Good. Glad to hear it. Why don't you bring him along to the hall when we get back? Do him good to have some honest beer poured down him instead of that thin stuff you prefer.'

'He is involved in a delicate experiment. You know how these mages are. I fear he may not be disturbed.'

Courberall smiled without the slightest trace of humour. 'He will be disturbed for the sake of his King. Bring him, Tallimon – two days from now. And let that wench serve us at hall. We could do with a few more pretty faces there. The maids at the moment are as plain as horses. I shall look forward to the meeting.' He stood up in his stirrups, stretching his legs. 'The day is wasting; time we were off. Fare well, Tallimon.'

He raised a hand and his party broke into a canter. Tallimon sat on his horse like a sack of meal, his mind turning furiously. One rider from the King's group stayed behind, however, kicking his mount over to join him.

'Well brother, our father has set you a puzzle.' It was Madavar.

'A puzzle, brother?' Tallimon said. 'I don't know what you mean.' As always, he felt that he and his half-brother shared some secret or were privy to some joke that the rest of humanity could not share.

I could have loved this man, Tallimon thought.

'I hope Aimon can disengage himself from his *experiment* in time for his audience. The King looks forward to meeting him extremely.'

'No doubt I can prevail upon him to neglect his research for a few hours,' Tallimon said frostily.

Madavar laughed. 'A shame about Garran.'

'Yes,' Tallimon said. 'Taurberad is not happy about that. You really ought to be more careful with the prisoners in your care, Madavar.'

'You are right there. Strange, but the wench who smuggled him his beer died also – in convulsions just like his. Perhaps whatever he had was contagious.'

'He was a good man,' Tallimon said with feeling. He was not sorry Garran was dead, but he wished it could have been otherwise.

'Yes,' Madavar said. 'He was. I hate to see a good man die, Tallimon.' He hesitated – a rare thing for him. 'I want to see no more die, either.'

The two men stared at each other for a moment in perfect understanding.

'One cannot change fate,' Tallimon said.

'Why not? Men like us are the movers and makers in this world. If we cannot change things, who can?'

'Tell that to my father,' Tallimon said bitterly. 'It is easy to mouth platitudes, Madavar, when you have the gold ring of the King's heir on your arm.'

'There are more important things, Tallimon. The people, for instance. We must think about what is best for them.'

'I always think of what is best for them, Madavar.'

The openness of the moment was gone. They had laid down their shields for a second; now they had them back up at their chins.

'There is no talking to you, Tallimon. You were always the proud one.'

'And you were always the pryer, who needed to know everything.'

They were silent. It was too late, Tallimon realized. They were both set on their courses now, galloping towards a collision. It could not have been otherwise: there could only be one King in the land.

'Fare you well, brother,' Madavar said.

'Fare you well.'

Madavar galloped off in the wake of the King. Tallimon watched him go with that old twist of regret. For an instant he had almost been ready to throw it all away. Absurd. If Madavar became King after Courberall it would be Tallimon's head first on the block. It was the way these things were done. Courberall had done well to cultivate his aura of inviolability amongst the people – it had safeguarded him more than once in the trying times of the Greshorns. None of the nobles truly believed in it; at one time the King had been merely one clan leader amongst many. But the people did, and that was what mattered. Whoever came after Courberall would not have the same protection. It was a thing to be built up. A King, thought Tallimon, must make himself into a legend of sorts if he is to prosper.

They had been riding out for a rendezvous with Fferidan, he was sure. Courberall knew something of what was going on.

Now how, Tallimon wondered, am I going to produce Aimon in two days' time? And Merrin too, for that matter?

Merrin. Usually only unattached maids poured for the men in hall. Was Courberall trying to make a point?

But he had to smile sourly. This would have been Madavar's idea. Its barbed neatness smacked of him. While he had been talking in veiled terms of reconciliation he had known that Aimon's non-appearance would start a hare for the King to chase. It was his repayment for Garran's death – and it meant that Garran had not talked, Tallimon was positive.

He stood in his stirrups and looked north-west, where the green rumpled hills edged to the snowline, and the ranks of the mountains reared up like savage megaliths covering the far horizon. It was snowing there. There would be drifts on the hills, grypesh abroad, no doubt. Where was Cardillac now? It all hung on him.

Tallimon kicked his mount, and his troop followed him wordlessly as he made his way down to the city. There were things to do.

Sixteen

It was snowing, and had been all morning. A dark day, the cloud so thick that even the snow seemed grey, and the world was flat and monochrome, leached of colour.

It was a silent world, also. The steadily falling snow muffled their hoofbeats and even the metallic click of the harness was subdued. There was nothing to see but the shifting veil of flakes drifting down heavy and lazy, the anonymous pale curves of the endless drifts, the occasional dark facet of rock where the bones of the land showed through.

Willoby sat his horse heavily, uncomfortably. His stitches ached and stretched with every jolt and thud of their progress, and his head throbbed. He wiped his streaming nose once more — it was becoming raw to the touch — and flexed his numb toes in their boots. They had kitted him out again, but he was wearing a dead man's clothes this time and they were too small. He felt as though the crotch of his breeches and the pommel of the saddle were conspiring to split him in two. He buried his chin in his cloak, blinking snowflakes from his lashes.

I could have stayed in hospital, he thought, been tucked up warm and dry by a nurse. What the hell was I thinking of?

And how did I do it?

He still shied away from all thoughts in that quarter. It was easy enough to slip back into a dream if you really wanted to; and that was what this was. He had woken up briefly, but they'd put him out again and *voilà*.

How did I get these things, though? he wondered, touching his stitched chest gingerly with his good arm. Did someone in — in reality cut me up? Bastards probably mugged me — that's it.

They jumped me while I was doing my drooling imbecile bit. Jesus, what a world!

The dream isn't too hot now, either. Monsters and blood, snow and pain.

How many universes are out there, each one a mere figment of some madman's mind? Maybe that's what we are – with our missiles and hypermarkets and freeways. Just some loony's bad dream as he butts his head against the wall.

Don't be a pillock, Willoby. Get a grip, blast you.

They want me to kill a man – a king. Willoby the assassin. That's why I'm here.

You're here because you're a loony tune who has the daftest imagination . . . imaginable.

Too real – it's too real, too logical for a dream. Madness then, that must be it. Madness gives a sense to it, makes it seem more feasible.

Christ, there's reasoning for you.

He turned, groaning, in the saddle to peer at Merrin. She was haggard and hollow-eyed, and held herself unnaturally straight. A damned shame, making a woman in her state travel.

There was this urgency. Cardillac was like a driven man. He had a haunted look about him. Not fear . . . Willoby would have sworn it was more like guilt. Of them all only Aimon seemed unaffected, but he was a hard-nosed old sod.

There were seven of them. Three warriors accompanied Willoby, Cardillac, Merrin and Aimon as they slogged their way south and east across the snow-choked bluffs. Two of them were Neyr and the veteran, Gamran, whom Willoby had seen in the Rime Giant fight. The third, Mard, was a mere boy not much over eighteen who rode up front with Cardillac, his face aglow with pride and cold air. The men they had left behind had been glum, obviously unhappy. Willoby wondered if any of them would live to see the land beyond the snows.

They had been riding since the fall of the previous night – ten or eleven hours, Willoby thought – without a break. The horses were tired, stumbling far more often than when they had first set out. And some of the riders, he added to himself, were even worse. It had been like a kind of nightmare, the plodding along in the darkness across the paler shade of the snow, no talk except some whispered consultations between Cardillac and old Gamran. A night without end, until the slow grey seep of the dawn into the air, which had somehow made Willoby feel more exhausted than ever.

A lurch from his mount made him suck in air sharply. It was a willing enough beast, happy to follow the rump of Cardillac's steed without too much prompting. Its coat was matted with snow. They were like a series of stiffly moving white statues, lost and wandering in an empty world.

'Here.' It was Aimon, ambling beside him and offering a small wood flask. Willoby accepted gratefully. The barley spirit seared his throat and set a flame in his gullet, though his extremities remained cold-bitten and numb.

'We will stop soon. Are you in much pain?'

Willoby shook his head. 'It's this rotgut. Makes me catch my breath. Just don't ask me to dance a jig for a while, drunk or sober.' Or get off this bloody horse, he added to himself. Mounting it had been agony enough. 'What's the big rush? Is someone after us?'

'Yes. Many people are. In fact you could say that *everyone* is after us. And if you think this is bad, wait until we get out of the snows. You will see then what a horse-killing pace is.'

'I can't wait.'

He glanced back again. Merrin was sitting her horse like a mannikin, eyes closed. Poor little bint. She had guts, for sure.

Willoby remembered the warm smoothness of her in the dark, the exquisite give of a breast under his hand.

Well you can kiss that goodbye for the foreseeable future, mate.

'How much farther?' he asked Aimon, realizing with irritation that he had already asked twice since setting out.

Aimon's lips twitched. His beard was full of rime but his eyes were as dark and striking as coal on a snowman. He looked like a cadaverous Father Christmas.

'Maybe another night in the snows. And then another day after that to Courbisker.'

'*Courbisker?*'

'The city down in the plains. It is quite a sight, though I doubt if you will get to see much of it.' Aimon broke off and looked away with a frown. 'At any rate, we will probably enter it in the night, to avoid . . . comment. And then you will meet Tallimon.'

'*Tallimon?*' He knew the name, had heard it mentioned a score of times, but it meant little to him.

'You will know him when you meet him,' Aimon told him, as though reading his thoughts. 'And he will acquaint you with your . . . task.'

'Ah, right.' And here was the rub. 'So I'm to kill this king of yours.'

'We'll talk later of it.' And Aimon reined in his mount until he was with Neyr and Gamran at the rear once more.

They halted mid-morning. The warriors bent the horses' forelegs until the animals lay down, then covered them with snow. Everyone slept except for Neyr, who took first watch. They lay curled against their mounts for warmth, the snow covering them as effectively as a cloak. Despite the cold, sleep came upon them swiftly, and for Willoby it was black, dreamless.

He was woken by a rough shake from Aimon, opening his eyes to find that the world was blue with dusk. It was snowing again. He struggled upright, stiff as wood, his wounds aching. The cold brought a series of shudders out of him until he warmed fractionally.

'Jesus! Worse than bloody Brecon, this.'

'Eat,' Aimon said, thrusting something dark and unpleasant-smelling under his nose. He pushed it away. His stomach was shrunk and closed. 'Bugger off.'

'You must eat something,' he heard Merrin say. Straightening, he saw her pale face in the gloom, the black hair surrounding it. She looked nun-like, otherworldly. Obediently, he ate, forcing down leathery venison and swallowing snow to wash it down. His throat ached and his head felt as thick as dough. He wanted to go back to sleep, to bed, anywhere.

'Some bloody assassin,' he croaked.

The darkness grew thicker with the falling snow. Cardillac gave a signal and they mounted in the windless murk, both Merrin and Willoby needing help to clamber on to the tall horses. When he was finally up there, Willoby thought that for the second time in his life he might faint; the world was a gently swirling haze of colour. But the lights trickled away, and his eyes blinked the dim figures of the others into focus. They were on their way again.

An eternity of dark cold that ate into the depths of his very bones. The night was moonless, starless, and still the silent snow fell on them. But it was lighter now; smaller flakes, almost a powder. Willoby could make out more shapes in the darkness: naked boulders, the black thatch of trees. There were chuckling rivers underfoot carving their way downhill. The sound of water flowing, dripping, coursing was everywhere. And there was a smell in the air of wet soil and green things. They were coming to the end of the snows at last.

Dawn, bleeding into a black sky, and the snow was gone. The ground was boggy, sucking at the horses' hooves. They halted and snatched sleep on the wet ground: grim, mud-covered scarecrows with red-rimmed eyes and drawn faces. Then they were on the move again. It all merged into one unending blur of cold, wet, aching discomfort for Willoby. Twice Aimon had to stop him from toppling senseless out of the saddle, while Cardillac took Merrin in his arms across his pommel. She was boneless as a cloth doll.

Willoby hardly remembered their entry to the city, except that it was night and raining – another battering misery to add to the others. There were lights ahead in the darkness, and they climbed up and up in garlands and necklaces until it seemed they were a fairy-light rope bridge to the moon. Numberless pauses, crouching deep in the mud of ditches as horsemen rode past, shuddering in freezing water. Torchlight spangling across a wide expanse of murmuring river, stippled by the steady rain. And then they were launching into it, Willoby sucking in air with a hoarse cry as the chill liquid stole the breath from his lungs. He was gripping his mount's mane as it forged out in the water, struggling. Aimon was there, his hard fingers gripping Willoby's arm until the feeling left it. And they were struggling ashore with a dark stone wall rearing above them, water streaming from them and the night breeze cutting them like a blade.

A light, a gleam of flame quickly hidden, and they were labouring steeply upwards through a gap in the great wall. The familiar horse and humanity smells, woodsmoke rank in the rain, cooking meat and the sound of voices laughing, talking. Tents hulking like bent giants in the night, an intolerable period of waiting, scurrying – the horses gone now. Neyr and Gamran grabbing his arms and propelling him from shadow to shadow.

And finally an end to the rain, and firelight. They were all there, standing dripping in a warm, close dimness with men coming and going and the smell of food. Someone peeled the sodden clothes from Willoby. His flesh felt waterlogged, dead as soaked meat. A warm cloak over his shoulders, blessed dryness. People were talking in low voices. He saw Merrin being laid on a low cot next to the firepit. Smoke stung his eyes as he slumped beside her. Clean straw under him, a soft tangle of furs and blankets. Cardillac and Aimon were bustling about, looking like filthy clockwork toys wound up too tight.

Willoby stared at Merrin's face. There were rings under the eyes and the cheeks seemed sunken, hollow. She was as white as a sea-scoured bone, black hair straggling in muddy tails across her temples. But her eyes opened.

'We're in Courbisker.'

'Yes, the city. We made it, Merrin. You'll be all right now.'

But she did not relax. 'Be careful here, Willoby. Watch what you say. He doesn't mean you to survive.'

'Who?'

But she was gone again, eyes closing and speech fading to a slurred whisper. With a sort of convulsive dart her hand fastened on his shoulder. He kissed her blue lips, full of a desperate tenderness.

Aimon crouched beside them. 'She's awake?'

'She was.'

'She's a brave lady, a heart like a man's.' Then he took Willoby's chin between skeletal fingers and stared at him. 'And you, Turnkey – are you whole?'

Willoby jerked his head free of the thin grasp. 'I'll survive. I take it we sneaked in successfully?' Without warning he yawned. The firelight was caressing him, filling his head with dreams of slumber. He wanted to burrow down into the straw and play dead for half a day.

'We were successful. The rain helped. It was a miserable night.'

Aimon was soaked and filthy. Cold water dripped from him, but he seemed unconcerned. Willoby wondered what kind of stuff the old bird was made of. Hard as nails, for all his grey hairs.

'And now what, Aimon?' Willoby asked.

'Now? Get some sleep, as much as you like. When you are ready the Prince will probably want to meet you. But for the moment you are to get your strength back.'

Sleep. It beckoned to him like a temptress, muddled his thinking. One thought came to him amid the others: *Merrin is on my side.* He smiled at that and leaned back against the cot so his head was next to hers.

'Do you love her, Willoby?' Aimon. Willoby had almost forgotten he was there. His weariness disarmed him. 'I do, yes. By God I do.'

'If you want to help her then you must do as Tallimon asks, to the very letter. Do you understand me?'

'No. Tired. Sleep.'

'You have a beard of sorts now Willoby, a black beard. Do you know who you resemble?'

But Willoby was smiling in his sleep, his face close to

Merrin's. Aimon shook his head, then he creaked upright. Cardillac stood by him, watching.

'They look good together, Aimon. He is thinner than he was. His face; it reminds me— '

'I know. It is eerie, is it not? He might be Courberall's brother.'

Tallimon was afire when they met him, pacing his new hut like a caged panther. It was odd, Aimon thought, to see someone clean, energetic, wholly awake. But then Tallimon had always had that light about him, that impression of crackling energy.

He and Cardillac slumped on stools by the fire, sharing a jug of barley spirit. Their clothes steamed in the warmth. Cardillac was nodding as he sat.

'So how bad are his injuries, Aimon? Will he be up to the deed in two weeks' time?'

Aimon dragged his fingers through his beard, wincing. 'Hard to say. It is his arm that worries me. It has been well looked after and will heal nicely if the last few days have not turned it bad. But there will be little strength behind the blow, Tallimon. One clear strike is all he will be capable of – and your father is a strong man. Our friend had best strike true, for if the ruse is to succeed he must be unaided, entirely alone.'

'Indeed, indeed.' Tallimon was still pacing up and down, up and down. The firelight glittered off the gold circlet that adorned his temples. His restlessness irritated Aimon. He nudged Cardillac privately and the Decarch's head snapped up.

'And Merrin, how is she?' Tallimon's voice had fallen, become awkwardly casual.

'She has the beginnings of a fever. Her wounds are not deep, but they are ugly.' Aimon aimed the blow deliberately. 'She will be badly scarred, but she will live.'

Tallimon paused, staring into the fire. 'How are they together? Has she . . . has the ruse worked?'

'Undoubtedly. He is in love with her.' And she becoming so with him, perhaps. The thought came into his mind, startling, unlooked-for. Perhaps tiredness was twisting his thinking. The impression remained, however.

'So there is no question of him refusing. We can be sure of that hold on him.'

'We can be sure,' Aimon said, keeping the creeping disgust carefully out of his voice.

'Excellent. There is no word yet of Fferidan's command – they are probably still chasing Caridan's decoy in the mountains – but I think the King met him yesterday, on the pretext of a hunting expedition. No doubt my father has his suspicions about what is happening – Madavar certainly has. But they do not know about the Turnkey. Courberall will still believe himself personally invulnerable, and thinks the majority of the clans unquestionably loyal. He will leave the rest to Madavar. Nothing major enough has happened to warrant a change in plans. You and Merrin are summoned to the hall tomorrow night.'

Aimon started. 'What?'

'The King expects it. This is glorious luck, you turning up here now. We can forestall Madavar. It will look as though I am unjustly suspected – to the other clan leaders, at least.'

'I may be in a condition to show my face at the hall, Merrin certainly is not.'

'She must. It is expected. She must pour for the King.'

Aimon flushed, anger brightening his eyes. But he said nothing. He and Cardillac looked at each other. The Decarch was wide awake now.

'What of Garran?' Cardillac asked. 'He made it through, I take it.'

Tallimon hesitated. 'Yes and no. Madavar caught him on the threshold of the city. He died under interrogation.'

Colour fled Cardillac's face. He clenched his fists, whispering, 'Bastard.'

'Yes. But at least his clan leader, Taurberad, has come over to us as a result. I have the loyalty of almost half the clans.'

'What of my uncle?' Cardillac asked, still pale.

'Surbadan? He is with us, not surprisingly. He has agreed to provide me with one Amon to seal off the lower city on the day of the founding. I will have one and a half thousand men at my command. It will be enough.'

'Has the occasion been planned out yet?' Cardillac asked.

'Not yet. But we know the King will be laying the first stone of the new citadel on the summit of Courbisker hill. It is then that we will strike. The Turnkey will be hidden in the crowd, with some of our own people nearby. He will do the deed, and I will ask, publicly, what clan he belongs to. No clan will claim him, and he will be disposed of, given over to the mob. Madavar and Idramon will be taken care of by you, Cardillac.'

Cardillac nodded slowly.

'And Surbadan's men will saturate the upper city so no loyalist clans can bring their forces to bear. There will be confusion, uncertainty. I will be the only leader visible, with five clans supporting me. I will be suitably grieved, of course.'

'Of course,' Aimon said.

'And will claim the regency for as long as it takes the people to accept the idea of a new king.'

'Will the people swallow it?' Cardillac asked. 'It is obvious you are the beneficiary of all this. They are bound to link you with the King's death.'

'They will have no evidence. Madavar and Idramon they will not care about – only their own people will we need to watch, the Royal Clan, and Madavar's personal retainers. Ordachar will hold a force in readiness for that purpose. But it is the King that matters. So long as there is nothing linking me with the assassin, they are as likely to blame any one of half a dozen clan leaders. They know I am not the only man of ambition among the Kristill, and they will not believe that I would commit parricide as well as regicide.'

'And they will leave it at that,' Cardillac said doubtfully.

'You exaggerate the affection of the people for Courberall, Cardillac. They believe him inviolable, yes, but they do not love him as once they did. The Greshorns did that, and his policy since. So long as we prevent any organized resistance on the day, we can prevail.'

'I wish I had your confidence,' Cardillac said.

Tallimon stared at him closely. 'You are tired, Cardillac, or you would not speak so. Both of you need rest. We can talk more tomorrow.'

'It is almost tomorrow already,' Aimon said. 'I feel a thousand years old.'

'Where did you enter the city?'

'Through the Surbadoi lines. Cardillac has contacts there. We swam the river – and damned cold it was, too . . . You wish to talk to the man Willoby at some point?'

'Yes – no. No, I don't.' Tallimon seemed oddly confused by the question. 'It is better if he never sees me. Harder for him then to point a finger before he dies.'

'All he has to do is shout your name.'

'He will not get the chance. My men will make sure of it. He will remain dumb once he has struck his blow; and then death will shut his mouth for good. You must impress upon him, Aimon, that the fate of Merrin depends upon his actions on the day.'

'And if he fails entirely in his mission – then what?'

'Then we will have war. Courberall will be taken alive and my forces will hold the city. A bloody business it will be, but we can still prevail. I would rather it were otherwise, though. War is always an uncertain business.'

'So be it. With your permission, Prince, we will leave you now. I cannot think straight, and Cardillac is as good as a sleepwalker. There is much to do tomorrow.'

'Of course. My apologies for keeping you, Aimon, but I was impatient to hear the news. It is going to plan – more than that, I think we have luck on our side also. Now all we have to do is keep this pot simmering for the next few days without letting it go off the boil.'

'Where will you accommodate Willoby and Merrin? He will have to remain hidden, and no doubt you wish them to be billeted together.'

Tallimon flushed. 'They can stay in the Surbadoi lines for now. I will post men by their hut to deflect the inquisitive. You

have both done well, remarkably well. I am in your debt.'
Tallimon smiled uncertainly. 'It is good to have my friends
about me again.'

'Yes,' Aimon said. 'It is. And you are.' He saw with
satisfaction that Tallimon was not pleased with the remark,
and wondered at himself. Was he becoming disenchanted? It
had seemed such a good plan not so long ago, but now he
disliked the taste of it in his mouth. The tiredness maybe.
Cardillac was very quiet, too: he seemed deep in thought.

Probably thinking on the men he had left behind in the
mountains. Only a miracle would bring them out alive. But
they had known that the night they left.

Sleep at last. Aimon and Cardillac were billeted in a hut
close to Tallimon's. They threw themselves down and lay like
corpses until the dawn broke open the sky of another morning.

Seventeen

The rain had stopped, and a gleam of sunshine touched the high slopes of Courbisker hill, kindling the building city to life. The job of construction went on apace, everywhere men forging through the deep mud and the sun-touched pools of standing water. The new buildings disclosed their first leaks, and in places the outer wall crumbled as the shallow foundations sank into the soft soil. The wood and stone trains slogged through glutinous muck that bogged them to their axles, the North Road a brown ribbon spangled with long shining puddles where the ruts had filled. The King was still in the hanging woods to the north, hunting, it was said.

Willoby woke once before the dawn, somehow aware that there was a change in the hut. It was a small, draughty structure with only he and Merrin occupying it. Neyr, Mard and old Gamran had been billeted with the rest of their Rimon, what was left of it. The fire had sunk and it was almost dark. On the cot beside him Merrin breathed quietly. But there was someone else there, bending over her. A tall, slim shape with a shine of gold about the forehead. Willoby did not move. The shape touched her face tentatively, lifted the covers to look at her naked torso. There was a hiss of sucked-in breath.

Willoby stirred, deliberately, yawned and turned over. The shape straightened. He could not see the face in the dim light. It paused a second, and he felt the eyes upon him, a hatred that was almost palpable. Then it turned on its heel and padded away noiselessly, shutting the thick door behind it. For some reason Willoby felt relieved. He fought himself upright, groaning at the pain and stiffness that seemed to crucify him through and through. He tugged Merrin's coverings over her bare shoulder and she whimpered a little in her sleep, shifting towards the edge of the cot. He nuzzled her like a cat smelling its young, relishing the smooth warmth under her chin.

'Tallimon,' she murmured, and her lips curved in a smile.

He withdrew gently, his face twisted and ugly. Fool, he thought. That was what she had called him and that was what he was. A fat fool, lost in someone else's world. Damn them; her too. He was alone in this place, no friends. I'm just a cog in their machine, part of the big picture. And she's the oil that keeps this cog turning smoothly, so they intend.

But Christ, he hadn't felt like this since he was a boy. Was it show on her part – the role she had to play? He remembered the fierce joy of her under him, her glad cry as they had joined. He smiled into the dark. Women can fake anything, that most of all.

I don't care. Even if this is just one more lie amid the dream, I'll take what I can get from it.

He wondered how long he had left here, and what Jo was thinking to see her husband comatose in a hospital bed. Would it grieve her? Maria, too? Would she weep if her father died? He didn't know. He didn't know anything about his family, he realized, any more than he knew anything about the people here, the ones who populated his hallucination. It seemed that there was nothing in his life he could be sure of. Except death and taxes. He felt suddenly poor, poverty-stricken as a pauper, rudderless. It's always been like this, he thought. I just never noticed before.

Damn her.

He leant and kissed her again. Her lips were warm now, soft as the petals of a flower. A shame her back would be scored and scarred after this. It was like seeing a work of art wantonly vandalized.

Maybe it's just my prick convincing my brain. It can't be love; I hardly even know her and, besides, she doesn't really exist. Not really.

She felt real enough, though, as he stroked the satin of her cheek, the hollow of her shoulder. He wanted to make love to her, not out of lust but to splice himself further into her life, perhaps, to plant his seed in the dream. He could not explain it, even to himself. The feeling could not be translated into any words he knew without coming out trite and tawdry.

The bitterness kept him awake until after sunrise, despite his weariness.

Preparations for the King's return were well under way. Hunting parties were ranging out into the hills in search of boar, deer, oxen, wildfowl, and the birdcatchers were spreading their lime on tree limbs in the woods in anticipation of larks, blackbirds, thrushes. On the river, men in hide-covered coracles set aside their scruples and fished precariously for the excellent white-fleshed pike that abounded there, and freshwater clams were prised from their beds by the hundred. Down by the gates, the belch and reek of the brewery rose as men stirred the great, raw-built wooden vats of yeast-bubbling beer, and the wild vines of the southern-facing hills had long since been stripped bare for those who preferred the thin, insipid wine they produced.

Barley bread was being baked by the hundredweight in stone ovens, the surrounding valleys scoured for any remnant of the crop growing wild. The women were digging for tubers and plucking herbs from thick-growing copses while watchful horsemen patrolled the skyline. Thyme and rosemary, parsley and sage were cut and plucked and sent in fragrant bundles to the city. And all the while the timber and stone from the cuttings and quarries rolled along in the mud, and the artisans laboured to have Courbisker looking like a true city for the setting of the citadel's foundation stone.

In the evening, the King and his party returned from their hunt.

Merrin woke in the middle of the afternoon feeling stale and unwashed. She levered herself up from the cot. The fire was burning brightly and sunshine lanced in the roof hole, heavy and thick in the twisting smoke. She rubbed her eyes. Aimon and Willoby were there, squatting before a display of food, plates, cups and jugs. Hunger sprang to life in her at once, but she felt too grimy to join them. Willoby smiled at her, seeing her awake. The flesh seemed to have been pared from his face and there was a colour in his cheeks. His beard was growing heavier, and he was wearing clean clothes. He looked almost handsome and she smiled back. Aimon turned.

'So, the maid awakes. Good afternoon. How do you feel?' He was beside her in a flash, examining her back, pressing his palm to her forehead.

'I'm fine, I think. I feel better.'

'The fever has broken, and you're healing well. Excellent. Are you hungry? We have been laid a princely feast here.'

'Yes, but a wash first.' She winced at the black dirt crammed under her nails, the mat-like consistency of her hair. And she was oddly conscious of Willoby's gaze. It made her blush absurdly.

Aimon clapped his hands, and two serving girls appeared. One drew back a hanging from the far end of the hut, and there was another glint of firelight and a curling wisp of steam. Aimon grinned. 'Your bath awaits, lady – and mind that back.'

Afterwards, clean, perfumed, and clothed in a long gown of sky-blue linen with amber beads about her throat and lapis lazuli pinning up her hair, she joined them at their meal. Her back was stiff and sore, making every movement awkward. Aimon had salved it for her before she dressed, treating her as impersonally as if he had been doctoring a horse. She liked that in him. Any other man would have been ogling her – as Willoby was now. She caught his eyes again and he looked away, the gesture almost coy, strange in such a hulking figure.

'Do you like my hair? I put it up as you described,' she told him. He nodded, speechless. Her hair was piled on her head leaving her neck bare. He had told her it was how ladies wore it formally in his world. Aimon laughed, and crammed his mouth with more venison.

There was something different, she thought. She felt as shy

as a courting girl in Willoby's presence. What had changed? Was it that he looked like one of their own people now? He suited his clothes: fine leather breeches, a woollen tunic over a linen shirt, fur-trimmed boots and a broad belt on which hung a long-bladed knife in a wooden scabbard. The sight of the knife marred her mood. Suddenly the food tasted less wholesome. She struggled out of a maelstrom of conflicting thoughts. Aimon was speaking to her.

' – tonight, then, we must make our appearance. We will be on display, Merrin, as proof of Tallimon's innocence if you will. The King requested that you especially be there to pour for him.'

'In the hall? We must be there? But— '

'It is a nuisance, I know, but it will help allay suspicion. Madavar believes us to be out in the hills yet. It is why he prompted the King to ask for us, to embarrass Tallimon. We can foil him by appearing.'

She felt instantly weary at the prospect. Willoby's eyes were switching from her to Aimon and back again, taking in everything. He had frowned at the mention of Tallimon's name. She wanted to ask Aimon if the Prince had enquired after her, but did not dare with Willoby present. The wheels were turning: she must remember the task in hand. She smiled at Willoby, but he did not return it. He knows she thought. He knows the fool we play him for.

'What about me?' he asked in his deep, even voice. 'What do I do while you lot are off feasting in your hall?'

'You stay here for the time being,' Aimon said easily. 'You must remain unseen for the moment.'

'So those men at the door – they're my jailers?'

There was a pause. Merrin saw his face harden, that sneering smile she did not like playing about his lips. Her fingers were shredding bread in her lap and she stilled them with a conscious effort.

'Yes, they are,' Aimon said with a shrug.

Willoby nodded. 'Just so long as I know.'

*

225

The Great Hall was crammed full to bursting. Along the walls the long trestles had been set up for the nobles, whilst at one end the King and his kin sat on the dais. In the middle the firepit glowed, black, glistening shapes turning slowly about it on the spits, worked by sweating pages. The air was thick with smoke and the roasting smell, the reek of beer and close-packed men. A small army of attendants went to and fro with heaped wooden platters. Merrin's head swam. Her body was smarting and sore under the robe. She had donned a bronze-pinned shawl so they would not see the blotted lines where the blood had oozed on her back. She held a heavy jug in each fist, and the effort it cost to move easily under the King's gaze made the perspiration break out on her forehead. They must love this, she thought, to see the whore whom Tallimon made into a lady transformed back into a serving wench.

They were all here. Courberall sat on the dais with his sons – his legitimate sons – placed on either side of him. The firelight made their gold arm-rings glitter. Madavar caught sight of her and gaped, making her grin. It was good to see him off-balance once in a while. The King's look was friendly, however – more than friendly. She felt a chill, wondering if he would try to claim her tonight now that it was clear she was no longer Tallimon's favourite. His eye moved on, though, up and down the tables. He had other things on his mind tonight. She saw his cyclopean gaze fix where Tallimon, Aimon and Cardillac made a subdued, barely drinking trio. Ordachar was further down the hall, singing already. He had always liked his beer.

Tallimon. He was watching her, noting the new set of her hair, the strain fighting through on her face. She pictured a marvellously swift series of images: past intimacies, his eyes smiling down on her as they loved, his rare laugh at a gibe of hers. Then they were gone. Another woman was pouring for him, gazing into his face with adoration.

Aimon winked at her but her face was too stiff to respond. She moved down towards the cooking end of the hall, weaving in and out of pages moving the other way. And then, some-how, Courberall was there again. He was standing at the doors looking keenly about him, but with the hood of a cloak pulled half round his face. How— ?

Willoby. The breath stopped in her throat as she recognized him. He watched her as she approached.

'What do you think you're doing? You shouldn't be here!' His resemblance to the King had thrown her completely. She had never consciously noted it before.

'You sound like my wife. I came to have a look at the fun.'

'How did you get out?' Her wrists were quivering under their load. He relieved her of a jug and drank deeply from it. There was a shine to his eyes. He leaned against the wall as if needing its support.

'Drank my guards under the table. They're a soft-headed bunch. This is quite a sight, this place. Like something out of the Round Table, except for the stink.'

'You can't stay here. Someone will see you. Go back, Willoby. You don't know what you're doing.'

'Yes, I do. Drop that gnat's piss and come with me. I need some air.'

He dragged her out by the wrist, and in moments they had left the hall, the keen, clear outdoor air filling their heads, the stars visible overhead. Merrin's sweat turned cold on her. He pulled her into the deeper shadow between two buildings.

'We'll be seen— '

'Hush.' Willoby was drunk, or nearly so. He was huge in the dark night. His eyes seemed to take fire from the stars. She was afraid, and yet not afraid.

'What do you want?'

He kissed her clumsily. His bulk pushed her against a wooden wall so that the half-healed scores on her back cried out. She moaned slightly, but he took it the wrong way and pressed his body hard against her. What was he going to do – take her here, now? What should she do? Accommodate him?

But he drew away. His breath was foul with alcohol.

'I love you, Merrin.'

Had anyone seen her leave with him? She had to get back. 'I

have to go, Willoby.' What had he said? She had not been listening. Panic beat black wings about her head.

'God-damn you,' he snarled, but his voice ended on something close to a sob. 'I know it doesn't fucking matter, but I wanted you to know. I love you, damn it.'

Love. His eyes glimmered even more brightly, she noticed with astonishment. He was near tears. She caught one drop as it brimmed over on to his cheek, and felt a sudden pang, unidentifiable. Compassion? Regret? A vision of Willoby fifteen, twenty years younger, a tall man with a grin on his face, those frown lines not quite so deep. In all her short life she had never before been offered unconditional, selfless love. It bewildered her.

She drew close to him, knowing he was wounded, and buried herself in his embrace. His arms hurt her, but she was glad of the pain. It was like a reminder, or a punishment. She was party to this man's murder, and yet he loved her. Of them all, he was the only one who had ever been willing to offer her something for nothing.

'It doesn't matter,' he said. 'I know it's not the same for you. I'm no Apollo. But I wanted you to know. I don't care if it's all for show, it's still something . . . Ah, Christ, I'm no good at this.'

'It's all right, Willoby. I know.'

'Your back. I forgot — I'm sorry; I must have hurt you. See what I mean? Clumsy bastard.' His fists were clenching and unclenching at her shoulders.

She felt pity for him, for herself. They were similar in some ways, both misfits, used and abused. But the hard, practical side of her still had an ear out for approaching footsteps, and wondered how long her absence from the hall would go unnoticed. It was half a mile down the hill to his hut. Dare she risk getting him there? She hated herself for her thoughts. The childish, lost part of her felt somehow safe in his arms. I know what it's like now, she mused. I thought I did before but I was wrong. And far down in her a voice asked: could I love him also? She didn't want to know the answer — there was no

228

helping it. She had a job to do; in a short while he would be dead.

That made her cling tighter, and there were tears in her own throat.

Footsteps, coming closer. They were purposeful, not the wandering stagger of a reveller. She and Willoby drew deeper into the shadows. He loomed over her like a great, protective bear.

'Merrin?' Whispered. It was Cardillac's voice. He was standing peering into the deeper darkness where they were hiding. Merrin felt a rush of relief and moved out to meet him, Willoby trailing after.

'Moon and stars, Merrin – what's going on? The King is asking for you . . . and what is he doing here? He should be under guard.'

'He came to see me.' She took Willoby's arm and pressed it. 'He's going now.' She reached up and kissed him. 'I'll see you later.' And then she turned and ran into the hot hubbub of the hall, hoping her tears had not blotched her face.

Willoby stood irresolute, confused. It was that damned beer.

A hand on his shoulder. Cardillac looking ruefully at him. 'Come on, let's get you back. If you want to drink with someone you can drink with me. I couldn't get drunk tonight if I tried.'

They made their way down through the darkened huddle of the city. The place was an unholy maze of tents and raw-built buildings, the trenches of new foundations, the skeletons of huts black against a vast, starlit sky. Few people were abroad in the lower city but flickering lights were everywhere, campfires by the score ringing the upper reaches of Courbisker hill, and lower down the place was so quiet they could hear the lap and gurgle of the Great River in the night's stillness.

Cardillac had a swift way with Willoby's guards. He kicked them awake and got rid of them in short order, calling others to take them away and dump them in the river. Then he and

Willoby sat in front of the rekindled fire with a flagon of beer each. The journey down the hill had cleared Willoby's head somewhat. He blinked at the bright chiaroscuro of light and dark in the hut, the leaping shadows, and passed his fingers through his rapidly thickening beard. It itched. He craved a shave, though he had a feeling it made him blend in more. Most of the men he had seen in this place were bearded, except for that bloke Tallimon, of course.

He was unsettled, his spirits in a strange flutter. I'd almost swear she's serious about me, he thought. The way she looked . . . God, she's young. She might be my daughter. And he smiled sourly.

Cardillac was drinking steadily, two points of high colour burning on his cheeks. He seemed to be a man intent on unconsciousness.

But I can respect that. Willoby chuckled aloud mirthlessly, refilling Cardillac's rapidly emptying flagon from the jug nearby.

'Do you remember Garran, Willoby?' Cardillac asked thickly.

'Nope.'

'A good man, one of the Serradai – Taurberad's clan. He could track a man across blank rock, outlast a horse. That's why I sent him as messenger to Tallimon.'

'Bravo,' Willoby muttered. He was not especially interested. He was wondering if Merrin would join him after the feast. They'd have to be careful, of course, with their mutual wounds, but it must be physically possible.

'Garran,' Cardillac went on, 'was caught by Madavar's men, however, a scant mile from the city. Tallimon told me he had been tortured to death, or else he had broken under interrogation and was then quietly got rid of.'

Could she love him? Was it possible? The damned thing about drunkenness: it gives credence to wishful thinking. All things become possible, a nuance becomes an acknowledged gesture. Damn head wants clearing, Willoby thought. And then the image of her moving across that hall. She looks good with her hair up like that. That lovely long neck, and those jewels shining. Like a duchess.

'But Garran died of poisoning, on Tallimon's orders – so he would not talk. And also to turn his clan leader against Courberall. He was murdered.'

The word caught Willoby's attention. 'Murdered?'

'Ordachar told me, thinking I knew already. He has never been the brightest of men. My Prince killed one of his own – and for what? And he would have me believe that Madavar did it. What kind of man is he, Willoby?'

'How the hell should I know? I've never even spoken to him.' Though perhaps he had once. A strange kind of meeting.

'He plots to kill his own father. He will let nothing get between him and the kingship. Even Merrin he— ' Cardillac stopped suddenly, darting an anxious glance at Willoby.

'What about her? What about Merrin?'

'He – he loved her once, and she him.' Cardillac's words came out in a rush. The colour had fled his face. 'But he discarded her like a threadbare cloak. He made her into a lady, and then threw her back again. He ordered her to prostitute herself, to take you as a lover and gain your trust. That is the kind of man he is. But he was not always like that. He was my *friend*, once. Perhaps he thinks he is yet.'

Willoby was sitting very still. The ramifications of Cardillac's words were unfolding in glorious Technicolor within his brain. He had known she must be acting, that she could not truly care. But to hear it from someone else's lips like that, the fact that she had been acting under orders all this time. What was she? A whore, yes, but what else? Could she be such a consummate actress?

The castles in the air that he had been hesitantly building that evening crumbled and disappeared. He felt entirely sober, and sick to his stomach. Of course he had known; it had been too swift, too easy. Absurd, even. But one stupid, *stupid* part of him had been spinning out this hope. *Damn* her.

'You people are full of shit,' he said disgustedly, and he

drank his beer in swallow after swallow until the blood seemed to be pounding a rigid tattoo in his head and his throat ached.

'I'm sorry,' Cardillac slurred. 'I was a fool to say that. I'll regret it when my head clears.'

'It doesn't matter. Nothing matters except waking up and getting on with my life. This is all bullshit; it's not happening.'

And yet it hurts. It fucking hurts.

He stood up. 'I'm going outside. Don't try to stop me.'

Cardillac was already halfway to his feet. He looked into Willoby's face and sank down again.

'Be careful where you go. She cares for you, Willoby – she truly cares. I think you're the first man ever to have treated her decently in her life.'

'Bully for me.'

'You have to do it. You have to go through with it, or she's as good as a corpse. Remember that.' Cardillac was glassy-eyed, the words sliding as they left his mouth.

'Drop dead.'

He was outside again in this starlit, impossible world of his dreams. He made his way steadily downhill to where the river plopped and muttered by the incomplete city wall. There were men there, spear points gleaming. He avoided them easily – he had always been quiet on his feet – and reached the riverbank itself, under the huge shadow of the stone works. He sat there on the damp ground, the alcohol in his system keeping the cold at bay, and listened to the nightfowl crying out to each other across the quiet water. It was peaceful, wholly beautiful, the stars a great spangled band of speckled light across the sky. He watched one shoot and vanish in a streak of light towards the horizon, and smiled up at the vast vault.

It's lovely here, despite everything . . . She was right to call me a fool; she was just being honest. Not so fat now, though.

But what to do? Keep trundling along and see what happens? Murder this man like they want?

He grimaced. Not my style.

What would happen if he refused to go through with it? He should have asked Cardillac that. They'd kill him, surely.

And Merrin too, it seemed. *She's as good as a corpse.* That was why she had been ordered to seduce him: so they would have that hold on him. Poor kid. Now the odd moments of fear he had seen on her face made sense. She was terrified that he might *not* love her.

Damnation!

Too late now – he could not help his feelings.

'They've got me by the short and curlies,' he said aloud to the quiet river and the night birds. 'Bastards.'

There was this talk of some great occasion in a few days' time: the city founding. Each time it was mentioned everyone tensed up. He smiled. That must be it, then.

He slid his dagger out of its sheath, turning the long blade in his hands. It was double-edged, a stabbing weapon. An assassin's tool. He remembered another knife, another world, him throwing it out over the moors in a fit of pique.

Wonder if some archaeologist will stumble across it and be flummoxed.

Wonder what Jo's doing, how she's taking my coma, or fit, or whatever it is.

Wonder what Merrin truly thinks of me.

He sheathed the knife again, though he had been half inclined to pitch it out over the dark river, and listen to the plash. Not so simple any more.

I can't really die in a dream, can I?

He does not mean you to survive.

This Tallimon, a real Machiavelli. But Cardillac's not too chuffed with him. Nor Merrin, I think, even though she . . . loved him.

He hung his head. The mud was chilling his backside, but the discomfort focused his mind, cleared the last of the beer fumes away.

I'll do it anyway. Why not? It doesn't matter to me in the end, it's not real. And it might help Merrin. That'd be something good out of this.

233

He tried not to peer too closely at the logic of his thoughts, but stood up. That's it, then. That's the way it'll be. Might as well enjoy this place while I can.

He went back up the hill, hoping Cardillac had not quaffed all the beer.

Eighteen

All morning they had been pouring into the city. The North Road was clogged with them. Men, women and children of all sizes, shapes and ages. They had churned the wet ground to muck in their wake, cut a swathe across the land on their journey south. The Host of the Kristill had come to Courbisker in its tens of thousands for the day of the City-Founding.

Sentries watched them from the new walls, waving and grinning at relatives or friends as they waited to pour through the gates. For some this was their first glimpse of the new city. The throng buzzed with a thousand conversations, and faces were uptilted in awe at what the builders had accomplished. A city, the first they had ever known.

Willoby watched them come in from a spur below the summit. With him were Aimon, Cardillac and Merrin. He had never seen so many people. It was like a biblical epic, the parting of the Red Sea or something. Their noise carried up the hill as a formless surf of sound, waves breaking on a distant beach.

The Big Day. Well, he thought wryly: I'm dressed for it. He wore a buckskin tunic trimmed with fur, for all the world like Davy Crockett. His boots were light leather – suitable for running – and a cloak of dark, inky blue was draped over his left shoulder and arm. Hidden in the folds of the cloak was the knife. Its presence was like a weight over his heart.

Cardillac had tried to teach him how to use it in the days leading up to this. That was a laugh. Willoby knew every knife move in the book, and several out of it. He had lost count of the times he had faced a man with a blade in his hand.

Two inches, between the ribs that lay over the heart. That

was all it took. Or a slice down in the angle of the jaw, shredding the jugular. One blow was all he would have time for.

This is my last day on earth, he thought. Dream or reality, it didn't matter any more. Willoby no longer cared – the distinction had lost relevance. There was only this bright morning, the crowds roaring below, the trio who stood silently with him looking down.

He flexed his wounded arm experimentally. It had healed well. Not so strong as once it had been, but it would serve.

Pictures running through his mind: the stored-up memories. Breakfast with Merrin, sitting and gazing out across an immense expanse of space, clear across the plains to where the white mountains towered eternally on this world's horizon. Staring down on the Great River, coiling like a broad silver snake that wound away south into the unknown lands. Seeing a thousand horsemen come thundering to the city in column of fours, the sunlight catching every nick and boss on their armour, the guidons cracking in the sharp wind.

Watching Merrin's face as he moved inside her, seeing the tears gleam full of firelight, the pair of them moving as slowly and carefully as if it were their first time, drawing out every sensation.

How long have I been here? he wondered. Less than a month, anyway. And yet he felt he had crammed in more to these few short days than he had known in all the long, even-pacing years that had preceded them. There was that life, that sense of living, which he had not known for so long. Every-thing was different: the food, the drink, the texture of the clothes, the smells, even the air he breathed. And the lady.

Maybe it's death approaching that does this, the knowledge that it can't last – it'll be over soon. Maybe.

For he was sure now that he would not see this day's sun go down. No one had dared tell him in so many words, but he read it in their faces – especially Merrin's.

She likes me, she truly does. That's better than nothing, I suppose.

It was for her that he would do this thing. No other reason. Unless it might be a chance to change history – this land's history, anyway. To be the little cog that finally fucks up the whole machine. He grinned to himself. How many people get to do a Lee Harvey Oswald?

Even if he wanted to back out, he could not. Men followed him everywhere, discreetly but implacably. They were watching him now. Surbadan's men, Cardillac had told him. They would shadow him to the end; perhaps they were even the ones who were meant to finish him off.

Never thought I'd end up going to the slaughter like a lamb, but these things happen.

He'd take one or two with him before the end though, out of sheer bloody-mindedness if nothing else.

'Time we were in position,' Aimon said gently behind him.

He nodded but did not move, still staring down at the vast crowds, then out and up at the eternal mountains. He'd have liked to climb one of those, take a horse and ride into the passes once summer came.

A hand on his arm. Merrin. She looked beautiful this morning. Her eyes were green-brown, he noticed for what seemed like the first time. Blue suited her, and he liked the paler sash that belted her slim waist. He winked at her, and the foursome started for the summit of the hill.

For Tallimon, the morning had been strangely tranquil. He had risen, eaten and dressed with particular care, unflinching even when the clumsy page had scraped his chin almost raw with the pumice-stone. There was a fatalism in the air, almost as though the vast pageant that was to ensue was a tragedy already mapped out by onlooking gods. The pieces he had spent so long manoeuvring were at last in place: they had their tasks to fulfil, he was a spectator.

Fferidan had returned only three days earlier, his men exhausted and horseless for the most part. That had been perhaps the most perilous moment. Caridan had eluded him, and was now in hiding among his own clan. The men Cardillac had left behind were all dead, a litter of corpses trailing down out of the hills with grypesh carcasses surrounding them. Cardillac had been right to abandon them, though Tallimon knew he hated himself for it. *Perhaps he hates me also,* he thought. The Decarch had been colder these past days. A hard thing, to learn for the first time the value of expediency. No matter. He would be amply rewarded for his loyalty once the thing was done.

So, the illustrious Fferidan had come trailing back to Madavar with empty hands and not a few empty saddles. Madavar knew something had been going on, up in the foothills, but not what. Despite the skirmishing between his men and Tallimon's, he had not had enough evidence to go before the King.

Luck, Tallimon decided, *has been on my side, most definitely.* Even the messenger he had sent, fruitlessly it transpired, to find Cardillac had returned safely.

He almost laughed aloud as he remembered Fferidan's face, Madavar's glowering frustration, as he, the King's bastard, had made peace with the former in the King's presence. Fferidan had actually been pleased, thinking it a victory. Madavar had seen the gesture for what it was; a morsel to keep Courberall off the scent.

And yet it had all been so close, ruination a mere heartbeat away.

Not that it was any farther away now.

Be calm, Tallimon told himself, as he buckled his belt with steady fingers. *The plan is intact. The hardest is over. One bloody deed and the thing is accomplished. I will be king by the time the sun sets tonight.*

And the thought immediately following that: *So long as this Willoby does what he is told.*

A great square had been marked out at the highest part of the hill, and the peak itself had been levelled. On four sides, trenches marked out the foundations of the new citadel. A dais had been constructed and long tables stood in rank on rank, empty as yet.

All down the long way from the summit to the very gates of the city tall poles had been set up and garlanded with flowers and greenery. It was almost as though the road were shaded by well-spaced saplings. Standing between the poles were spear-armed men, the sun setting alight the metal studs and rings on their armour as they turned and shifted, exchanging banter with the gathering crowds.

There were hundreds here already, standing a dozen deep along the lines of the square, hopping good-naturedly in and out of the foundations. Hundreds more had clambered up on the frameworks of the half-finished buildings and were throwing blossoms on the serried heads below. They had grandstand seats for the occasion, and shouted what they could see to their less fortunate comrades down in the press.

And still the people kept coming. They poured up the hill in a steady stream, kept clear of the main roadway by the over-worked spearmen. They filled all the available space between the new halls, houses and barracks that clustered on the hillside, raising a haze of dust into the clear air so that men on the nearby ridges saw the City enmeshed in a cloud, like a pale smoke-pall. Here and there a spear-point caught the sun and flashed, like a tiny lightning from a dun-coloured thunderhead.

Cardillac was sweating in the growing crush. Willoby loomed at his shoulder, stolid and emotionless as a statue. He wondered what was happening in the big man's head, and admitted a grudging admiration for his coolness.

A headache filled his own temples with ceaseless throbbing, and his mouth was dry and foul with dust. Am I afraid? he wondered. Afraid of treachery, perhaps. This was a different thing from facing an acknowledged enemy with a sword in his hand. And yet it was just another method of warfare. Tallimon had told him that. More, Tallimon had made him learn it. How could he condemn his Prince for having Garran killed, when he, Cardillac, had left his own men to die in the hills?

Whatever happened today, a new era would be ushered in, a new set of rules concocted by Tallimon and Madavar.

I am doing what men of middle ability have always done, Cardillac told himself. Rising by clinging to the cloak of another. That knowledge tasted worse than the dust in his mouth.

He studied the crowd intently, finding what he was looking for in the great multitude of faces and forms. There were armed men among the populace, warriors from the Royal House who would act as the King's bodyguard. But there were Tallimon's men also; almost his whole Penton, five hundred strong, had infiltrated the throng. It was easy to pick them out: like himself, they wore heavy cloaks despite the warm sun, the better to hide the swords hitched up under their left armpits. Cardillac wondered who among them had been given the job of dispatching Willoby, once the blow had been struck. He himself intended to be away from here before the moment came. He had no great desire to see either Willoby or Courberall in death.

I am becoming over-nice about blood these days, he reflected. Unlike some. He glanced left at Merrin. She was very pale, standing straight as a spear with the dust settling on her hair.

Mayhap we are all just flies caught in Tallimon's web.

Merrin steadied herself against the jostle of those around her. The trumpets would sound soon, signalling the start of the King's procession, and then she, Cardillac and Aimon would depart – if the crowd would let them – and Willoby would be alone in the midst of the whole Kristillic nation, waiting to do his deed.

She dared not look at him, for fear her mask would slip. Never had she felt so confused, so bereft. Not even on the night Tallimon had discarded her. If only they had had more time!

She had led this man who loved her to his death, and he did not blame her for it. The weight of that burden bowed her spirit. All that kept her from sobbing was the bright, glowing ember of hatred for Tallimon. It kept her face composed, stiffened her backbone. She wanted to destroy him, to bring

him down into the dirt where he had thrown her, and let him
know it was she who had accomplished it. She no longer cared
about becoming a lady again: the mark Tallimon had placed
on her would remain for ever.

Impossible. She would play out her part to the end, watch
two good men murdered, and have her part in the sharing out
of the spoils.

She bowed her head, clamping her teeth tight on the tears.
The hatred smouldered on in her breast, waiting to catch
flame.

Willoby fingered his beard. It was a fair length now – it had
always grown quickly. This place was good for him. He was
thinner, fitter, and he no longer had that smoker's shortness of
breath. He felt younger. Pity it wouldn't last.

A nod from Cardillac. Time to move forward, to get into
position. He lurched into movement.

Even now, an absence of fear. There was only that buzzing
excitement, the first tricklings of adrenaline. It was that going-
into-contact feeling. As egocentric as any human being,
Willoby knew he did not yet quite believe in his own mortality.
He knew the fear would come at the last, but hoped to hold it
off as long as he could. These people valued courage: he
wanted to look well in their eyes.

His thoughts hopped from one thing to another as he
nudged and pushed his way to the forefront of the crowd. He
had been told where to stand, what to do, when to do it. They
had even told him how he would be spirited away to a safe
place, prior to being magically sent home. Cardillac had not
been able to meet his eyes on telling him that. They knew he
knew. He thought they were puzzled at his nonchalance, his
unworried attitude, and that only made him more determined
to keep up the facade. He'd die with a smile on his face just to
baffle the buggers.

Not that they were a bad bunch. He liked them. He and
Cardillac were similar in many ways and Aimon, despite being
a hard case, was not a bad bloke at heart. Merrin he was in

love with – no point beating about the sodding bush. He adored her, even while knowing she could never feel the same way. Perhaps it was as well it should end here, with everyone's masks in place. It was still bright and interesting and alive, a pageant of people and things to fascinate him. He would take those memories with him untarnished when he went.

For a moment he thought of Jo, Maria. One last attempt to reconcile it, make sense of what had happened to him. Did he really lie yet in his hospital bed, or had he disappeared like some tasteless ghost? He hoped they would be all right; for a second he even prayed that they would.

Horns blowing down in the lower city, the tall curving trumpets they called *lurs*. That was the signal for the fun to begin. The lines of spear-carrying men pushed back the packed crowds even farther, forcing a clear way from the square right through the city. The roadway there was a real one paved with stone slabs. The masons had worked like dogs to get it finished on time; already men called it the Royal Way. The King would ride up it very soon, his sons – all three of them – and the clan leaders behind him. It was to be a day for rejoicing, an occasion to mark the beginning of a new era. He would not be armed, and would wear no armour. So Cardillac had said.

The crowd swayed and lurched, people packing closer into the press. It would become hard to move soon. Willoby had to get right up to the front, so he could step out swiftly, but he had to stay unnoticed also.

A hand in the small of his back. Aimon, motioning him forward again. There was sweat on the old man's face; he was as pale as paper.

Merrin, here beside him. Soon it would be time for them to leave, and he would be on his own but for the wary warriors with their hidden weapons, and the thousands of spectators. Willoby pushed his way to the first rank of the crowd. His heart was beginning to beat faster; he could feel the knife like some hard, malign serpent nestling under his collarbone.

Cardillac, lifting his hand in salute or farewell. They were supposed to be more discreet, but Willoby was glad of the gesture. Then the Decarch had turned, and was lost in the throng. Willoby knew he would never see him again.

Merrin's fingers linked in his. He gripped them reassuringly, then bent to speak in her ear. He had to raise his voice to be heard over the clamour of the crowd.

'You'd best go now. Someone might see you with me.'

She nodded, and he saw to his astonishment that though her face was hard and set, her eyes were filling with tears. Her beauty wrenched at something in his breast.

'Don't do it,' she said, and he thought his heart would stop.

'It's not worth it – *he's* not worth it.'

He smiled at her, a wide, pure smile of sheer happiness. 'I have to. But it doesn't matter. This is a dream for me, remember?' The lie sounded forced even to his own ears.

'No,' she said brokenly. 'That's not true. You'll die, Willoby – they'll kill you.'

'It doesn't matter,' he repeated. Again he felt that he had lived his lifetime in just a few days. He had seen a new world, made new friends, fallen in love. And now it was over. He felt little regret; he knew, far down, that it was his death that made her weep and perhaps even made her believe she cared for him, but it could not last, not in the normal, humdrum way of things. Best to leave it while it was still in full, brilliant flower.

'Go now, go on. Remember the plan.'

She hugged him tight. He could feel the seams and lines of her scarred back. Then she turned and was gone; a distant dark head amid a hundred others. He was alone.

And then there was one. He felt momentarily wretched and afraid, starting to realize that it really could be the end. No way out of this. But he snarled and growled at himself like some apoplectic sergeant-major. Those nearby saw the big, powerful man with the dark beard straighten to his full height and smile a cold, unnerving smile as the internal battle was won.

I was a soldier once, and by God I'll finish like one.

Outside the gates of the crowded city the collected nobles stood by their horses and waited for the King. A special pavilion had been set up for him so that he could spend the night outside the walls and enter in triumph on this day of celebration.

Tallimon caught Surbadan's eye. The clan leader stared at him as stonily as if he were a stranger. That was good.

Madavar stood nearby, calm as a windless lake. He bowed his head slightly as Tallimon met his gaze. It was like the opening flourish of a duel. Yes, Madavar knew . . . something. But Tallimon was sure he had no idea of the real danger. He had expected an attack on the King's pavilion in the night, a dagger in the dark. That was why two hundred men had surrounded it throughout the lightless hours. Did he believe now the danger was past? Tallimon doubted it.

'A fine day for the occasion – not a cloud in all the sky,' Madavar said.

Fferidan was beside him, looking as puffed up as a young gamecock. He believed himself the hero of the hour, the ass.

'Today a dynasty is being established, sire, the beginning of a royal line that will last a thousand years. As long as this city will endure.'

Madavar had the grace to look slightly embarrassed. Tallimon smiled though.

'I'll drink to that, later today.'

'We all will,' Madavar told him.

A commotion, guards snapping upright. The King emerged from his pavilion, a huge figure glittering with gold. He belched, grinned at the assembled notables, shouted for his horse.

'Let's get this damned thing over with, then,' he said gruffly, once he had hauled himself into the saddle. 'We're wasting good drinking time.'

There was a splurge of laughter. The thin tension of the morning was broken. The crowd of horsemen mounted, gave way before the three sons of the King, and then the entire assemblage followed in Courberall's wake towards the City gates. As they approached, the whole lower circle of the city erupted with a roar.

*

That cheering, lower down in the city. The King's procession must have started. Willoby looked round. The cloaked men were all about, dotted in the crowd. He could count fifteen without moving his eyes. Cardillac and Aimon standing well back – he thought it was them, though he could not be sure. They were two more blurred faces among the many. There was no sign of Merrin.

More people were climbing on to the roofs, children were being hoisted on their fathers' shoulders. Some of the lesser nobles sat on horses made restive by the teeming people.

A louder roar, rippling up the hill like a line of falling dominoes. Horn calls blew challenge and counter-challenge. Willoby felt he was attending some anachronistic oddity; like being a modern-day spectator at Rome's circus, catching a glimpse of an alien world.

There: a line of horsemen moving slowly up the new road. The man at the head of the procession was lifting a hand in response to the cheers. Willoby could see a black beard, the glint of gold – something odd about one eye. Courberall, the High King. Only a few hundred yards away. The crowd gave a convulsive heave. A spear butt pushed against Willoby's chest, forcing him back. He stared at its wielder: a mere youngster in chain mail, and the man drew back with widened eyes.

Others shoving and shifting behind him. Suddenly there was one of the cloaked men almost at his shoulder. Their eyes met; they nodded fractionally at each other, like men agreeing on some silent contract. A tall man with a blond moustache and a reddish cast to his hair. He'll be first on the scene, Willoby thought. Maybe he's even the one ordered to shut me up.

Not long now. Willoby recognized Tallimon in the slowly advancing procession. He was white-faced, but smiling and waving at the crowd.

Someone jostled him and he glanced irritably aside. It was Merrin. She was breathing fast and her hair was flying wild over her shoulders.

'Jesus God, Merrin, get the hell out of here!'

'*No*. I won't let you do it.'

'What?' The adrenaline was beginning to pump. He could feel his heart starting to race, the tiptoe readiness of his muscles. 'Go away, for God's sake. You'll get yourself killed here.' He felt blond moustache's eyes on the back of his head. The procession was scant yards away. People were throwing flowers at the King, and he was grinning, his one eye ashine.

Merrin gripped his arm. Her face tilted up to him, wild with fear and determination.

'You mustn't do it. Let Tallimon do his own killing.'

'Are you mad? Do you think he'll let either of us away alive? I have to, Merrin – at least that way you'll be safe. I *want* to do it. Let me go!'

The King was level with them. The noise of the crowd rose to a great, suffocating roar. Arms were upraised, the air was thick with the tossed flowers, the early blossoms of the river meadows. Their scent hung heavy and sweet over the stink of the packed masses. A voice was shrieking in Willoby's head, the voice he knew from those times in combat. It was the over-the-top voice and could not be ignored.

Merrin clung to him desperately. Blond moustache was pushing towards them. He saw Tallimon's bright, hate-filled glare. People were shouting Courberall's name; the hooves of the procession were deafening on the stone roadway. Willoby fought for breath.

'I love you, Merrin. Forgive me.'

He dealt her a short, savage blow to the side of the chin with his left fist.

A vision of Jo's head snapped back by the blow of his hand.

She crumpled. He caught her as she fell, and threw her into the astonished arms of blond moustache.

The King was moving past, still waving. Willoby put his head down and charged.

People were scattered like skittles. He knocked aside those few who had pushed in front of him and came up against the young spearman. A shattering blow to the middle of the youth's face, then one shoulder cannoning into his chest. The man flew ten feet across the roadway. Horses reared and neighed shrilly.

The way was clear. Willoby ran. Never had he felt so absurdly alive, so full of strength and energy. Already men were converging on him from all sides, but he was invulnerable, invincible. A laugh came out of his throat, sounding manic even to himself.

The King turned. Horses were galloping up. A vast, thunderous noise. Some people were still cheering, others crying out in alarm as they realized something was wrong.

Now. This is it.

Courberall looked at him, and for an instant their eyes met. He saw the King's face fill with surprise, even puzzlement. Then Willoby had leapt forward and set one huge hand under Courberall's boot, shoving upwards.

The King toppled over on the far side of his horse.

Willoby whipped out his dagger. The handle was hot in his palm, taking heat from his body. The King's horse bucked and circled. Courberall was lying on the ground clinging to its reins. Willoby loomed over him like a cloud.

A massive blow in his back sent him to his hands and knees, sprawling at the King's feet. A horse had charged into him.

He lost the knife. It skittered away across the stones.

Or had he thrown it away, into the dark stretch of the moors?

He scrabbled for it, but someone had seized his cloak – many hands were grabbing for him. There were men all over him. He fought madly. One attacker was thrown clear, but the others hung on like dogs worrying a bull. Then a spear butt smote Willoby full on the forehead.

An explosion of light. For a second he was deaf. The world was a heaving turmoil of kicks and blows and snarling faces. He thought he heard Merrin's voice, and fought ever more fiercely.

There was the pain of a blade entering his thigh, being punched down into the flesh. Another in his shoulder. They were stabbing him. Weakness flooded his veins like water. His struggles waned. Another blow, under his ribs this time. He saw a scarlet spurt. Blood everywhere.

The King stood over him as they held him down and stabbed. Blond moustache stood with a bloody knife and way back Tallimon, his face like stone. *Removing the evidence,* Willoby thought.

But the big, one-eyed man pulled them off him as he lay there in a pool of his own life's blood. Willoby was able to move; he felt no pain as yet, only that sense of his strength ebbing. He struggled up; the one-eyed man kicked him down. He was shouting something but Willoby could not understand the words; they were in a language alien to him.

I'm dying, he thought.

They stood round him like pedestrians at the scene of an accident, while his blood flowed out to thicken the dust. The King seemed transfixed by Willoby's face, and lying there, Willoby suddenly grasped why.

We look the same. We might be twins.

He wanted to say something, to reach out to the one-eyed man who stood over him, but there was a commotion, a ripple in the bystanders. Somehow, bewilderingly, Merrin had burst in on them. There was something in her hand that glittered. The surrounding warriors were caught by surprise. The King straightened—

'This is for Tallimon!' she screamed.

—And the knife was plunged to the hilt in Courberall's neck. He stood à moment, shocked, with the hilt protruding grotesquely. All around, his men looked blankly at him and there was almost a silence. Then he fell forward on top of Willoby.

Willoby tried to push the body off him, but had not the strength. He saw Merrin's face, the eyes searching for his as they caught her, the bruise at her jaw where he had left his mark. Her visage was a blaze of triumph and hatred.

Then she went down under the swinging blades. He closed his eyes.

The clash of weapons, men screaming, horses in agony. He was buffeted as he lay, but Courberall's body protected him.

His blood ran warm and free in the road to mingle with the King's.

Someone tugging at him. Suddenly the weight on him shifted. He was being pulled along by his arms, his heels rattling on the stones. There was a press of men everywhere, the flash of swords. He saw a glimpse of blue on the ground, a head of dark hair matted with blood, before the trampling hordes engulfed it. He wept as they dragged him away.

They halted. The skeletons of buildings reared up on all sides. The sound of the fighting was farther away, a distant cacophony of noise. Aimon's mouth had bled into his beard and Cardillac had a gash clear down the front of his face. One nostril flapped bloodily as he breathed. They were pushing ripped portions of their own clothing into Willoby's wounds. Tears on Cardillac's face cleared streaks through his blood.

'Help me up.'

They aided him into a sitting position.

'What's happening?' he asked in a whisper.

'War,' Aimon told him 'Madavar lives. His men are fighting for survival. And there is a battle down by the walls. Surbadan's Rimons are striving to keep off reinforcements.'

'War,' Willoby said. It meant nothing to him. She was dead, and he had survived. He had accomplished none of the things he had set out to do.

Dead.

'Why did she do it, Aimon?'

'Who knows? I think she loved you, Willoby, but she realized too late. I think – I think also she wanted to bring down Tallimon more than she wanted to live. She did not want to go back to the way it was before you came.'

'God forgive me,' Willoby said.

He grew dizzy, and they laid him on his back again. This world was becoming darker – and yet it had been a bright morning such a short time ago. I meant to die today, Willoby thought, to go down like a soldier. Maybe I'll go yet. He was tired, and becoming cold. He had to make a conscious effort of will to speak.

'What will you do now?'

Cardillac answered him, his voice distorted by his wound. Aimon was doing something with a phial, sprinkling things and muttering to himself.

'I'll fight on – there's nothing else for me.'

'With Tallimon?'

'Yes. He is my Prince, after all. I'm almost glad it's come to an open battle. A hopeless one, perhaps, since Merrin has now implicated him in the assassination. But it is the warrior's way. I wish, though – I wish it could have been different.'

'Bury her for me, Cardillac, or burn her or whatever you people do. Don't leave her lying like that in the street.'

Cardillac nodded, unable to speak.

Aimon rejoined them. 'We are ready.'

'For what?'

'Sending you home, Willoby. You may yet live, if they can patch you up like last time.'

He drew a painful breath. Home. He could hardly even remember what it was like. The other things were too strong in his mind.

'Is Tallimon going to lose, Aimon? Was it all for nothing?'

'I don't know. I think he will take the city – he has Surbadan's men to fall back on. But I do not think he will ever become King. I don't think the Kristill will ever have another King.'

'That's why you found me in the first place. Because I was Courberall. He is what I would have been, had I belonged here.'

Aimon stared at him, speechless.

The battle-roar rose and fell like a storm-whipped sea. Cardillac clasped his hand. 'We do not have much time. You must go back now. It – it has been good knowing you, Willoby.'

'Call me Will. All my friends do.'

They smiled at him out of their battered faces. Aimon took his other hand and spoke again but once more Willoby could not understand the language. He closed his eyes as his stomach turned. The noise eased, the sounds of fighting drawing off. He could not recall at what point they let go of his hands, but knew only that they had gone. He was alone, drifting in some desolate emptiness between worlds with nothing but the images from his memory for company. Merrin's face, alight, the gems shining in her hair. Sunshine bright on snow-deep mountains. A teeming city on a high-sided hill. And a burly, one-eyed man who was himself, and was a king.

They glowed like jewels in his mind, and he smiled as he viewed them. Such beautiful, impossible things.

But eventually they, too, faded, and he sank, deep into the welcoming blackness.

Epilogue

The young doctor pushed his glasses up his nose. It shone in the light of the overhead fluorescents.

'I don't understand, Sister. What kind of ward are you running here? You let a patient waltz out like it's some kind of open house, and then you let him waltz straight back in again, critically ill. And no one's seen anything. What kind of nurses do you have?'

'No one saw a thing,' Sister hissed at him. 'It was as if he had vanished into thin air. The first we knew of it was when his wife came in, almost hysterical, and the police behind her. We searched everywhere – he wasn't in a condition to get far – and then here he was again, in his own bed but wearing fancy dress *again* – some kind of cowboy outfit, I think – and suffering multiple stab wounds.'

'Unlucky man, mugged twice in twenty-four hours.'

'The police are treating it as attempted murder. He's stable now, but we almost lost him for a moment.'

The doctor rubbed his eyes behind his glasses. 'The shit will hit the fan over this one. I've already had the local rag on the phone. They're sniffing for a scandal.'

'Yes. His wife was speaking to them.'

'Is that her, sitting beside him? She seems very young.'

'No, doctor, that's his daughter. She's been here quite a while, dry-eyed, just staring at him.'

'Pretty, isn't she?' The sister looked at him with contempt.

The doctor coughed uneasily. 'We've had his prison on the blower, too. They're working on the theory that an ex-prisoner did this to him.'

'Is he a criminal?'

'No, a prison warder. Hasn't been well, it seems. Between you and me, I've been informed that he's being treated for a psychiatric disorder.'

'Maybe that explains the dressing up.'

'Maybe. But we'd best keep a close eye on him when he wakes. Make sure he doesn't go off on his travels again.'

'He's not going anywhere,' the sister said. 'Not for a long time. He seems peaceful enough now, though. Look -- he's smiling.'